BOOMER'S BUCKET LIST

Also by Sue Pethick

Pet Friendly

Published by Kensington Publishing Corp.

BOOMER'S BUCKET
Sue Pethick LIST

ZEBRA BOOKS
KENSINGTON PUBLISHING CORP.
www.kensingtonbooks.com

ZEBRA BOOKS are published by

Kensington Publishing Corp.
119 West 40th Street
New York, NY 10018

All Kensington titles, imprints, and distributed lines are available at special quantity discounts for bulk purchases for sales promotion, premiums, fund-raising, and educational or institutional use.

Special book excerpts or customized printings can also be created to fit specific needs. For details, write or phone the office of the Kensington Sales Manager: Kensington Publishing Corp., 119 West 40th Street, New York, NY 10018. Attn. Sales Department. Phone: 1-800-221-2647.

Zebra and the Z logo Reg. U.S. Pat. & TM Off.

First Kensington trade paperback printing: January 2017
First Zebra mass market paperback printing: June 2023
ISBN-13: 978-1-4201-5602-7
ISBN-13: 978-1-4967-0905-9 (eBook)

10 9 8 7 6 5 4 3 2 1

Printed in the United States of America

To all the animals whose lives have
touched and enriched my own

PROLOGUE

The summer she turned thirty, three things happened that changed the course of Jennifer Westbrook's life. She landed her dream job, got a divorce, and adopted a dog.

"How old are they?" she asked, staring at the bouncing, squirming mass of puppies in the pen.

Betty, the woman who was selling them, smiled.

"Four months old today. That's Trixie, their mama, over there."

She pointed toward a frazzled-looking yellow Lab who watched them anxiously from a few yards away.

"And the father?"

The woman scowled.

"A golden retriever, lives about half a mile down the road. Got out one day and made a beeline for this place." She shook her head. "They tell me he's purebred, but he's got no papers and my business is selling registered dogs, not mutts. Every litter that can't be sold for top dollar is money out of my pocket."

Jennifer looked around at the neat and orderly kennels that surrounded the woman's modest farmhouse and nodded sympathetically. No doubt, a batch of mixed-breed pups was a nuisance to a small-time dog breeder like Betty, but the truth was, a mutt was exactly what she was looking for. Jennifer had spent half her life being told that everything about her had to be perfect. Now that she was finally on her own, she wanted nothing more than to lead a normal, "imperfect" life.

"I'll say this for him, though," Betty added. "He makes good pups. They may not be purebred, but they're lookers." She gave Jennifer a sidelong glance. "So, you want to take a closer look?"

"I think so, yes."

Betty held the puppies back as Jennifer stepped into their pen. From the other side of the fence, it had been hard for her to tell one pup from another, but now that there was a stranger in their midst, the difference in their temperaments began to show.

Five of the six ran to her immediately, jumping and sniffing, giving gentle nips when Jennifer reached out her hand. Remembering the tips she'd read about choosing a good-natured puppy, Jennifer gently rolled each one onto its back and held it there briefly to see its reaction. All but one tolerated the treatment with good humor; now the choice was down to four. Next, she spent some time petting and picking up each one, but instead of helping her narrow the field, it only left her wishing she could take them all. She stood up, shaking her head.

"I don't know," she said. "They're all so sweet. Which one do I choose?"

Betty gave her a knowing smile.

"Give it a minute," she said. "In my experience, people don't choose a dog. The dog chooses them."

Jennifer was doubtful. Surely there were more scientific ways of choosing a companion animal, she thought: boxes to check, tests to perform. But there she was, having checked the boxes and done the tests and all it had done was make her head spin. She decided to give it a try.

It took less than a minute for two of the pups to wander off and begin roughhousing, then a third bounded across the pen and knocked his little sister onto her back. They were losing interest, Jennifer thought, and who could blame them? The stranger's novelty was wearing off.

Then the last pup let out a contented sigh and leaned against Jennifer's leg. She glanced down and saw a pair of chocolate-brown eyes looking up at her, their outer edges creased in an affectionate smile.

"Looks like you've got your answer," Betty said.

"I think you're right." Jennifer looked up. "Does he have a name?"

"Well, the kids call him Boomer, but you can name him anything you like."

"Why Boomer?"

The woman chuckled. "He doesn't say much, but when he does, you can't miss it."

Jennifer nodded. "Boomer it is, then."

She plucked the little guy off the ground and gave him a cuddle. As he settled into her arms, Jennifer felt as if the last piece of her new life was falling into place. A whole world was out there just waiting for the two of them to discover it.

"You and me, Boomer," she said. "We're going to have a lot of great adventures."

CHAPTER 1

It was a glorious late-summer day in Chicago. The humidity that had made August so unbearable had finally relinquished its hold on the city, and the breeze blowing in from Lake Michigan held the promise of a perfect weekend. As Jennifer stepped out of her office, she couldn't believe her good luck. There'd been no last-minute snafus, no clients demanding her personal assistance, and no out-of-town conferences to attend. Other than a few errands to run on the way home, in fact, her calendar was blessedly free for the next forty-eight hours. She couldn't wait to pick up Boomer and get started.

The doggie day care was a block and a half away. Boomer enjoyed spending time at Waggin' Tails, but romping indoors wasn't the same as being outside in the fresh air, and Jennifer wanted to take him with her while she made her rounds. The woman who taught their obedience class said it was good for dogs to get experience with different people and situations; a walk would give Boomer a chance to practice his good manners and tire him out a bit before dinnertime.

The bell on Waggin' Tails' front door rang as Jennifer stepped inside, setting off a riot of barking in the back. The door separating the boarding area from the front room opened and Hildy, the co-owner, stepped out.

"Jennifer! You're here early. Going out to enjoy this lovely weather?"

"Yep," she said. "Just thought I'd swing by and pick up your favorite client first."

The "favorite client" comment was something of an inside joke: Jennifer's way of acknowledging that, sweet as he was, her dog could be a bit of a handful.

Hildy buzzed the back room and asked them to bring Boomer up front.

"Boomer's been doing really well lately," she said. "I think maybe he's starting to settle down in his old age."

The door opened, and Hildy's assistant brought out the Lab/retriever mix.

"Seems a little early for that," Jennifer said as Boomer bounded toward her. "He just turned five last month."

Hildy looked abashed.

"Oh," she said. "Well, maybe he was just tired then."

"Or maybe"—Jennifer smiled—"the obedience classes are finally starting to pay off."

"Yes, I'm sure that's it," the woman said. "Well, we'll see you two on Monday. Good-bye, Boomer."

"Old age," Jennifer grumbled as they stepped outside. "You're lucky you're not a woman, Boomie. After a comment like that, you'd be dying your hair and getting Botox."

Downtown was crowded with office workers trying to get a jump on the weekend. As she and Boomer headed down the sidewalk, Jennifer noticed how often the strangers who passed them smiled when they saw him, and she congratulated herself for adopting such a kind and loving animal. Boomer might not be the best heeler in the world, but he didn't snarl or jump on people, and he was a good listener whenever she'd had a tough day at work. In the short time they'd been together, in fact, Boomer had become her best friend.

Their first stop was at Altimari's Cobbler Shop to pick up a pair of shoes Jennifer had taken in for repair. The slingback pumps had been the sole casualty of Boomer's chewing phase as a puppy, and it was just bad luck that they'd been the most expensive pair she owned. In a strange way, the fact that he'd picked out the Manolos had earned him a grudging respect in her eyes; Boomer obviously knew quality when he tasted it. Nevertheless, she'd never quite worked up the nerve to toss the shoes out, and when she told Mr. Altimari that she still had them, he'd encouraged her to bring them by the shop and let him see if they could be salvaged. Considering how long they'd been sitting unworn in her closet, Jennifer figured she had nothing to lose.

Lucio Altimari was at his workbench behind the counter when Jennifer and Boomer walked in. Mallet in hand, a leather apron secured to his wizened frame, he looked like an older version of St. Crispin, the patron saint of cobblers, whose picture was prominently displayed on the wall behind him.

"Hello, Mr. Altimari," Jennifer said as the door swung closed behind her. "I got your message."

The old man looked up and waved.

"*Ciao bella!* Yes, I fix them," he said, in an accent redolent of Tuscany.

He set aside the boot he was working on and stood, slowly working the kinks out of his back as he approached the counter. At barely five feet tall, the tiny, white-haired gentleman was almost a foot shorter than Jennifer. Nevertheless, with his powerful forearms and piercing blue eyes, he could be something of an intimidating figure. The eyes narrowed when he caught sight of Boomer.

"Ah," he said. "*Il distruttore di scarpe.*"

Jennifer's Italian was rusty, but she was pretty sure he'd just called Boomer a shoe destroyer.

"That was a long time ago," she said, "and he's really, really sorry he did it. Aren't you, Boomie?"

Boomer hung his head, and Mr. Altimari shuffled into the back of the shop to retrieve her shoes. When he set them on the counter, Jennifer gasped. They looked as good as new.

"These are amazing," she said, picking one up to examine it. "You'd never even know they were damaged."

"I do my best," the old man said modestly. "Not perfect, but not so bad, either, eh?"

He showed her the bill, and Jennifer gave him her credit card. It wasn't cheap, she thought, but it was a lot less than a new pair of Manolos would be. As he handed her the receipt, the old man shot Boomer an admonitory look.

"I forgive you this time," he said. "But you no touch the Ferragamos or we gonna have words, *capisci?*"

"Don't worry," Jennifer said. "I think Boomer's learned his lesson."

Mr. Altimari wrapped the shoes in tissue paper and laid them carefully in a plain shoebox that he slipped into a paper bag. Satisfied that her dog had been sufficiently chastened, he could now move on to his favorite topic of conversation: helping Jennifer find a husband.

"So, you have big plans for the weekend, yes?"

"Not yet," she said. "To tell you the truth, it's been so long since I had an entire weekend off that I've forgotten how to plan for one."

"You should go out, have some fun." He shook a gnarled finger at her. "You not gonna meet anybody at home."

Jennifer smiled and nodded, trying not to feel irritated. Mr. Altimari meant well, and if he knew nothing of her past, it was her own fault. After leaving Vic, she'd gone out of her way to remake her life—new town, new friends, new job. Maybe if she hadn't been so eager to disavow her old life, things would be different, but there was too much at stake now for her to take the chance. Unless and until she wanted to open that Pandora's box, Jennifer told herself, she'd just have to put up with a little well-intentioned meddling.

"Don't worry, I'll think of something," she said. "And if I can't, I'm sure Boomer will."

Boomer looked up and wagged his tail happily.

"I know, I know," the old man said. "Not my business." He handed her the bag.

"Buona giornata."

"Molto grazie, Mr. Altimari."

The L clattered by as they stepped back out and headed for the grocery store. Jennifer felt a whoosh of air as the train passed overhead and shut her eyes against the dirt and leaves that rose up in its wake. Just two more errands, she thought, and they could go home. If she picked up dinner on the way, there'd be nothing to cook and no dishes to wash. There was still plenty of daylight left. Maybe the two of them could go down to the beach and play "catch the Frisbee." And tomorrow, she thought, they'd get up early and take a jog around Lincoln Park. She and Boomer hadn't done that in an age.

Jennifer ducked into Trader Joe's while Boomer waited outside, cadging pats from passersby and watching the cars make their way through rush-hour traffic. When she returned, he searched her pockets for the dog treat she always bought him as a reward, then devoured it quickly and waited while she bent down to untie him. As Jennifer grabbed his lead, she saw the hackles rise on the dog's back.

"What is it, Boomie? What's wrong?"

She looked up and saw a man she recognized coming toward them, talking on his cell phone, briefcase in hand.

"Oh, no," she groaned. "It's Phil."

She ducked her head, wondering what to do.

Oh, boy. This is awkward.

The two of them had been on a date the month before that ended when Phil, who'd been drinking, came on too strong and Boomer jumped to Jennifer's defense, baring his teeth and all but chasing the guy out of her house. Admittedly, it wasn't Boomer's finest hour, but Jennifer had had a hard time blaming him. The way she figured it, the guy had it coming.

Phil was only a few feet away now—she'd know that self-important blather anywhere. She glanced up and their eyes met. Phil's gaze went from Jennifer to Boomer and back again. Then, without missing a beat, he quickly changed course and crossed the street. As he scurried away, Jennifer smiled. Boomer wasn't just a dog, she thought. He was a big, fluffy bodyguard.

Probably best not to mention it to Mr. Altimari, though.

After a quick stop at Chipotle for a burrito and chips, they walked through the door of Jennifer's town house. Purse, leash, and shoes were abandoned at the door as she took the bags into the kitchen and set them on the counter. Boomer made a beeline for his water bowl.

"What a day," she said, taking a plate down from the cupboard. "Just once, I'd like to work for a client who knows what he wants before I finish my entire ad campaign."

She poured herself a Bud Light and set the chips on the table.

"I told Derek he's going to have to hire another AE if this keeps up, and you know what he said?"

She took another sip of beer and plunked her plate down on the table.

"He said half our clients would walk if he tried to steer them to another AE. Yeah, right," she said. "Like that's ever going to happen."

Jennifer continued filling Boomer in on the latest down at Compton/Sellwood while she ate her burrito and finished off the chips. It wasn't until she got up to get herself another beer that she realized Boomer was no longer in the kitchen.

"Hey, dude. Where'd you go?"

She walked out into the living room and found him lying on the couch. Boomer lifted his head and thumped his tail once, not bothering to get up.

"Poor guy. You really are tired, aren't you?"

Jennifer placed her hand on his side and gently patted the silky coat.

"All your buds at day care must have been running you ragged."

Jennifer frowned. They'd been home almost half an hour, and Boomer was still panting. It could be the heat, she told herself, but his heart, too, seemed to be beating a little faster than usual. Remembering Hildy's comment about Boomer's being more tired than usual, she wondered if he might be coming down with something.

"Tell you what," she said. "Why don't we just stay in tonight? I'll take a shower, put on my pj's, and join you here on the couch. Maybe we can find something good on Netflix."

She slipped her hand under his collar to make sure he wasn't feverish, then started upstairs. Boomer was going in for his annual checkup the next week anyway, Jennifer thought. She'd ask Dr. Samuels about it when she took him in then. In the meantime, she wasn't going to let herself get freaked out about this. The fact was, it was probably nothing.

CHAPTER 2

People do a lot of different things when they're nervous. Jennifer was making her already too-busy life even busier. As she sat in the veterinarian's office that morning, waiting to hear Boomer's test results, she was answering e-mails, checking her phone messages, and balancing her checkbook—anything to keep from imagining the worst.

She reached down and gave him a reassuring pat.

"It's probably nothing," she whispered. "No need to worry."

But Jennifer was worried. When she'd brought Boomer in for his yearly checkup and casually mentioned that he seemed more tired than usual, she'd been expecting Dr. Samuels to give him a shot of vitamins. Instead, the vet had urged her to have a battery of tests done on Boomer that had lasted half the day and required a specialist's interpretation. She suspected that Samuels was overreacting, but he'd been so insistent that she'd agreed to have them done. Now sitting in his office a week later, Jennifer almost wished she hadn't. After all, Boomer was just a kid. There couldn't be anything *seriously* wrong with him, could there?

The examination-room door opened, and Dr. Samuels's new assistant called them in. A well-endowed brunette in her thirties, the woman dressed like a teenager and spoke in a giggly voice that went up at the end of every sentence. Just the type, Jennifer thought sourly, that her ex-husband, Vic, would have slobbered over. Boomer looked up, growling low in his throat as Jennifer shut down her computer. She might not have been so quick to judge, she thought, but Boomer didn't seem to like the woman, either, and Boomer was an excellent judge of character.

"Looks like it's our turn, Boomski," she said. "Let's go."

The door had barely closed behind them when Dr. Samuels came in. From the look on his face, Jennifer could tell it was bad news. Her heart began to pound, and she reached out for Boomer as if to shield him from what was coming. Samuels shook her hand and gave Boomer a friendly pat.

"Thanks for coming in again. I know it was hard having to wait, but I wanted to make sure I hadn't overlooked anything before we discussed the test results."

He glanced at Boomer's chart, then cleared his throat and set it aside.

"This isn't the kind of news I like to give my patients," he said sadly. "I like to think I can save every animal who comes in here. Unfortunately, however, that's just not the case."

Tears sprang to Jennifer's eyes and a lump formed in her throat as Samuels continued.

"When you brought Boomer in last week, I detected a systolic murmur and suspected there might be something wrong with his heart. Your comment that he'd been more tired than usual added to that suspicion, but without further tests there was no way to know for certain what was wrong."

Jennifer took a deep breath and willed herself to calm down.

"So, what's the problem?"

"Boomer has HCM, or hypertrophic cardiomyopathy," he said. "It's a thickening of the heart walls that reduces the amount of blood ejected during its contraction phase. As the animal's body begins to starve for oxygen, the heart pumps harder, stressing it further. Eventually, the animal develops heart failure."

He paused, waiting for Jennifer to ask another question, but her mind had gone blank.

"But he doesn't even look sick."

"I know," Samuels said. "And Boomer probably doesn't feel sick, either, at least not the way you or I would. He may not be able to jump or run around like he used to, but the chances are he doesn't really notice, and the good news is he's not in any pain."

All right, Jennifer told herself, this might not be the outcome she was hoping for, but it wasn't the end of the world, either. At work, she had a reputation for solving the biggest problems for the toughest clients. All she had to do was apply that talent to fixing Boomer's problem and everything would be fine. Heart failure was treatable, and she had money in her savings account. Whatever it took—a special diet, medicine, exercise—she'd pay for it, and gladly. She'd do anything to keep her boy alive.

"Okay," she said. "How do we fix this and get Boomer back to his old self?"

The vet gave her a pitying look and slowly shook his head.

"I guess I didn't make myself clear. You see, Boomer's condition is very advanced; he's past the stage where diuretics or any other type of intervention might have helped. All you can do now, I'm afraid, is to make sure he stays comfortable and enjoy the time you have left with him. I'm sorry."

"That can't be right," she snapped, sounding angrier than she meant to. "My grandfather lived for years with heart failure."

Samuels nodded patiently.

"I imagine he did, but human hearts are different. Look, if you'd like to speak with the canine cardiologist, I'd be happy to arrange a phone consult for you, but he and I went over the test results very thoroughly and there was really no doubt in either of our minds. At best, we think Boomer has perhaps a month left."

Jennifer found herself struggling to breathe, as if all the air had suddenly been sucked out of the room.

"A *month?*" she said, fighting to keep her voice steady. "But that's just not enough time. There are so many things we haven't gotten around to doing yet, stuff I promised him we'd do someday."

She knew she was babbling, but she couldn't seem to stop.

"Work's been a grind and I know I've put some things off, but Boomer's only five and he's my best friend, and, and"—tears were spilling down her cheeks—"and he's all I've got."

Samuels, too, was fighting back tears. He stepped forward and gave her a gentle hug.

"I know how you feel; I lost my Boston terrier to HCM when she was only two. It's a rare condition in dogs and I hoped like hell that I was wrong. The only positive thing I can tell you is at least you know it's coming now. With most cases, the first symptom is cardiac arrest."

Jennifer nodded, wiping away her tears, and forced a weak smile.

"Thank goodness for small favors, I guess."

"Exactly."

She glanced at Boomer, who was watching her with a look of concern.

"Is there anything else I should do?" she said. "What about changing his diet?"

Samuels shook his head. "No, just keep an eye on him. If he starts passing out or you notice his gums turning blue, you'll want to give him some extra rest. Other than that, I suppose you could try not to get him too stressed out. When the end comes, though, I promise it'll be quick and relatively painless."

Jennifer walked out of the vet's office with Boomer in tow, as oblivious to the world around her as a sleepwalker. She always knew she'd lose her dog someday; it was realizing how much of his short life she'd already missed that she regretted. While she'd been spending nights and weekends at work, Boomer's time on earth had been dwindling. Now it felt like every dream she'd put off had been snatched away. When they got back to her truck, she slipped behind the wheel and wept.

"I'm sorry, Boomie," she sobbed, hugging him. "I'll make it up to you somehow. I promise."

An hour later, Jennifer was back at home, already halfway toward keeping that promise. Dry-eyed and determined, she was working on a plan. She took out a pad of paper and grabbed a pen. At the top of the first page, she wrote: *Things to Do with Boomer*. If her boy had only a month left, then she was going to make sure that it was the best month of his life. She'd pack the truck, and they'd hit the road, just the two of them, doing all the things she'd planned for them to do "someday."

As far as taking the time off from work, Jennifer thought, she was lucky. Her job as an account executive at one of the toniest PR firms in Chicago was a big plus, and with all the overtime she'd been putting in, they owed her. The CEO, Derek Compton, would pitch a fit, of course, but the way she saw it, he didn't really have a choice. There were two CLIOs, one regional ADDY, and a Cannes Lion sitting in his trophy case that were generally acknowledged to have been won through her efforts. He could give her the time off or she could quit and go to work for one of his competitors when she got back.

With that problem solved, the question became what she and Boomer should do during their month together. Hildy told her he'd been slowing down the last couple of weeks, and Dr. Samuels said to expect more of the same in the time ahead. Jennifer glanced over at her dog, happily ensconced in his favorite chair and gnawing a rawhide chew.

"Sorry, Boom-Boom. Looks like hiking the Appalachian Trail is out."

She sat back, searching her memory for the times when Boomer had enjoyed himself the most. Like any dog, he loved eating, playing, and chasing squirrels, but what was it, specifically, that made his tail wag?

Well, she thought, he loved cars—the ones that drove by on their street, of course, and the souped-up NASCAR racers on the TV—and he went wild whenever they took a drive and Jennifer let him stick his nose out the window so he could savor all the good smells that flew by. He loved the roar of loud engines and sniffing the puddles of oil he found in the street. He even had a squeaky toy that looked like Lightning McQueen from the movie *Cars*.

"Okay," she said, writing the number "one" on her list. "'Something to do with cars.' What else?"

After ten more minutes of brainstorming, though, Jennifer was stumped. She kept thinking of things they *could* do, but none that seemed big or important enough to make up for what she felt had been her neglect of Boomer. As her confidence slipped, she began to feel discouraged again. Tears had begun welling in her eyes when she heard Boomer jump down from his chair and start rooting in his toy box. Seconds later, she heard the familiar *squeaky-squeak* of Lightning McQueen. Jennifer turned and saw Boomer walking toward her with the toy in his mouth, the hopeful look in his eyes daring her to try and take it away.

"Yes, I know," she said. "I've already got cars on my list, but what else, Boomster? We can't just get in the truck and drive around the block a hundred times. If we're going to take a road trip, we have to take a trip *to* somewhere."

And then it hit her: *Cars!* The movie was about driving Route 66. Which, as it happened, started in Chicago and went west all the way to the California coast. If she and Boomer drove Route 66, they could see some interesting sights, gorge themselves on regional foods, and romp in the Pacific Ocean when they reached Santa Monica Pier. She could probably even find maps and guidebooks showing all the places they could visit along the way. She grabbed the squeaky toy, and the two of them started a tug-of-war.

"What do you say, Boomer? Want to get your kicks on Route 66?"

CHAPTER 3

Jennifer's prediction about her boss came true the next day
when she told him about her plan to take a month off. She
knew he wouldn't be happy about it, but she hadn't expected
a flat-out denial of her request, either. By the time she and
Derek Compton had finished screaming at each other, the
entire office was in the loop. Nevertheless, she'd been right
about his not wanting to lose her. When she mentioned that
the stress of losing Boomer was forcing her to "reevaluate
her priorities," he'd given in, correctly interpreting it as a
threat to quit. As she stepped out into the hallway and
headed back to her office, she felt like a boxer leaving the
ring: bruised, battered, but victorious.

Stacy Randall watched Jennifer walk by her desk, feeling something akin to awe. As the department admin, Stacy
had been the target of Compton's wrath on more than one
occasion, and the fact that someone was finally getting the
better of him seemed like nothing short of a miracle. That it
had been Jennifer Westbrook, a beautiful ex-model with a
mysterious past, was just icing on the cake. When Jennifer

called her into her office, Stacy grabbed a notepad and hurried down the hall, hoping for a gossip-worthy tidbit.

"By now, I'm sure everyone within earshot knows that I'm taking the next month off," Jennifer said as she closed the door. "I'm going to need you to take care of a few things for me while I'm gone."

"Of course." Stacy took a seat, her pen poised.

"Since I'll be leaving on short notice, anything on my calendar for the next month will have to be either rescheduled or given to one of the other AEs."

"No problem."

"Mike Kuby can handle the presentation to Bewick's without me. I'll e-mail him my notes before I go."

Jennifer sat down, looking frazzled as she pawed through the papers on her desk, and Stacy wondered if there were any personal details she'd overlooked.

"What about things at home?" she said. "You know, like stopping the paper, the trash, having the post office hold your mail. . . ."

"Oh, God," Jennifer said, putting her head in her hands. "I didn't even think about that. I suppose I'll just have to try and take care of those things before I leave in the morning."

"I can do it for you," Stacy said hopefully.

"That's sweet, Stace, but I really couldn't impose on you like that."

"Oh, it's no problem," she said, smiling. "I'd be happy to. You've got enough to think about with Boomer . . . um . . . you know."

She shrugged, hoping she hadn't given offense.

"I could water your plants and stuff, too, if you want. I've done it for my neighbors before and they'd vouch for me."

Jennifer looked at Stacy's imploring gaze and sighed. She'd been aware for some time that her admin was a bit stagestruck by the high-profile clients who passed through the doors of Compton/Sellwood. Maybe she'd even been foolish enough to listen to some of the wilder rumors about Jennifer that had been passed around the office and thought some of that magic would rub off on her. As much as she could use the help, though, she hated to take advantage of the younger woman's girl crush.

"Are you sure?" she said.

Stacy grinned. "I'm sure."

"Okay, but only if you let me pay for your time."

"You don't have to," Stacy said. "But thanks."

Jennifer nodded. "I've got a second set of house keys in my locker. Make sure I give them to you before I leave this afternoon."

With that settled, Jennifer felt instantly less harried and it occurred to her that Stacy's offer might have solved a problem she'd only been aware of subconsciously. She was about to dismiss her admin and get back to work, when Stacy said:

"Have you given someone your itinerary?"

"What?"

"You know, a list of where you're going and when. Then if something happens to you along the way, the police will know where to look for your body."

Jennifer tried not to laugh. Clearly, Stacy had been watching too many episodes of *Law & Order*.

"I don't really think that's necessary," she said. "Boomer and I will be fine on our own."

"But what if your car breaks down in the middle of nowhere and you can't get a signal on your phone? You could be stuck for weeks without food or water before anyone even notices you're missing."

Jennifer was about to insist that there were plenty of people who'd notice if she went missing when it occurred to her—with a twinge of sadness—that that might not be the case. Her father had passed away when she was still in high school, and her mother was in a nursing home, barely able to remember what day it was. She and Vic had split up almost six years ago and he and his new wife lived somewhere up in Michigan and wouldn't bother to check on her in any case. One of her neighbors might notice if she was missing long enough, but like most city apartment dwellers, she barely knew any of them except to say hello. As the reality of her barren personal life sank in, Jennifer felt heat rise in her face. No wonder she spent so much time at work. It was the only life she had.

And now she was losing Boomer, too.

"No, if I had an itinerary, I'd have to stick to it and I was thinking Boomer and I would just wing it. Besides," she added sheepishly, "I really don't have anybody to give an itinerary to."

Stacy looked up from her note pad. "You can give it to me."

Jennifer shook her head, trying not to let her irritation show.

"I appreciate your concern, but there's really no time for me to make one up, thanks."

"Well . . . maybe you could just take pictures of your trip and send them to me. That way, someone will know where you are and you won't have to write anything. Please," Stacy said. "I'd feel a lot better if you did."

Exasperation was quickly souring Jennifer's mood. Nevertheless, she had to concede that Stacy had a point. She'd already been planning to take pictures of Boomer to remember their trip by and forwarding them to her admin wouldn't take any extra time. Plus, she had to admit that the thought of being on the road with no one back home even knowing where she was gave her a creepy feeling. A woman alone—even if she had a dog with her—could still be pretty vulnerable.

"All right. If it makes you feel better, I'll send you some pictures along the way, but that's it. I promised myself that this trip was just for Boomer and me. For the next few weeks, I'm off-line: no e-mail, no text messages, and no social media. If there's an emergency, I'll have my cell with me, but don't you dare call me for anything less than a nuclear war over the North Side of Chicago." She paused. "And not even then."

Stacy grinned. "What if there's a nuclear war over the *South* Side?"

Jennifer shook her head. "I don't live on the South Side."

The rest of the day passed by in a blur. Once word got out that Jennifer Westbrook would be incommunicado for the next few weeks, every team member with a question and every client who wanted his hand held called, texted, or barged into her office demanding attention. Stacy ran out and brought back a kale salad so that Jennifer could eat at her desk during a conference call from Boston and tried to redirect the flood of people demanding to speak to Ms. Westbrook *now*. By the time Jennifer walked out of her office at six, she was vowing to kill anyone who stood in her way. She grabbed her purse, tossed her spare house keys on Stacy's desk, and sprinted down the hall.

Derek Compton was waiting for her by the elevator.

"So, you're leaving us," he said.

"Don't make it sound so final," Jennifer said, pressing the down button. "Unless, of course, you've changed your mind about firing me."

"Of course not. I'm just not looking forward to the next few weeks without you. Stacy tells me you won't even be online."

"That's right," she said, wishing the elevator would hurry up.

He nodded, working his mouth in a way that suggested he was holding back a string of expletives.

"Well, the circumstances aren't the greatest, of course, but I hope you and Boomer have a good time."

Jennifer nodded. The numbers above the elevator doors were counting down very slowly. The darned thing must be stopping at every floor.

"Thank you."

"I know you said Boomer likes cars"—he reached into his breast pocket—"so I got you both a little going-away present."

She glanced at the envelope in Compton's hand, and her eyes widened. It looked like a VIP ticket to the Chicagoland Speedway.

"Is that what I think it is?"

"Yep. Cal Daniels invited me, but when I told him about your dog, he agreed to let the two of you watch Sunday's race from his private box. He even offered to have his limo driver take you there and back."

She opened the envelope and took out the ticket, watching the hologram on the front flash the letters "VIP" in gold. The speedway was right on Route 66, and Boomer would adore watching the stock cars whizz by, she thought. And if they went on Sunday instead of tomorrow like she'd planned, that'd give her an extra day to get packed up and ready. As she tucked the ticket back into the envelope, Jennifer had to fight to keep from spilling her tears. Say what you want to about Derek Compton, but the man had a good heart.

"Thank you," she whispered. "From both of us."

CHAPTER 4

Nathan Koslow pressed his ear against the telephone receiver, straining to hear his brother's voice. Between the lousy connection and the clamor coming from the people in the newsroom, he could barely make out what Rudy was saying.

"Hang on a sec," Nathan said. "There's too much noise in here."

He put his hand over the mouthpiece and began searching the cavernous room for a place that offered some peace and quiet.

The *Trib*'s bull pen was a hive of activity at that hour. With deadlines looming, reporters hammered out stories and barked at the interns who scurried between the rows of half-height partitions. Printers and fax machines spit out paper, ringing telephones went unanswered, and section editors paced, their faces drained of color by the fluorescent lights that buzzed overhead. It was a vibrant, hectic space, and Nathan loved it, but it was no place to hold a private conversation.

He glanced over at his section editor's empty office,

one of six glass-walled niches that lined the walls of the bull pen, and smiled. Julia Mikulski didn't like having reporters invading her space while she was out, but this was an emergency.

"I'll call you back in a minute," he said, and hung up.

Nathan paused at Julia's door, knocking before he entered in case she'd snuck back in and was on the floor doing one of her stress-relieving yoga poses. Julia practiced yoga like a drunk practiced sobriety: It was something to turn to when the chips were down, but not much fun for the long haul. When no one answered, Nathan slipped into the office, turned on her computer, and picked up the phone. Rudy answered on the first ring.

"Did you go to the Web site?"

"Not yet." Nathan scowled. "I have to get into the system first."

Julia's desk was covered in papers, layered like sediment that had accumulated during the years she'd been working at the *Trib*. The top layer consisted of handwritten notes and phone message slips; under that were the copyedited articles that the newspaper would be running that week, then ideas for stories they'd be working on in the coming months, going further into the future the deeper you went in the pile. Anything beneath that was probably best left to an archaeologist.

He signed in to the central computer system using the username and password that Julia had helpfully left on the Post-it Note she'd stuck to the screen.

So much for security.

"Okay," he said. "I missed about half of what you said before. Start from the beginning. You bought a car. . . ."

"Not *a* car, Nate, a freakin' Mustang GT. It's got a 435-horsepower V-8 engine, a top-of-the-line audio system, leather seats, navigation system, the works. It was a steal, too. I don't think the guy who owns the dealership is all that bright, to be honest, but hey, that's not my fault."

"A convertible?"

"Are you kidding? 'Course it's a convertible. You don't think I moved all the way to California so I could drive a sedan, do you?"

Nathan rolled his eyes. It seemed as if everything his brother purchased these days had to be in service to his new-found West Coast lifestyle. Since moving out to La La Land, Rudy had begun directing low-budget, blood-splattered horror movies with titles like *Hollywood Zombie Hookers* ("They Never Eat and Run!") and *Massacre on 34th Street* ("Putting the 'Black' in Black Friday"), and judging from the amount of money he had to throw around, movies with no redeeming social value were paying pretty well.

The system had accepted Julia's password. Nathan launched the browser and entered the Web site address. When he hit "return," the screen filled with a three-quarter shot of a sapphire-blue sports car, its diamond-bright finish gleaming in the sun. He could almost see Rudy tooling along Sunset Boulevard with the top down.

"Oh, man," Nathan sighed. "That is one fantastic car."

"I know, right?" Rudy said, obviously pleased that it had made an impression. "I can't believe I had to go all the way to Chicago to find one like it."

"So, why not just fly out here and drive it back yourself?"

"I told you—I'm in preproduction for *Cousin Betsy Is a Bloodsucking Vampire.*"

"Can't the dealer ship it out there?"

"He could," his brother said. "But that'd cost me a few grand and he can't even promise me when it'll get here. If you drive it to LA, all it'll cost me is gas money and a couple nights in cheap motels."

Nathan smirked. "So, you're a big spender *and* a cheap-skate."

"Come on, little brother, help me out here," Rudy whee-dled. "Besides, you'll love driving it; the thing's a chick magnet. If you keep your smart mouth shut for a change you might even get some action."

Nathan looked at the computer screen, clicking through the pictures of the Mustang that the dealer had posted on his Web site. Rudy was right; it was a beauty, and beyond anything Nathan could afford. Still, the comment about the car being a chick magnet grated. He might not have the kind of legendary love life his brother bragged about, but Nathan did all right. He was just between relationships at the moment . . . everybody had a dry spell once in a while. The problem was, Nathan's dry spells seemed to be lasting longer and longer.

He chewed his lip. It wasn't just relationships he was between, either. Since losing his regular column, Nathan had been bottom-fishing at the *Trib,* and steady assignments were hard to come by. If he could sell Julia on the idea of a travel series he could write from the road, he'd guarantee himself a week's worth of work and some fun in the sun.

"Okay," he said. "Tell the dealer I'll pick it up tomorrow."

Julia Mikulski's eyes narrowed. "You want to do *what?*"

Nathan's editor had returned to her office in a foul mood, made worse by the suspicion that someone had been using her computer without permission. As she sat behind her desk, reeking of the Marlboros she'd been sucking down while huddled out on the sidewalk with the rest of the pariahs, she seemed cool to the idea of letting one of her Life & Style reporters take a week off no matter how many travel articles he promised to send her. As her glare hardened, Nathan gave her his most winning smile.

"Drive my brother's car out to LA. He bought it from a dealer here in Downer's Grove and the guy won't ship it out there."

Not exactly the truth, but Nathan didn't think she'd be fact-checking his story.

"And how long will that take?" she said.

He shrugged. "A week? Depends on how many good stories I can scare up along the way."

The overhead lighting made Julia's long face look even more haggard than usual. Working at a newspaper was stressful. Competition from the Internet and the 24-7 news cycle on TV meant that even papers like the *Trib* were struggling, but smoking and an indifferent attitude toward her health was making her old before her time. She sat back and gave her computer a significant look. Nathan knew she suspected him of using it, but short of having the cops come in and dust it for fingerprints, she wasn't getting a confession. Twelve months spent feigning interest in everything from ladies' knitting circles to galas at symphony hall had given him a heck of a poker face.

"All right," she said. "You can go."

Nathan let out the breath he'd been holding.

"Thank you."

As reluctant as he'd been to sign on to his brother's scheme, once he'd agreed to go, the prospect had become downright irresistible. A week in a sports car, feeling the wind in his hair, a beautiful blonde at his side. . . .

"As it happens," Julia said, digging through the sediment on her desk, "I have an idea you can work on while you're on the road."

His face fell. "You do?"

She scrabbled through the layers for a few more seconds, then pulled a piece of paper from the depths, flourishing it like a magician extracting a rabbit from his hat.

"Route 66," she said, reading the note in front of her. "You can drive it from here to Santa Monica Pier. Lots of interesting things along the way, too, apparently. You should be able to find plenty of human-interest stories."

She tossed the paper in his direction. It made a graceful arc across the desk, then stalled just out of reach, fluttered, and landed at his feet.

Nathan snatched it up and placed it back on her desk.

"No."

"Why not?"

"Because it doesn't exist, for one thing, and I'd rather stick to the Interstate."

"What do you mean it doesn't exist? People talk about driving Route 66 all the time. Are you telling me someone's taken it?"

He slumped forward, shaking his head. How could he explain this to a woman who'd never left the city she was born in, much less driven a car?

"No, it's still there," he said. "But when the Interstate system was built, the old Route 66 became obsolete. Parts of it fell into disrepair. I'm not even sure you can still drive it all the way from here to the West Coast."

Julia snatched up the paper and studied it carefully.

"It says here you can."

"Well, maybe you can, then, but I guarantee it'll take me a lot longer to get to California that way."

The grin she gave him was feral.

"Well, why not give it a try and see how it goes?"

Nathan's eyes narrowed. What was going on? When he walked in and asked for permission to take a week off, Julia had acted like the entire division would collapse without him, and now she was all but pushing him into an assignment that might take him away from his desk for the better part of two weeks. A note of suspicion crept into his voice.

"I thought you couldn't spare me for that long."

"That was when I thought you'd be enjoying yourself out in La La Land," she said primly. "This way, I know you'll be getting some work done."

"All right, fine," he said, snatching the paper out of her

hand. "I'll take Route 66 and see what there is worth report-ing on. Just don't blame me if it's a bust."

"Agreed," she said. "When are you leaving?"

"I told Rudy I'd pick the car up tomorrow, but I don't know how much time that'll take. Maybe tomorrow, maybe the day after."

"Make it the day after. Morty's got the flu and we still need the piece he was going to do on that girl who's driving at Chicagoland on Sunday. I'll e-mail you his ticket."

Nathan smiled. He hadn't been to the Chicago Speed-way in years; it'd be fun to watch the boys in the press sec-tion turn green when they saw him drive up in the Mustang.

"Okay. I'll watch her race and write the piece as soon as I get back to my motel."

He got up and headed for the door.

"This brother you're going to see," Julia said. "He's the movie director, right?"

Nathan nodded. "Rudy, yeah."

"Tell him if he's looking for a screenplay, I've got a few ideas rattling around."

She smiled sweetly, and Nathan felt his stomach lurch. According to Rudy, there were more wannabe screenwriters in Hollywood than there were cars on the freeway at rush hour. Besides, did she even know what sort of movies his brother directed?

"Sure thing," he said, trying to sound upbeat. "I'll be sure and tell him when I get there."

He'd almost made it across the threshold, when he heard Julia's voice again.

"Oh, and Nathan? Keep your paws off my computer."

CHAPTER 5

If Nathan had harbored any illusions about impressing people with his brother's Mustang, they were quickly dispelled when he reached the speedway. Never mind what was out on the track; every car and truck in the parking lot had been customized with aftermarket features that made a mockery of the term "street legal." Driving to the press parking area was like maneuvering a dinghy past a group of aircraft carriers.

He was just getting out of the car when a limo cruised by. People in the crowd cast discreet glances as it passed, hoping to catch a glimpse of the person or persons behind its darkened windows. *It could be a starlet or a visiting dignitary in there,* Nathan thought—maybe both in the same car—and wouldn't that be something to write about? As he crossed the parking lot to get a closer look, he slipped a hand into his pocket and took out his iPhone, ready to take a picture in case he got lucky and it was someone famous. The limo pulled up to the VIP entrance and stopped. Then the chauffeur got out, put on his cap, and opened the rear door.

A woman stepped out, steadied by the chauffeur's hand.

In spite of her dark sunglasses, Nathan didn't think she was anyone famous. She was certainly good-looking, though. Her auburn hair, parted on the side and tucked behind one ear, grazed the shoulders of her fitted bomber jacket; slim-fitting jeans showed off a trim figure; and the high-heeled booties she was wearing accentuated her long legs. Nevertheless, when she straightened up, people closest to the limo began to turn away. As Nathan lowered his phone, he understood why: A golden retriever had exited the limo behind her wearing the distinctive saddle blanket and harness of a dog in service to the blind.

A large man in a tweed blazer stepped up to greet the woman and usher her and her dog toward the VIP entrance. As the three of them passed through the gate, the dog tugged the woman forward, excited by the crowd that pressed in around them.

The chauffeur got back behind the wheel, and the limousine drove off. No one seemed to have given the woman or her dog a second thought. She wasn't famous or even infamous, and although she was very attractive, there was nothing about her that had satisfied their hunger for excitement and celebrity. Perhaps it was disappointment or even pity for her disability, Nathan thought, but he'd be willing to bet that no one else who'd witnessed her arrival was as curious about the woman as he was.

There was something about her little performance that didn't add up.

By the time she and Boomer arrived at the luxury suite, Jennifer was ready to call off the whole charade. Rude looks from the men who felt free to ogle a blind woman were bad enough, but the pitying glances were the worst. More than once, she'd been tempted to take off the dark glasses and declare herself cured, like a suppliant at a revival meeting. She might have done it, too, but for one thing: Boomer was having the time of his life. Straining against his harness, his tail whipping like a wind sock in a gale, he'd spent the walk in from the parking lot jerking her from one side to the other as he took in his surroundings. No one who'd been watching closely would ever have mistaken Boomer for a real service dog, and she'd been half expecting someone to call her bluff, but no one said anything and the trip to the third floor had been mercifully brief. If anyone had noticed that he wasn't as attentive or well behaved as he should have been, they'd probably attributed it to the effect of the unfamiliar surroundings.

Of course, it didn't hurt that she and Boomer had been shown to the suite by Cal Daniels, a man whose company logo decorated more than one of the cars down on the track that day. Cal was a big man, not just tall, but beefy, with a large head, broad shoulders, and a ruddy complexion that darkened ominously in a confrontation. That, and his solicitous attention to her, had probably deterred anyone who might otherwise have been tempted to stop a person entering the stadium with a dog. Jennifer suspected he'd also been using her supposed blindness as an excuse to take her arm on the way to his suite, a suspicion that was confirmed when he was reluctant to release her once they'd arrived.

"Can I offer you a drink?" he said.

Jennifer removed the glasses and smiled for the first time since exiting the limo.

"I'd love one," she said. "Diet anything would be great."

The third-floor suite was impressive. A private, climate-controlled room overlooking the start-finish line, it had three tiers of thickly padded grandstand seats in the middle with a 180-degree view of the track below. On the left, red leather stools crowded a small wet bar and a smattering of tables provided space for those not wishing to eat in their seats. Mounted on either side of the room were flat-screen televisions broadcasting a warm-up show in anticipation of live race coverage. Other than the two of them, there were about a dozen people inside. Derek Compton had mentioned there'd be people from Cal's company joining them that day, but he'd assured her it wasn't a business meeting, just a thank-you from the boss.

Daniels returned from the bar and handed her an icy can of Diet Coke.

"You can let your doggie go now," he said, nodding at Boomer. "As long as he stays in here, he's free to roam."

"Thank you," she said. "He loves to explore."

Jennifer released the harness and Boomer took off. Sniffing the floor with a wet and curious nose, he worked his way past the tables and the leather barstools to the vast expanse of glass in front, accepting pats from the folks who were still arriving.

She popped the top of her soda and took several large swallows, the sting from the carbonation as it went down making her eyes water. Until then Jennifer hadn't realized how nervous she'd been about her fraudulent performance. Now that she and Boomer were in the clear, she was surprised at how dry her mouth had gotten.

The door opened again and six more people—five men and a woman—arrived. Daniels told them to help themselves to the bar, then introduced them to Jennifer as they walked over. As she sipped her drink, Jennifer found she was only half listening, keeping one eye out for Boomer as he continued his survey of the room. In spite of Cal's assurance that her dog was free to roam the suite, there was always a chance he'd slip out whenever anyone opened the door. With more people arriving and the room getting crowded, she'd have to stay alert lest Boomer escape and blow their cover.

"Is anything wrong?" Cal asked.

Jennifer shook her head. "Just trying to make sure my dog doesn't slip out the door."

"Don't worry, he'll be fine. My people know all about his situation. They'll keep an eye on him."

Jennifer nodded and turned toward the monitor, feeling a prick of irritation. How much, she wondered, had Cal told everyone about Boomer's condition? Had he simply said there'd be a dog in the suite that day, or had he also mentioned that her dog was dying? It made her angry somehow to think that word about Boomer's illness had spread, as if more people knowing about his diagnosis made it more certain that her dog would die.

You're being irrational, Jennifer told herself. Cal hadn't done anything to hurt her. Furthermore, he was doing her a big favor by inviting Boomer to see the race. So what if the people there knew about his condition? It didn't change anything.

She'd been watching the prerace show for several minutes, when a man on her right said: "What do you think about that, Jen?"

Jennifer turned and was surprised to find Cal and one of her own colleagues staring at her expectantly. Jason Grant had been hired to run the social media team at Compton/Sellwood six months before and was rapidly becoming a thorn in her side. Quick to come up with proposals that promised much and delivered little, he was also a good salesman and eager to the point of mania, which often made her more judicious suggestions seem stodgy by comparison. Rumor had it that Jason also referred to her as "the Workhorse" behind her back, but at least that was an improvement over the sobriquet some of the other men in the company had saddled her with: "the Ice Queen."

"I'm sorry," she said, shaking her head. "I wasn't paying attention. What's the question?"

"We were talking about the upcoming promo that you and your team are putting together for us," Cal explained. "Jason has a couple of ideas of his own and I thought, as long as you're here, he could run them by you, see what you think."

Jennifer felt her stomach tighten. So, Derek Compton

had lied; this was a business meeting after all. Nevertheless, it wasn't Cal's fault and there were still several minutes to go before the race started. As long as Boomer was all right, she figured it wouldn't hurt to answer a few questions.

"What sort of ideas?" she asked, doing her best to feign interest.

As Jason shared his suggestion that Daniels Shock Absorbers go all-in on social media, adding Twitter, Tumblr, and Instagram messages to their Web site and Facebook pages, Jennifer felt her smile begin to cool. She and her team had done a lot of research before putting together their marketing plan for Cal's company, and none of it had indicated that an expanded social media campaign would bring in enough business to justify the cost. She could understand Jason's point of view, of course. He was a young guy trying to impress the client with the latest whizbang approach to capturing hearts and minds, but the truth was that not every approach produced results. Unless Cal Daniels had money to burn—which she sincerely doubted—it wasn't worth paying for what this kid was proposing.

Jason finished his spiel with a flourish, and the two men waited for her response. Jennifer nodded thoughtfully, stalling for time. How should she put this?

She was still trying to come up with a diplomatic way of telling them what she thought, when the door swung open and a waiter came in pushing a linen-covered cart that was laden with food. Before the door could swing shut, she saw Boomer slip outside.

"Boomer, come back here!" she yelled, startling the people around her. "I'm sorry," she told Cal. "I have to go catch my dog."

Forgetting the ruse that had allowed her to bring a dog into the stadium, Jennifer charged out the door, searching the broad, carpeted passageway for her wayward animal. With the start of the race only minutes away, the area was crowded with people jostling one another as they headed for their seats. A woman stepping out of the restroom ran into her, and the child in her wake trod on her foot. Jennifer peered over the heads that passed her on all sides. There was a stairwell fifty feet to the right. Had he gone in that direction, she wondered, or back the way they came in? If she didn't find Boomer soon, they'd be evicted before the race even started.

Then she heard a voice above the din.

"Here he is! I've got him."

A sandy-haired man in a blue shirt was waving at her from across the aisle. Jennifer waved back and began pushing her way through the sea of bodies. As the crowd parted, she saw Boomer standing there, the man's hand securely on his harness. The relief she felt brought tears to her eyes.

"Thank you so much!" Jennifer said as she hurried over.

Boomer's hindquarters were wiggling, and before she could stop him, he stood on his hind legs and licked the man's face.

"Boomie, get down! I'm so sorry," she said, reaching for his harness. "He's usually better behaved than this."

The man laughed. As Boomer's paws hit the ground, he bent down and ruffled the dog's fur playfully.

"That's okay," he said, glancing up at her. "He's just excited. After all, it's not every day you witness a miracle."

"What?"

He pointed. "You can see."

Jennifer's hand flew to her face.

"Oh, my God. I forgot the glasses. We'd better go."

The man looked over her shoulder and grimaced.

"Better not. There's a security guard coming this way."

"Oh, no," she said. "He's going to throw us out."

"Hold on, don't panic." The man reached into his front pocket and handed her his sunglasses. "Put these on and take Boomer's harness like he was leading you somewhere."

Jennifer did as she was told.

"Okay, now what?" she whispered.

"Now," he said, glancing back over her shoulder, "you act like you're really ticked off at me."

"What?" She shook her head. "No. Why would I be mad at you for catching my dog?"

He gave her an exasperated look.

"Because," he hissed. "People aren't supposed to pet service dogs. It distracts them from doing their job. A blind person like you ought to know that."

"But I'm not—Oh, yeah," she said. "Point taken."

"Okay, here he comes." The man winked. "Just pretend you weren't hitting on me."

Jennifer stiffened and drew back just as the security guard arrived.

"Excuse me," he said. "We don't allow dogs—"

He paused, seeing the harness and special blanket.

"Oh, sorry, ma'am. I didn't know he was yours."

"That's quite all right," Jennifer said, staring vacantly into space. "Apparently, you're not the only one who doesn't recognize a seeing-eye dog when he sees one."

She reached down and patted Boomer's head.

"Would you mind showing us back to our suite? I'm afraid we've gotten turned around."

As the guard took her arm, leading her back the way she'd come, Jennifer saw her Good Samaritan smile and wave.

CHAPTER 6

Jennifer sat in their motel room that night, swiping through the pictures she'd taken at the speedway and trying to decide which ones she should send to Stacy. Technically, she wasn't on the road yet, but she thought her admin would enjoy them and it would be good to get into the habit. Once she and Boomer were underway, she wanted to be able to do it automatically. After all, what good was an itinerary if you didn't keep it up-to-date?

When the security guard had returned them to their suite, Cal apologized for the distraction and urged her to get something from the buffet table, sparing Jennifer from a confrontation with Jason, the social media fanboy. There'd been just enough time for her to grab a sandwich before the drivers started their engines and the roar of forty-three stock cars sent everyone scrambling for their seats.

She and Cal sat in the front row, overlooking the starting line, while Boomer staked out a place by the window. Up on hind legs, his front paws braced against the lower sill, he'd watched the cars approach the rolling start like a bird dog waiting for a duck to fall. Then as the leaders passed the start-finish line and the whine of their engines shook the stadium, Boomer went crazy. Back and forth he ran along the window, "chasing" the cars down on the track in a barking frenzy. Cal's people seemed to have gotten as big a kick out of Boomer's antics as she had, but looking back Jennifer knew she'd been lucky that no one in the adjoining suites had complained about the noise. Daniels Shock Absorbers might be an important sponsor, but they'd still be in trouble if anyone found out that Boomer wasn't really a seeing-eye dog.

She swiped back to the video she'd taken of Boomer as he tried to follow the cars on the other side of the window, and smiled. Watching him leap and lunge, determined to catch the race cars as they zoomed by, it was hard to believe he was really sick. Maybe she'd send it to Stacy, she thought. It would give the poor girl something to laugh about when Jennifer's clients started bellowing on Monday morning. Adding it to the rest of the pictures, she hit "send" and reminded herself to thank Derek again for giving her his ticket. It had been a long time since she'd seen Boomer so energetic.

If only it had lasted, she thought, as she slipped the phone back into her purse. Instead, as the cars continued to whiz by, Boomer's bark had grown weaker and, a few laps later, he'd stopped running in pursuit as they passed. By the time the winner had crossed the finish line, he was lying on the floor at her feet.

Jennifer glanced down at her dog, softly snoring on the bed beside her, and bit her lip. He'd been so tired after the race that he could barely walk, and for the second time that day she'd been afraid that their cover would be blown. It had been risky enough having a seeing-eye dog that didn't pay attention; if she'd had to carry him back out to the limo, too, even her Good Samaritan wouldn't have been able to save her.

She reached over and picked up the sunglasses that

were sitting on the nightstand, wondering about the man who'd covered for them back at the speedway. Boomer had always been protective of her, and it often took a while for him to warm up to people he didn't know—especially men—so it surprised her when he'd run over to a stranger rather than taking off on his own. She was grateful that he had, of course. If the guy hadn't grabbed Boomer's harness when he did, the security guard might have spotted him first and they'd have been tossed out. Still, it had given her an odd feeling to see her boy take to someone else so quickly. Whoever the man at the stadium was, Boomer must have thought he was pretty special.

With the pictures sent off to Stacy, and Boomer sleeping soundly, it was time for Jennifer to get to work. She dragged her suitcase from the closet; took out the maps, guidebooks, and travel brochures she'd picked up at the Auto Club; and spread them out on the desk. Dr. Samuels said that Boomer had a month left, and she was determined not to waste it. First, they'd explore every historic landmark and scenic byway from Joliet to Santa Monica. Then, when they got to California, she'd promised Boomer that he could romp in the surf. She was going to plan this trip like she planned her projects at work, right down to the last detail. Every second would be filled with interesting things to do and every day would be better than the day before. They'd have fun, and lots of it! As she opened up the first map, she felt like a general devising a battle plan.

An hour later, though, Jennifer was exhausted, and she'd barely planned a thing. There were so many variables to consider, so many competing interests to juggle, that it was overwhelming. Even worse, she'd developed a crick in her neck, and eye strain was giving her a headache. This would be so much easier to do online, she thought, pushing the guidebooks aside.

Jennifer glanced longingly at her iPhone, wondering if

there were any important e-mails in her in-box. Her self-imposed prohibition against electronic media was going to be a tall order for someone as connected as she was; she could hardly even remember what she'd done before the Internet. Could she really go an entire month without it?

Yes, Jennifer told herself, feeling her spine stiffen. She owed Boomer that much, at least. A month free from the constant distraction of social media would be good for her, and there would be plenty of time to catch up with things once he was gone. She'd done enough for one night, she decided. She put everything back in her suitcase, got ready for bed, and crawled under the covers with the new book she'd bought to read on the trip. Halfway through the second chapter, she was fast asleep.

Jennifer woke up the next morning in a panic. She'd been dreaming she was back in college, trying and failing to get to a final exam. It was a familiar dream; she must have had it dozens of times over the years, but this time it was different. This time, she was confident she'd get there because Boomer was leading the way.

Then Boomer died and she was lost.

Gasping for breath, dread roiling her insides, she sat bolt upright and looked around. Light was streaming through a gap in the curtains. Was it morning already? Why hadn't Boomer woken her? He always got up before she did. She turned, saw him lying in the same place he'd been the night before, and felt her throat constrict. Was this it? Had the dream been some sort of omen?

She held her breath, waiting until she saw the rhythmic rise and fall of his side, then released it slowly. It had just been a bad dream, nothing more. Boomer was still with her, still sleeping peacefully by her side. She crept closer and gently set her ear against his side, hearing the steady, reassuring beat of his heart.

"Please don't leave me, Boomie," she whispered. "Not yet. I'm just not ready."

By the time Jennifer had showered and changed, Boomer was up and pacing the floor. Dream or no dream, he was ready for a walk. She put on his leash, and the two of them headed out to the dog park in back. While Boomer sniffed the relief area for inspiration, Jennifer flipped through a pamphlet called *Discovering the History of America's Mother Road.* She'd been planning to take him on a hike that morning, but after all the excitement they'd had at the speedway, she thought it might be better to just do some sightseeing.

"What do you think?" she said, as he circled a particularly promising spot on the yellowed grass. "We could view 'iconic examples of Dust Bowl–era architecture and memorials celebrating twentieth-century American car culture.'"

Boomer ignored her, busy as he was with the task at hand.

"How about 'a well-loved statue of Paul Bunyon,' or 'the Gemini Giant, pride of Wilmington, Illinois'? Could be fun."

Still no reaction.

"Or . . ." she said, putting the pamphlet aside. "I could just roll the window down and let you stick your head out while I drive. What do you think? Should we go bye-bye?"

That got his attention. After a few purposeful seconds scuffing up the grass, Boomer began tugging on his leash, pulling her toward the truck.

Jennifer shook her head.

"No, Boomster, not yet. I meant after breakfast."

The look he turned on her was baleful. How *dare* she mention that magical phrase if they weren't going bye-bye right *now?*

"You're right," she said. "I shouldn't have said anything. But we still have to eat. What do you suggest?"

The desk clerk told them that the Joliet Route 66 Diner

served takeout breakfasts and it was only a few blocks away. As Jennifer walked back across the parking lot with two clamshell containers in her hands, Boomer waited impatiently in the truck, his nose wedged into the two-inch crack at the top of the window.

"Hold your horses," she said, setting the Styrofoam boxes on the ground. "I want to record this for posterity."

Jennifer lowered the tailgate and put Boomer in the back, then took out her phone, grabbed the boxes, and climbed in next to him. The dog's bottom quivered as he watched her pick up the first box and lift the lid.

"Who ordered the chicken-fried steak with scrambled eggs?" she said.

Boomer whined and pawed the truck's bed as if to say his patience was wearing thin. Jennifer nodded and changed the setting on her phone to video.

"I asked them to cut it into small pieces," she said. "But that doesn't mean you can just snarf it down."

She set the box down in front of him and hit the "record" button, trying not to laugh as Boomer devoured the food like he hadn't eaten in days. Scrambled eggs and bite-sized pieces of breaded beef were sucked up like dirt in a vacuum cleaner; Boomer's whiskers had so much gravy on them he looked like he'd grown a mustache. When the show was over, Jennifer set the phone aside and picked up the second box. That was another video she'd have to send to Stacy, she thought. Nothing like watching a dog slurp up an entire breakfast to give you the giggles.

"Pardon me," she said, unwrapping her plastic fork, "whilst I savor my own repast."

While Boomer snuffled around, looking for any overlooked morsels, Jennifer dug into her blueberry pancakes. It wasn't long, though, before two things became apparent. First, although they were delicious, there were way too many pancakes for her to finish, and second, they would not go to waste.

Jennifer set down her plastic fork. "Want to finish these up?"

Boomer, who had been following every bite that went into her mouth, needed no encouragement, and it wasn't long before Jennifer's box, too, was spotless.

"Nothing like a hearty breakfast to start the day, huh?"

She took out a package of baby wipes, cleaned the last of the gravy from his face and paws, and returned Boomer to the backseat while she discarded their trash. Then she cracked open the passenger's side window, strapped Boomer into his harness, and started down the road.

"Look out, world," she said. "Here comes Boomer!"

CHAPTER 7

There are few things more exhilarating than a NASCAR race. As the drivers approach their rolling start, the rumble of forty-three engines shakes the ground, touching something primitive in the human mind. Close your eyes and you could be standing in the middle of a buffalo stampede.

—"Gentlewoman, Start Your Engine,"
by Nathan Koslow, staff reporter

Rudy Koslow might have been two thousand miles away, but his irritation was coming through the telephone loud and clear.

"Route 66? What the heck are you thinking? It'll take you twice as long to get my car out here that way."

Nathan was working on his article for the *Trib,* typing away at the narrow desk in his motel room while he listened to his brother rant. He'd known this was going to happen, which was why he hadn't bothered telling Rudy about the change of plans before leaving Chicago. So it took him a little longer to get out to LA. What difference did it make?

"It's the deal I made with my editor," he said. "I send her travel articles on the way out there and she doesn't hire someone to take my job while I'm gone."

"Seriously? Nate, I don't know why you're still working for those people. First they take away your column and now they're making you scrounge for work. Who needs that kinda crap?"

"It was a business decision; times are tough."

"Maybe in Chi-Town they are, but not out here in Cali. Listen, I've got a script that needs a page one rewrite: *Vampire Sluts from Mars*. It could be your first screen credit. What do you think?"

"That's okay," Nathan said, rereading the last line of type. "I'm good."

"No, you're not. You've been moping around ever since Sophie dumped you."

"How would you know?"

"Are you kidding? Every time I get a call from the family, it's 'Nate's depressed,' and 'He looks so sad.' Blah-blah-blah. I'm sick of it."

"Uh-huh." Nathan deleted the word "primal" and replaced it with "primitive." "Tell them to mind their own business."

"No, *you* tell them," Rudy said. "I've got a movie to shoot."

Nathan glanced at the time: ten forty. Checkout time was eleven, and he had to get his article sent off to Julia before he left. He'd spent the night before writing about the trip to Chicagoland Speedway, but it still needed a little polish—something that wouldn't get done as long as he was stuck on the phone, talking to his brother.

"Look, I don't like this any better than you do," he said. "You asked me to drive the car out there and this was the only way I could get the time off. My boss says Route 66 is hot right now, so that's what I'm writing about. Besides, we're only talking about a few days."

Rudy wasn't buying it.

"There's tons of stuff along the Interstate. Why can't you write about that?"

Nathan shrugged and almost dropped the phone. He

couldn't believe he was defending this miserable assignment to his brother. Oh, the irony.

"The stuff along the Interstate is all the same," he said. "Fast-food joints, gas stations, and cheap motels."

"You're telling me Route 66 doesn't have any of those?"

"No, I'm telling you they're different—older, more authentic."

Rudy snorted, clearly unconvinced.

"Okay, so when *will* you get here?"

"Depends on what condition the roads are in and what I find along the way. Eight, maybe ten days."

"*Ten days?* Geez, I thought you were going to save me some money. Now I gotta pay for a bunch of extra nights in a motel?"

"No, no." Nathan stopped typing and took the phone in his hand. "That's the upside of this whole thing. Since technically I'm on the job, I can expense the trip. I'll be showing up later, sure, but it won't cost you a dime."

His words had the desired effect. When he realized that his good deal had just gotten even sweeter, Rudy's fury suddenly vanished. Getting his Mustang a little later and a lot cheaper suited him just fine.

"All right," he said. "Go write some stuff for your editor, and call me as soon as you know when you'll be here."

"Thanks, bro."

"But listen, that road's pretty old so be careful; it could be dangerous. I don't want my car getting dinged."

"Got it. Fine. Good-bye."

Nathan hung up and tried to clear his head for the final push. Only a couple of paragraphs to go, and he'd shoot this thing off. He just needed to get into the zone. If he could just focus on the words in front of him, he thought, the rest of the world would fade into the background. The lost column, his lousy personal life, even his family's concern about his low mood could be shut out through the simple process of putting one word after another on the page. Whatever issues he had at the moment, he'd deal with them the same way he always dealt with the problems in his life: Ignore them until they went away. That's what Sophie had done, hadn't she?

It had been a long time since Nathan had been to a NASCAR race, and he'd almost forgotten what a thrill it was. He wanted to convey to his readers how the raw power of the cars vying for position on the track stirred the crowd and made the atmosphere crackle with emotional energy. It wasn't just about seeing how fast a bunch of high-octane cars could go around a banked oval; there were strategies involved, grudge matches to settle, and personal rivalries to contest. For the drivers and their teams, the stakes were astronomically high. A win could mean endorsements worth millions; a loss might snatch those millions away. Sitting in the stadium, watching the cars as they battled toward the finish line, he'd felt that. Nathan wanted his readers to feel it, too.

Satisfied at last with his story, he wrote a quick e-mail to Julia, reminding her what a good turn he'd done filling in for Morty, and sent it as an attachment. He'd kept up his end of the bargain; now it was up to the guys in the Sports section whether to use it or not. He hoped they would, of course. Nathan took pride in his work and hated it when anything he'd written had to be scrapped, but there was always another story out there. The truth was, since losing his regular column, he'd been pretty much indifferent to the fate of anything else he wrote.

It had been a pretty heady experience, getting his own byline. Having his own column gave him a chance to stand out from the crowd. It was a reflection of his personality, a statement of how he saw the world. Was it possible he'd gone too far poking fun at the high and mighty? Sure, but that was the point, wasn't it? Controversy sold newspapers. Besides, some people deserved to be taken down a notch.

He stood up and started throwing his stuff back into the duffel bag. It was a cheap motel, not one with the kind of charm and history he'd be writing about on this trip. Julia might have been willing to pay for his accommodations, but that didn't mean he'd be staying at the Ritz. The way Nathan figured it, the per diem she'd allowed him would barely cover two meals a day. Even so, he was happy to help his brother out and it would be good to get out of the city for a while. The last few months, his life had been locked in a routine he couldn't seem to break out of. Most days it was just get up, go to work, come home, watch sports on the tube, and go to bed. It felt as if he were walking through life on a treadmill.

As he zipped the duffel closed, grabbed his keys, and headed out the door, Nathan could almost hear his old man telling him to stop sniveling and get over it. He still had a job, after all; still wrote stories that people enjoyed, or said they did; still had a decent place to live and even a few friends—though fewer, now that Sophie was gone. Was he depressed? Maybe, but so what? Join the club.

He threw his duffel into the Mustang, jumped inside, and heard the tires squeal as he peeled out of the parking lot. The problem, he thought, was that he was thirty-five years old and the life he'd always imagined his thirty-five-year-old self living was still nowhere in sight. Big stories were expensive to cover, and budgets were tight. There were no mysteries to solve anymore; no clandestine meetings in darkened car parks à la Woodward and Bernstein; no feeling that you were doing anything at all besides selling entertainment and ad space to an increasingly indifferent public. With very few exceptions, the life of a newspaper reporter had become a soul-sapping grind; most days they just handed out assignments and you completed yours without much enthusiasm.

The corner of Nathan's mouth quirked up. He had gotten a peek at one mystery recently: the blind woman at the speedway. Or rather, the woman with the phony guide dog who was pretending to be blind. What was her story? he wondered. At the time, he'd supposed she just wanted to get her dog inside, but he'd never heard of a dog that enjoyed watching NASCAR. Maybe if the security guard hadn't shown up when he did, Nathan could have gotten a chance to talk to her and find out. His reporter's instincts told him there might be a very interesting story there.

Yeah, right, his inner voice said. *Like that was all you cared about. What are you, a monk now? You meet a beautiful woman and all you can think about is whether or not she's got an interesting story. Come on, who are you trying to kid?*

Nathan frowned. He hated being reminded that his love life stunk, even if he was the one doing the reminding. He'd always been able to bounce back quickly when a relationship ended, but losing Sophie had knocked him back on his heels. At the time, he hadn't really cared all that much. The *Trib* had just eighty-sixed his column, and Nathan was too busy trying to recover from that deathblow to deal with any problems there'd been between the two of them. When Sophie finally called it quits, he told himself he'd get over it, that he just needed some time, but it had been almost a year now and he still wasn't back in the game.

The clouds parted as he left the city limits, and Nathan smiled. What was he worried about? He had a hot car, perfect weather, and miles of open road ahead of him. As the Mustang picked up speed, the sunlight dazzled, making the sapphire-blue finish gleam. Now, he thought, all he needed were some new sunglasses.

CHAPTER 8

A drive along Route 66 is a trip back to a time when American power was in its ascendancy. We were a newer nation then, rich beyond imagining, and we wanted the world to know it. The Appian Way was in ruins, we had the Mother Road; the horses of the Light Brigade had been buried at Balaclava, we had horses made of steel; the Colossus of Rhodes was a faded memory, we would build our own giant men.

—"They May Be Giants,"
by Nathan Koslow, staff reporter

It was a beautiful day to be out on the road. As Jennifer drove southeast from Joliet, freshly mown fields replaced the concrete, brick, and steel of the city, and the depthless blue sky grew wider, creating the illusion that they'd left the ground and become airborne. She stole a glance at Boomer, who was resting his chin on the edge of the window, his tongue lolling, and felt a pang. He hadn't been interested in anything they'd seen so far that day.

Their first stop had been in Wilmington to see the Gemini Giant. Jennifer, who'd grown up listening to her grandfather's stories about the space race, thought that the pictures she'd seen of the thirty-foot statue were charming. She'd been certain that Boomer would love it. Seeing it in person, though, had been a disappointment. Not only did the Giant's silver helmet look more like a welder's mask than anything from NASA, but the pint-sized rocket in his hands could have easily passed for a torpedo. Even worse, Boomer had all but ignored it. After snuffling in the grass at the statue's feet, indifferent to the giant man staring down at him, he began tugging at his leash, eager to get back into the truck. Jennifer took a couple of quick photos for Stacy, and the two of them drove off.

Another big item on her list—the Paul Bunyon statue in Atlanta—was also a bust, and when Boomer lifted his leg to pee against the giant man's foot, Jennifer had begun to panic. Of course he didn't like the statues, she thought. What kind of person takes a dog to see a couple of big plastic men? Sure, they were interesting in a kitschy, old-fashioned way, but since when did a dog care about aesthetics? Maybe if they'd been carved out of butter like that cow at the Iowa State Fair, then yeah, but for the moment there was nothing about them that a dog could get excited about. From Boomer's perspective, Paul Bunyon's enormous legs might as well have been a pair of blue telephone poles. After a quick stop at a nearby dog park, they'd gotten back on the road.

Jennifer wished she'd been able to make better plans before they left home. It had been such a shock when she found out how little time Boomer had left that she'd just decided to throw caution to the wind and trust that she could figure things out along the way. Now, in hindsight, she was realizing that the things she found charming or memorable held little attraction for a four-legged animal. What if they never found anything that Boomer liked? Would the entire cross-country trip turn out to be nothing more than an extended car ride?

"Okay, smart guy," she said. "What do *you* want to do?"

Boomer lifted his chin and looked around for a moment, then glanced over at her and licked his chops.

"*Already?* I'm still full from breakfast."

He swallowed and gave her a significant look.

"All right," she said. "I guess I shouldn't have asked if I didn't want to know the answer. But after that, we're going to walk off some calories, Mister. I can't afford to buy a new wardrobe."

And before that, she thought, checking her dashboard, she needed to get some gas.

Generally speaking, Nathan enjoyed doing research. Back when he'd had his column, following leads and tracking down people who, with the right incentive, could be persuaded to divulge incriminating information was a rush, like being a con man without the possibility of serving any jail time. But sitting in the Historical Preservation Society's cramped, airless office that morning was excruciating. The docent, Mabel, had been droning on about the history of Route 66 for almost an hour, and Nathan was no closer to uncovering an interesting detail than he'd been when he walked through the door. The only rush he was looking forward to would be the one that swept him back outside.

It wasn't that he didn't appreciate the effort. The more she talked, in fact, the more Nathan suspected that Mabel herself would make a more interesting story than the information she was imparting. Plump and apple-cheeked, with pale auburn tresses swept up in a bun and made stiff with a generous application of hair spray, she seemed like the quintessential Midwestern farm wife: sturdy, devout, and nononsense. Try as he might, though, he couldn't steer the topic onto anything of a personal nature.

Mabel got up and went looking for the file of surveyor's reports that they kept in the back room, and Nathan checked his watch, stifling a yawn. This interview had already been both too much and not enough, he thought. Too much technical detail and not enough of the human drama that made for an entertaining article. Rather than waste any more of the woman's time, he decided to cut things short. When she returned with a three-inch-thick file in her hands, he stood up.

"This has been great, Mabel, but I think I've taken up enough of your time for one day. I'd better let you get back to work."

The docent's smile flickered, but she was savvy enough to know when her audience had had enough. There was no sense in beating a dead horse.

"Of course," she said. "You've probably got a lot more places you want to check out. Can I get you anything before you go? We've got pop in the fridge."

"No, thanks. I'm fine."

"All right, then, but if you have any more questions, don't hesitate to call. We're always happy to help."

Nathan felt like a reprieved convict as he got back in the car and checked the GPS for a gas station nearby. The Mustang was not only a gas-guzzler, but judging from the spots it had left in the motel parking lot that morning, it was leaking more oil than his *babcia*'s potato pancakes. If, as he suspected, the car had a leak in its head gasket, Rudy was going to hit the roof. He'd better hurry up and write some good stuff for Julia, or the entire trip was going to be a disaster.

Of course, it didn't help that he was starting to obsess about the woman at the speedway. Or rather, the mystery of what she'd been doing there. Why had she gone to all that trouble—the limo, the dog harness, the dark glasses—just to get her dog into a NASCAR race? Had she done it on a dare? It did seem more like a prank than anything else. Or maybe it was a test of some sort, a way to check and see if the security guards were on their toes. Like a puzzle he couldn't solve, the problem kept nagging at him whenever his mind wandered. What was it about her, he wondered, that had captured his imagination?

Was she good-looking? Sure, in a prim, I'm-so-perfect

way, but the hair, the clothes, the makeup? Definitely not his type. Women like that were too high maintenance, too controlling to be much fun. Take her out a few times, and the next thing you know, she'd be buying you a day planner and organizing your sock drawer. He'd take a blowsy blonde with less on the ball than she had in her bra over that any day.

So, if it wasn't the woman he was obsessing about, maybe it was her dog. Nathan smiled. He'd been standing outside the press area when Boomer came bounding over. Seeing the wayward retriever running toward him, his first thought had been that it was Dobry, and as he bent down and embraced the velvety golden coat, he'd felt a lump in his throat. It was like taking a step back in time.

Being an Army brat hadn't been easy, and Nathan took the long separations from his father especially hard. As the jock of the family, Rudy spent most of his time either working out or on the field—football in autumn, track in the spring—and Nathan's sister, Amelia, had little time for her annoying little brother. With their budget tight, his mother had had to pick up part-time work whenever she could, and money worries and her husband's deployments left her short of both time and patience. Everyone agreed that Nathan needed a dog.

He named him Dobry, which is Polish for "kind," and the people at the shelter said he was a Lab/retriever mix, but the only thing that mattered to Nathan was that he was full to the brim with unconditional love for a lonely boy whose life up until then had been a series of dislocations. From the day they brought him home, Dobry had been his best friend.

Nathan saw a Shell station up ahead and put on his signal. Thinking about Dobry always left him feeling a little downcast. When his parents had split up, the only apartment his mother could afford didn't allow pets, and Dobry had to be sent back to the shelter. The sudden loss of his home, his father, and his best friend had cast Nathan into a pit of depression that manifested itself as behavior problems at school. He was a smart kid—smart enough to know that picking fights would only get him beaten up, anyway—so he'd turned his sharp tongue and quick wit into cutting remarks that provoked as many tears as laughter, earning his teachers' censure and a grudging respect from his peers. It had been the perfect training ground for the kind of biting commentary that his column at the *Trib* had been famous for. Maybe that was why he'd taken its loss so hard. Without it, Nathan felt defenseless.

He pulled up to the pump and got out of the car. So, he thought, it wasn't the blind woman he'd been obsessing about at all—just her dog, and only because it had reminded him of Dobry. Nathan ran his credit card through the pay slot and grabbed the nozzle. Now that the mystery was solved, he felt almost giddy with relief. He had enough trouble in his life without mooning over some stuck-up princess.

As he removed the gas cap, he heard footsteps approach and stop next to the car.

"Hello, there," a woman said. "Remember me?"

Nathan looked up and nearly dropped the nozzle. It was her, the woman from the speedway, looking like a Midwestern farm girl in a chambray shirt, jeans, and work boots. Her auburn hair was pulled back into a haphazard ponytail, and a few stray tendrils had pulled loose, framing her bare face like a nimbus. The change from the day before was so complete that he might not even have recognized her if it hadn't been for those long legs. Nathan stood just over six feet, and the two of them were standing eye to eye.

"I was just thinking about you," he said, and winced. "Sorry. That didn't come out right."

"That's okay." She laughed. "It's not every day you witness a miracle, right?"

He stuck the nozzle into the gas tank and turned on the pump.

More often than you'd think, apparently.

"I'm sorry to come charging over here like this, but I didn't get a chance to thank you for rescuing me at the speedway yesterday. We would have been kicked out if you hadn't helped with that security guard."

Nathan nodded, trying not to stare. Without the makeup and the designer duds, there was a delicacy about the woman that was breathtaking. He'd thought she was good-looking before. Now she was stunning.

"No problem," he said, trying to sound as if rescuing damsels in distress was an everyday occurrence. "I take it you and Boomer got back to your suite okay."

"Yes. The escape actually helped me get out of a—Hey, you remembered his name."

"Of course. I'd remember yours, too, if you'd told me."

"I'm sorry," she said, and stuck out her hand. "Jennifer Westbrook."

He wiped his hand down his pants leg before offering it. Jennifer's grip was firm, businesslike.

"Nathan Koslow. Nice to meet you."

She was staring at the Mustang, obviously impressed. So, Rudy had been right about the sports car, Nathan thought. Too bad they weren't in Chicago. He might have screwed up his courage and asked her out for a drink.

"Did you stay in Joliet last night?" she said.

"I did."

"I thought so. When we were at breakfast this morning, I saw your car in the motel parking lot next door."

He cringed, thinking about the fleabag motel where he'd spent the night.

"Yep," he said. "That was me."

The pump shut off. Nathan hung the nozzle back up and replaced the gas cap.

So much for first impressions.

"Your sunglasses are in my truck," she said. "You want

to say hi to Boomer before you go? I'm sure he'd like to see you again."

"Sure, I'd like that."

Jennifer looked around at the other cars.

"We should probably clear out of here first. There's a dog park just down the road, if you'd like to meet us there." She hesitated, and a shadow crossed her face. "Don't expect too much, though. He's been kind of tired lately."

CHAPTER 9

Jennifer pulled into a parking spot and waited for Nathan to arrive. *Nathan Koslow,* she thought, frowning thoughtfully. Why did that name sound familiar? She met a lot of influential people in her job at Compton/Sellwood, but she didn't think he was one of them, and if he was someone she ought to know but couldn't place, she'd never let on. In her experience, most truly famous people were happy to be left alone; it was only the minor celebrities who hated to go unrecognized. Unless she could remember where she'd heard of him, it was probably best not to ask.

She saw the Mustang pull into the parking lot and reached back to untether Boomer's harness. A quick hello and then an easy walk might be best, under the circumstances. She grabbed his leash and walked around to the passenger side, expecting she'd have to coax him out. Instead, when she opened the door, Boomer leaped out of the truck and went barreling toward the Mustang. Before Jennifer could stop him, he'd launched himself into Nathan's arms. She stood there watching, dumbfounded. What had gotten into him all of a sudden?

"I thought you told me he was tired," Nathan laughed, dodging a lick to the mouth.

"He was," she said, hurrying over to attach his leash. "I guess all that resting on the drive out here must have helped."

Boomer leaned against Nathan's leg and stared up adoringly.

"Looks like you've made a friend," Jennifer said. "Care to join us on our walk?"

"Sure. Just let me lock up the car."

The park was busy that time of day. Mothers watching their children on the playground, joggers wearing earbuds and heart monitors, and businessmen on their lunch hour had all come out to enjoy the sunshine. While she waited for Nathan to return, Jennifer continued to rack her brain for where she'd heard his name before.

Nathan Koslow.

He wasn't a client—she'd have remembered that—nor was he someone from her former life. Maybe he worked at city hall, she thought. Every election seemed to usher in a batch of unfamiliar faces, and she could never keep them all straight. As he started back across the parking lot, Jennifer saw him glance at her black Toyota Tundra and raise an eyebrow.

"Is that thing yours?"

"Of course. Why wouldn't it be?"

"No reason," he said, swatting dog hairs from his shirt. "You just don't seem the type."

And what type was that? she wondered. She held out his sunglasses.

"Here, you don't want to forget these."

He slipped them on, and the three of them started down the path.

Even after being cooped up in the truck half the morning, Boomer was on his best behavior, staying close and gazing up from time to time at the two of them. The fresh air and sunshine felt good, and Jennifer felt her irritation begin to ease. Nathan Koslow wasn't the first person to comment on her choice of vehicle, after all, and Boomer seemed to be enjoying his company. A walk in the park might not be very special, but at least he wasn't begging to get back in the truck.

"Boomer usually tries to yank my arm off when we're out for a walk," she said. "He must like you."

"I like him, too. He reminds me of the dog I had as a boy."

"Really? What was his name?"

Nathan stared at the ground and shook his head. "It doesn't matter."

They came to the fenced-in area where dogs were allowed to run free. Nathan opened the gate, and the three of them stepped inside. A solitary white oak stood in the middle of the flat, grassy expanse, its massive crown of leaves already turning the distinctive brownish red of autumn, and acorns littered the ground. On their right were benches for people to sit down and relax.

"Looks like we've got the place to ourselves," he said.

"Yeah. Kind of surprising, considering what a nice day it is."

Jennifer removed Boomer's leash and lobbed the stick she'd picked up on the way there. The dog took off, caught the stick in midair, and brought it back, bypassing her outstretched hand at the last second and offering it to Nathan. After a brief game of keep-away, Nathan was able to wrestle it free. He drew his arm back and threw the stick again. It flew end over end, landing just inside the opposite fence.

"You should feel honored," Jennifer said as Boomer scrambled after it. "He doesn't usually like men. Or at least none of the ones I know."

Nathan took a seat next to her on the bench.

"He's obviously a very discriminating animal."

She smiled. "I've always thought so."

Boomer had lost his stick in the tall grass; Jennifer watched as he began a frantic search to recover it. Over at the playground, the happy squeals of delight had turned to wails of outrage. Someone had commandeered the slide.

"So," Nathan said, "I saw you at the speedway and you saw my car at the motel; now we're both here in Atlanta. What gives?"

Jennifer pursed her lips. Was this just an innocent question, she wondered, or was he angling for information? It would help if she could remember why his name sounded familiar. She could almost hear Stacy whispering a warning to her about serial killers.

Oh, don't be ridiculous.

"I'm on vacation," she said. "Boomer and I are taking Route 66 out to the coast."

He laughed. "Why, did your book club just read *On the Road?* Take the freeway; it's faster."

Jennifer felt her lips tighten. The sarcasm, coming on the heels of her own disappointment, felt like a rebuke. What business was it of his?

"It's not just about getting there *quickly,*" she said. "It's about appreciating the history, and the scenery, and the . . . the—"

"Broken asphalt, run-down buildings, cows?" He scoffed. "Come on. You're a little young to be nostalgic, aren't you?"

"I could ask you the same thing," she said coolly. "Since it looks like you're going the same way."

"Ah, but you see, I'm not on vacation. I'm getting paid to do this."

Jennifer turned away, pretending to watch Boomer as she absorbed this new piece of information. So, he was out here because of his job. Who did this guy work for, she wondered, the Department of Transportation? Public Works? If she didn't figure it out soon, it was going to drive her crazy.

Boomer came bounding back with the stick and started

teasing Nathan with it, pretending to give it up and then snatching it away again.

"So, what is it you do?" he said. "When you're not on vacation, that is."

He was awfully curious for someone she'd just met, Jennifer thought. Hadn't she read somewhere that Ted Bundy had seemed like a normal guy?

"Public relations."

Nathan threw the stick again, and Boomer took off.

"Oh, so you're a spin doctor."

"It's not the term I'd use," she said, watching as the dog went streaking away.

He smiled. "So tell me, what wonderful, historically significant things have you appreciated so far?"

After the spin-doctor comment, Jennifer wasn't sure she wanted to tell him. The truth was, most of what she and Boomer had been doing was pretty lame. Nevertheless, it seemed churlish not to answer.

"Lots of things," she said. "We ate at the Route 66 Diner, then we drove to Wilmington and saw the Gemini Giant—"

He grimaced. "What did you think of that? Disappointing, huh?"

"A little," she said, her teeth clenching. "We saw several covered bridges, too, and stopped at most of the scenic lookouts. Then we saw Paul Bunyon and now we're here."

"All of that just this morning?" Nathan whistled. "I'm tired just hearing about it."

Jennifer struggled to control her temper. Why was he being so snide? One act of kindness on his part hardly gave him the right to criticize what she was doing. When Boomer trotted back with the stick, she stepped forward and took it away.

"You know something? I think Boomer's had enough exercise for now. We'd better get going."

Nathan seemed nonplussed.

"Okay," he said. "I'll walk you back."

"No need," she said, forcing a smile. "I think I remember the way."

Boomer, however, was reluctant to leave.

Typical male, she thought as she snapped on his leash and started tugging him back out of the gate. He'd been showing off for his new pal, and now that she wanted to leave, he was sulking.

Jennifer gave Boomer the stick to carry, hoping to mollify him, but as they headed for the parking lot, he kept trying to turn around and go back, giving Nathan time to catch up with them.

"So, where are you heading to now?" he said, as they crossed the parking lot.

Jennifer closed her eyes and took a deep breath. Yes, he was annoying, but Nathan Koslow—whoever he was—had done her a good turn. She would not be rude, she would not be uncivil, but neither would she tell him anything more than good-bye. He had her thanks, he had his sunglasses—they were done.

"I don't know," she said, unlocking her truck. "I think we'll just wing it from here and see what happens."

She opened the back door and patted the seat encouragingly.

"Come on, Boomie. Drop the stick and get inside," she said. "We haven't got all day."

Boomer looked away. The stick stayed where it was.

"I said, drop the stick." Jennifer snatched it out of his mouth and tossed it aside.

"Maybe he's tired," Nathan said. "Here, let me help."

"No, don't do that," she said. "He can get in by himself."

"It's no trouble," he said, scooping Boomer into his arms.

Before Jennifer could stop him, Nathan had set her dog in the backseat and started securing his harness.

"If you're looking for something Boomer would enjoy, there's a fire hydrant museum about ten miles from here." He glanced back at her. "Twenty-two in a row and a fountain at each end. You should check it out."

She sighed. Just when she'd been ready to give this guy the heave-ho, he had to go and do something nice.

"Thanks. Maybe we will."

"There you go." Nathan stepped back and closed the door.

"I'm curious," Jennifer said. "How did you know about the fire hydrants? They weren't mentioned in any of my guidebooks."

"Oh, I'm full of travel info. It's what I'm doing these days."

As the penny finally dropped, Jennifer almost choked. *Nathan Koslow!* No wonder she hadn't figured it out sooner. She'd been thinking of him as the nice guy who'd helped her out at the speedway, not the *Trib*'s erstwhile attack dog. To read his columns, you'd think the man didn't have a heart.

"I just realized who you are," she said. "You write for the *Trib*. I used to read your column."

He nodded, but the smile had dimmed a bit.

"Thanks," he said. "It's always good to hear from a fan."

"Oh, I was never a fan," she said. "You've eviscerated more than one of my clients in the past."

Nathan shrugged. "Well, if I did, then they deserved it."

Jennifer wanted to wipe the smile off his face. Nathan Koslow had been a big deal around town before he started slinging mud at the wrong people. She'd be willing to bet that she wasn't the only one who'd breathed a sigh of relief when his column got pulled.

"No one deserves to have his public image manipulated like that," she snapped.

"Oh, but it's okay to manipulate it the way you do? Come on."

Jennifer was furious. Where did he get off comparing her job to the sort of snide, immature, muckraking that he'd engaged in? She didn't have to stand there and listen to this guy justifying his bad behavior. She yanked her door open and got into the driver's seat, but before she could shut the door, Nathan stepped forward and kept it from closing.

"Look, I'm sorry if I upset you," he said. "The fact is, it was nice seeing you again and I appreciate your returning my sunglasses. But it was my job to write those columns and I never went after people who were too weak or too poor to defend themselves—unlike your clients. You might think about that before you condemn me."

He stepped back then, and Jennifer slammed her door.

Boomer's nose was pressed against the glass, his eyes on Nathan as the truck took off. Nathan lifted his hand and waved good-bye, a cold lump of self-reproach settling in his stomach. He picked up Boomer's stick and threw it as hard as he could, then walked back to the Mustang. As he got into the front seat, he could hear Rudy's advice ringing in his ears.

Keep your smart mouth shut.

CHAPTER 10

Stacy sat at her desk, eating lunch and reviewing Jennifer's pictures on her computer, wondering how best to display them on the screen. If she was going to create a memorial page for Boomer, she told herself, it had to be really great. So far, though, the whole thing was turning out to be a lot harder than she'd expected.

The idea had come to her after Jennifer sent the video of Boomer eating breakfast. Seeing a dog inhale gravy-laden pieces of steak from a clamshell box was so funny that Stacy had watched it over and over, laughing harder each time. The stuff that went viral on the Internet wasn't nearly that good, she'd thought. Wouldn't it be fun to create a private page dedicated to Boomer so that Jennifer could enjoy it once he was gone?

Unfortunately, however, having an idea for a Web page and actually creating one were radically different things, with decisions to make every step of the way, and it hadn't taken long before Stacy was stumped. What should she call it? What template should she use for the background? How should the pictures be arranged, and which graphics, if any, should she include? As she took another bite of her sandwich, she felt her spirits plummet. Once again, it seemed as if her plans had outstripped her talent.

"Why the long face?"

She looked up and saw Derek Compton walking toward her desk. Stacy blanched. Was lunchtime over already? The truth was, she didn't know if using company property for something like this, even when she was on break, was okay. She set her sandwich aside and reached for the mouse, hoping to close the window before her boss could see what she was doing.

"Oh, you know," she said vaguely. "It's just this . . . thing I was trying to do."

"What thing?" He walked around behind her and took a look at the screen. "Hey, is that Jennifer's dog?"

"Boomer, yeah." Stacy gulped. "Jennifer promised to send me some pictures every day so I'd know where she was. You know, for safety's sake. Here, I'll just close this down—"

"Hold on." He leaned forward to get a better look. "These are good shots . . . great resolution. I wonder what kind of camera she used."

"Um, I think it was just her iPhone."

He nodded. "Mmm. What's the dog's name again?"

"Boomer."

Now that she knew she wasn't about to be chewed out, Stacy was happy to share her idea for the Web site. She pointed out a couple of her favorite pictures on the screen.

"That's him sitting in the limo on the way to the speedway and here he's standing in front of the Gemini Giant. She just sent that one a couple of minutes ago."

"Mmm-hmm." Compton pointed. "And these over here, are they GIFs?"

"Yeah," she said eagerly. "Want to see one? They're really funny."

The sight of Boomer slurping up his food made the boss

laugh even harder than she had. Stacy beamed, gratified that her instincts had been correct.

He stepped back and rubbed his chin thoughtfully.

"So, what is it you're trying to do with these?"

She felt her face redden, embarrassed to admit how flummoxed the attempt at building a Web site had left her. Derek Compton's media savvy was legendary. The man could probably create a prize-winning Web site in his sleep.

"Well," she said. "I thought it would be nice to make a Web page using all the pictures she's sending me. Something Jennifer would have to remember Boomer by once he's, you know, gone."

"A Web page, huh?" The man's frown deepened. "How far have you gotten? Have you picked a host for it yet? Do you have a domain name?"

Stacy shook her head. A domain name—argh! She felt like such an incompetent.

The elevator doors opened, and a few of the social media team members stepped out. Compton looked up at them and waved.

"Jason, you got a second? I want to ask you about something." He turned back to Stacy. "Have you thought about doing a Facebook page?"

She looked nervously from Compton to Jason and back again.

"Um, no, not really. I mean, I could . . . I guess." Her cheeks felt flushed. "To tell you the truth, I hadn't gotten that far."

Jason approached them, smiling broadly. He was a few years older than Stacy, but he was one of those people who had a really young face, and the way he talked sometimes made him seem a lot younger. They'd talked a few times in the break room, and she thought he was cute, but the only time he ever really flirted with her was when he needed a favor. Jennifer thought he spent too much time sucking up to the boss.

"'Sup?" he said.

Compton pointed to the computer screen. "Take a look at these pictures she's got and tell me what you think."

Jason walked around behind the desk and leaned in for a better look.

"Stacy, you know Jason, don't you?"

"Sure," she said, feeling like a trapped animal.

Compton grabbed the mouse and clicked on the GIF of Boomer eating his breakfast. As the steak and gravy flew, the two men guffawed.

"That's epic!" Jason squinted, examining the other photos on the screen. "Is that Jennifer Westbrook's dog?"

"Yeah. Apparently, she's been sending pictures to Stacy while she's on vacation."

"Uh-huh."

Jason took the mouse and clicked on one of the pictures to enlarge it.

"The resolution on these photos is insane." He looked up. "So, what's the plan?"

"A memorial page for Boomer. I'm thinking we do it as a Facebook page, manage it through the agency."

Stacy glanced at the remains of her sandwich, wishing the two of them would go away. The memorial page had been her idea, and they were talking as if she weren't there.

"I like it." Jason grinned. "Add in the backstory about the dying dog and it could be really impactful."

"My thoughts exactly," Compton said. "Listen, why don't you two put your heads together and see if we can't get this thing rolled out in the next couple of days?"

Stacy gasped. "That soon?"

She'd been thinking the memorial page would be something to show Jennifer when she got back from her trip, not now. It felt as if she were standing in front of a runaway train.

"Sure, why not?" Jason said. "This stuff is killer."

"But what about the rest of the pictures?" Stacy said. "If we do the Web page now, they won't be included."

"We'll add them as they come in. It'll keep the page current." He looked at the boss. "We need to jump on this. Once the dog kicks it, it's just old news."

Derek Compton nodded thoughtfully.

"I think Jason's got a point there, Stace, but it's your call. A private page is great, but getting Boomer's story out there could really help a lot of people who are in the same spot as Jennifer. As bad as losing her dog will be, it might make it easier if she could see how much he meant to other people."

Stacy bit her lip. She was starting to wish she'd never uploaded the photos in the first place. The point of doing a memorial page was to have it be private—a gift from her to Jennifer. Sure, the thought that Jennifer might love it and think it was worth publishing had been in the back of her mind, but that decision should be hers. And if Stacy agreed to let Jason help her with the memorial page, it wouldn't be just from her anymore, either. What had started out as a private exchange between the two of them would become a team effort.

"I don't know . . ."

"I'll tell you what," Compton said. "Why don't you send Jason the pictures you've gotten so far and we'll see what he and his team can do with them? If he comes back with something that knocks your socks off, great; we'll put it out there. If you're just not sure, you'll still have something to show Jennifer when she gets back. You'd like that, wouldn't you?"

"Yeah," she said, still feeling a flicker of unease. "But I should probably ask Jennifer about it first."

"Are you sure?" He seemed dismayed. "I thought you wanted it to be a surprise."

"Well, yeah. I did . . ."

"Then let's keep it that way," he said. "Trust me, no matter when this thing goes public, once Jennifer sees what a great job you did with it, she'll be thrilled."

Stacy nodded. What was she worrying about? The CEO of Compton/Sellwood had just offered to help her turn her idea into something a thousand times better than anything she could have done on her own. Before he walked over, she'd been ready to give up on the whole thing. How could she even think of turning down help from a professional? Besides, Jason wasn't going to just go off and make it public on his own; Stacy and Jennifer would still have the final say-so.

The more she thought about it, the more she was able to quiet the voice of caution in her head. This was exactly what she'd wanted. What could possibly go wrong?

"Okay," she said. "Let's do it."

"Excellent," Compton said, checking his watch. "In the meantime, lunchtime's over. Stacy, get those pictures to Jason so he can get started on it right away. And Jason, come by my office when you've made a first pass at it so we can talk about this idea some more."

CHAPTER 11

The engineer who designed the Old
Chain of Rocks Bridge started with a simple,
if challenging, goal: to build a roadway
across the Mississippi River, just north of
St. Louis, where it divides Illinois from Missouri. The reason for that is clear; the names
of those who decided it should span seven-
teen miles of rocky rapids are lost to history;
and the result is one of the world's most baf-
fling structures. Where else can you find a
mile-long span of steel and concrete with a
twenty-two-degree bend in the middle?

—"A Bridge Too Far,"
by Nathan Koslow, staff reporter

Dinner that night was beer and cheese fries eaten in a dark
corner of the Whoop-de-Doo bar in Troy, Illinois. Nathan
had been sharing them with a woman named Tiffany, whom
he strongly suspected was only sitting at his table because
she'd been impressed by Rudy's car. While he sat there getting quietly drunk, she'd filled the air with inanities, apparently unconcerned that he'd barely uttered a word since the
two of them walked in.

There'd been an e-mail message from Julia in his in-
box when he got to the motel; the *Trib* had decided not to
run his story about the speedway. She said it was due to an

ongoing turf war with the new Sports editor, but Nathan suspected it had more to do with his diminished stature at work. If Morty had written it as planned, would there still have been a problem? Julia had added that they might be still able to use the article as part of his Route 66 series if he could cut down on the racing sports information and punch up the wholesome family-entertainment angle, but it was probably just a sop to his bruised ego. Whatever.

He picked up his empty glass, frowned, and lurched painfully to his feet. The drive was killing him. His ears rang, his hands were numb, and the muscles in his back felt like they'd been beaten with a stick. Whoever had tuned the Mustang's suspension needed to have his head examined. If this kept up, Rudy would have to add physical therapy to the cost of having his car delivered.

Tiffany paused in her monologue and stared at him.

"Where you goin', Hon?"

"Getting another. You want somethin'?"

"Why don't you wait for the girl?" she said, looking around. "She'll be back in a minute."

He shook his head. "I need the exercise."

"Well, don't tire yourself out." She gave him a sly wink. "The night is still young."

The bartender gave him a skeptical look as he approached, and Nathan gave the man what he hoped would be a disarming smile. Sure, he looked a little shaky, but that was the Mustang's fault, and besides, his motel was only a couple of blocks away. Nathan could still drive with another drink in him. He just couldn't listen to Tiffany any longer without one.

"What'll you have?"

"The same." He set the glass down.

The man nodded, but made no move to pull another draft.

"What about your lady friend?"

Nathan glanced back at the table.

"She's not my lady friend."

Somewhere in the back, a timer dinged. The bartender held up his hand.

"Hold on a second."

As the man disappeared, Nathan slumped against the bar. His breath was stale, and his mouth felt like it had been stuffed with greasy, cheese-flavored cotton balls. Maybe he shouldn't have that beer, he thought. If he did, he might just do something stupid, like take Tiffany back to his motel room.

He glanced at the peroxide blonde sitting at his table and received a coquettish wave that made the cheese fries in his stomach congeal. He'd been enjoying watching her turn away the interested glances from other men in the bar in favor of sticking with him. Who cared if he was just basking in the unearned glow of his brother's car? Nathan hadn't gotten that much attention from a woman in a while.

But after listening to Tiffany's nonstop blather while she attacked his cheese fries with talon-like fingernails, his own interest had waned to the point where even getting lucky didn't sound all that great. Unfortunately, though, getting rid of her wouldn't be easy. The men who might have taken his place had found other interested parties, and if Nathan begged off, she was going to raise a stink. *Great,* he thought, that would make two women he'd pissed off that day.

Nathan opened his eyes and stared at the popcorn ceiling. He was lying on the bed in his motel room, a throbbing pain just behind his eyes. The place stank of mildew and stale cigarettes. He lifted himself onto one elbow and looked around. He was still wearing the clothes he'd had on the night before, and Tiffany was nowhere in sight. Whatever had transpired after that last beer, he had no memory of it. Never again, he swore. He didn't need that kind of trouble.

He sat up and waited until the room stopped spinning, then staggered into the bathroom to take a shower. The time was ticking away, and he still had work to do.

Hot water sluiced over his shoulders and down his back as Nathan waited for inspiration to strike. The agreement he'd made with Julia was starting to seem like a bad deal. He knew she was expecting him to entertain their readers with sightseeing tips and stories about the unending series of fascinating landmarks along Route 66, but it wasn't a tourist destination. It was more like a neglected museum with moldering exhibits spread out over miles of poorly maintained roadway. It might have been great in its heyday, but there was a reason the Interstate had made the Mother Road obsolete.

And there were other, more disturbing things about it, too. When the various segments that made up Route 66 were built, no thought had been given as to who or what was being destroyed in the process. That didn't make the road unique, of course, but it felt wrong to simply gloss over the facts so that readers wouldn't be discomfited. To give his editor the feel-good stories she wanted, Nathan would be ignoring some important questions that still echoed almost a century later. How do you separate the can-do spirit of the 1920s and '30s from the injustices of that era? Or the charm of tepee-shaped motels from the decimation of the native population? Could destroying the environment ever be justified in the name of progress?

Nathan turned off the water and grabbed a towel that was only slightly softer than a hair shirt. He knew what Julia would say. Railing about injustice and inequality was for the Op-Ed pages; people read the Life & Style section to get away from all that angst and hand wringing. His assignment was a series of travel articles, period. If the *Trib* had wanted his opinion, it wouldn't have canceled his column.

Now that he was finally clean, the smell inside the

motel room was making him nauseated. Nathan packed up his things, checked out, and drove to a bakery at the end of the block; their Wi-Fi was faster, and he could write as well there as he could in his motel room. He got himself a coffee and a bagel, found a table, and opened his laptop. As he looked over the notes he'd written the day before, though, his mind kept wandering back to Jennifer Westbrook.

Nathan still couldn't believe how quickly things between them had gone off the rails; he hadn't even had a chance to ask her about the seeing-eye-dog ruse at the speedway. One minute he was playing fetch with her dog, and the next minute she was slamming a truck door in his face. Even for him, that had to be some kind of record.

His fingers hovered over the keyboard. Maybe he'd just Google her, find out a little bit more about Jennifer Westbrook so he didn't have to keep speculating. Besides, a part of him was curious to see which one of her clients he'd blown the whistle on. Just telling her they'd gotten what they deserved sounded petty. If he'd known whom she was talking about, he'd have been able to give her chapter and verse as to why he'd called them out. Would it really matter if his next article for Julia was a little late? Chances were good that she wouldn't be using it anytime soon. He launched his browser and typed in *Jennifer Westbrook.*

The first two hits were paid ads for Compton/Sellwood, a PR firm that Nathan had a passing familiarity with. It was one of the smaller agencies in Chicago, but was known for keeping close tabs on its powerful political clients while maintaining tight control of their carefully cultivated image. The third hit was a link to a press release about the CLIO Awards and the next was a Wikipedia entry for Jennifer Marie Westbrook. He clicked on that one and started to read.

Born in Fulton, Illinois, to Wilfred and Ida Westbrook . . .

He'd been to Fulton once. It was a tiny town on the border with Iowa. One of the Quad Cities; economically depressed; lots of windmills. She probably grew up on a farm. He shouldn't have made that comment about her truck.

Crowned Miss Teen Illinois . . . Left college to pursue a modeling career . . .

That wasn't surprising. Not with those legs.

Married manager, Victor Ott . . .

Damn! Nathan grimaced, feeling his hopes begin to fade.

Acrimonious divorce . . . No children . . .

Okay, he was back in the running.

Named Ad Executive of the Year . . . Currently a senior account executive at Compton/Sellwood . . . Awards include . . .

His eyebrows shot up as he went down the list of honors and awards she'd won. Holy macaroni. This woman was waaaaay out of his league.

"Okay," he said, closing the browser. "Back to reality."

He spread his notes out on the table and set to work. Interviewing docents and visiting National Historic sites hadn't yielded much that he could build an article around, and he'd seen enough historic gas stations to last him a lifetime. How many more synonyms were there for "quaint"? The thought of going back and trying to wheedle some personal information out of Mabel was tempting, but he suspected the effort would prove fruitless. As strange as it seemed, not everyone in the world hungered for celebrity. That left the last place he'd visited the day before: the Old Chain of Rocks Bridge.

Two hours and four cups of coffee later, Nathan had a three-hundred-word article polished and ready to send to Julia. Once he added a few pictures, his editor would have more than enough to fill whatever spot she'd reserved for it. It wasn't until he took out his phone that he remembered: He hadn't taken any pictures of the bridge.

No matter; it wasn't far. He'd just swing by and snap a few photos on his way to the place he was visiting today: Purina Farms. After sitting in the Mustang for the last two days, it would be good to get out and stretch his legs for a while, and articles about pets were always a hit. Plus, with any luck he might run into Jennifer and Boomer there. Nathan still had some questions he'd like to ask her.

CHAPTER 12

Jennifer stood on the Old Chain of Rocks Bridge, holding fast to the guardrail as she and Boomer peered down at the turgid Mississippi. They'd just finished walking the entire length of the bridge and back—two miles—and it was time to take a break. Since leaving home, Boomer's energy level had been unpredictable. There were times, like yesterday at the dog park, when he romped and played like his old self, then others when it seemed that all he wanted to do was sleep. If they were going to make it all the way to the West Coast, she thought, they needed to pace themselves.

Boomer leaned forward, keeping an eye on the silvery shapes that wiggled just out of reach. The turbulent, oxygen-rich tailwater teemed with game fish that time of year. Jennifer pointed them out as they rose to the surface.

"These are mostly walleye," she said. "Oh, but that's a blue-gill . . . and there's a catfish. I used to catch those when I was a kid. We ate a lot of catfish back then."

Poor food.

That's what the kids at school called catfish: bottom-feeders, food for poor people. Even now, with all the money and success she'd earned, it still nettled. *The things that happen to you when you're young just seem to ripple out,* she thought, *touching everything else in your life.* If she hadn't been so ashamed of being poor back then, maybe her life would have been different. She might not have fallen under Vic's spell, or been afraid to take time off work to be with her dog, or say no to a client with questionable ethics.

Boomer reached his paw over the wooden trestle and tried to scoop a fish from the water.

"No, Boomie. Those fish are too slippery for you to catch. Come on," she said. "Let's go sit down."

It was peaceful there, and quiet. The wind had started to pick up, creating a tiny twister of fallen leaves that danced along the riverbank. Jennifer found a bench behind a windbreak of black haw and chokecherry and took a seat. Boomer jumped up beside her and put his head in her lap. She started stroking his fur, absently picking out the bits of leaf and twig that seemed to attach themselves by magic whenever he was out-of-doors. They had the place to themselves; the only sounds she heard were the water lapping against the shore and the soft rustling of the leaves. She should be enjoying herself, Jennifer thought. Instead, she was racking her brain for something to do.

Maybe they should just turn around and go back, she thought. Was there really anything along Route 66 that they couldn't see or do closer to home? Every time Boomer turned his nose up at something she thought he'd enjoy, Jennifer felt guilty, the voice in her head telling her that she should have known that if she'd spent more time getting to know Boomer and less at the office, he'd be having a good time now instead of lolling in the backseat while she dragged him from place to place. Then again, maybe she was just incompetent. Look at Nathan Koslow. He'd thought of something fun for Boomer to do, and he didn't even own a dog.

Jennifer winced, thinking about the way she'd acted

back at the park. It wasn't like her to be so rude to someone, even someone as deserving as he was. Nathan Koslow had never done anything to hurt her personally, after all. In fact, the opposite was true. Not only had he saved her at the speedway, he'd passed along a tip that had made for a special outing for her dog. Perhaps she was just angry with him for pointing out something that she'd been trying to ignore for a long time: Those clients he'd trashed *had* gotten what they deserved.

She heard a car engine and the sound of gravel crunching in the parking lot. Then a car door opened and shut. With the bushes behind her, she couldn't see who it was, but the heavy footsteps approaching sounded like a man's. Boomer's head came up, and she felt the fur along his backbone stiffen. Jennifer swallowed, trying not to think about the two girls who'd been raped and murdered on the bridge years before, their bodies dumped into the river. Suddenly, the solitude seemed ominous, threatening. Having Boomer with her wasn't the same as knowing there were human witnesses in the area.

Boomer jumped down from the bench and sniffed the air as the footsteps came closer. It was nothing, she told herself, probably just someone who wanted to see the bridge, but her brain had already switched into survival mode. Jennifer reached into her purse, grabbed her keys, and took out her phone. If attacked, she would use the keys as a weapon, take a picture of her assailant, and call for help.

This is silly, she told herself, but she still didn't put them away.

Then Boomer gave two short barks, and before she could grab him, he took off, tearing through the bushes. Jennifer heard the footsteps stop, then a scuffle, and a man's voice.

"Hey, Boomie. Whatcha doing here?"

As Nathan came around the corner, Jennifer collapsed back onto the bench.

"Oh. It's you."

"Yep," he said. "Just me."

Boomer was dancing around, beating Nathan with his tail and nipping at his outstretched hands.

Jennifer scowled. "I didn't say 'just' you."

"You didn't have to." He pointed. "What have you got there? Pepper spray?"

She held out her hands.

"Keys? Cell phone? Good thinking," he said. "I'm scared already."

As Jennifer put them back in her purse, Nathan looked around.

"I see you two are enjoying another outing full of fun and excitement. Did you walk all the way to the end of the bridge and back? That's almost too much mirth and merriment for just one day."

Jennifer shook her head. And there she was, feeling guilty about being rude to the guy. Why did he have to be so annoying?

"What are you doing here?"

Nathan showed her his phone.

"Taking pictures for the paper. Sorry if I bothered you."

He headed toward the bridge, Boomer tagging along at his heels, and started walking along the embankment, looking for a way down the steep slope to the shore below. Jennifer looked on resentfully. What was it about this guy that her dog found so appealing? It was like watching a canine version of the Pied Piper.

"How was the hydrant museum?"

"Oh, uh, it was great," Jennifer said.

She'd been so rattled by his sudden appearance that she'd forgotten to thank him for the tip.

"There were a couple of other dogs there, too. Thanks for telling us about it."

Nathan took a tentative step over the edge and started down toward the water. Boomer made a few halfhearted attempts to follow, then gave up and began pacing the area, whining fretfully. Jennifer walked over to the edge, put his leash back on, and the two of them watched Nathan continue his descent.

"I'm sorry about what I said yesterday. At the park, I mean. You're right; we were both just doing our jobs."

"Yeah, well, I lost mine," he said. "Tell your clients they can sleep peacefully now."

The embankment started to give way, releasing a small avalanche of dirt and gravel. As Nathan began to slide, Jennifer shortened the leash to keep Boomer from scrambling down after him.

"I thought about what you said. Maybe they did deserve what you wrote about them."

Nathan grabbed for a handhold to steady himself.

"I guess you earned your pay, then, huh?"

Jennifer pursed her lips. Why the nasty retorts? Couldn't he see that she was trying to apologize?

"I *said* I was sorry."

"I'm sure you were," he said, struggling to stay upright.

"Then why are you being such a *jerk?*"

Nathan had finally reached the firmer ground at the bottom of the bank. He took a picture of the bridge, then looked up at her thoughtfully.

"I suppose it's because that's what I always do when I'm nervous."

Jennifer drew back. "Why are you nervous?"

"Because," he said as he started back up the embankment. "You're a smart . . . successful . . . woman"—he grabbed a tree root and hauled himself up over the edge—"who is so much better looking than I am that I'm not even sure we're part of the same species."

The baldly self-deprecating comment made Jennifer laugh. It seemed that Nathan Koslow was not only a scathing commentator, he was an equally unsparing self-critic.

Boomer was greeting Nathan's return with a kind of

joyful scolding, grizzling softly as he nudged him away from the precipice.

"I think you've charmed my dog," she said.

He smiled. "Just your dog?"

"Yes." Jennifer hesitated. "For now."

"So," Nathan said, patting Boomer's side. "Where are you two going today?"

She shrugged. "Honestly, I think we're just going to head home."

"No, don't do that. Don't be a quitter."

"Why not? Boomer's bored and I'm fresh out of ideas." She felt her chin dimple. "You were right. This whole plan to drive Route 66 was just stupid."

"No, it wasn't," he said. "Come on, I'll prove it to you."

Purina Farms was having its annual Canine Games, and they were everything that Jennifer had been looking for. There were farm animals for Boomer to sniff, dogs for him to greet, and interactive dog food exhibits where he could sample and vote for his favorite flavor of kibble. He romped through an obstacle course, met Chops the pig, and got squirted in the face when he stepped too close to a milking demonstration. For a dog who'd spent his entire life in a three-bedroom town house, it was heaven.

"This was great," Jennifer said as they left the event center. "Thanks again for telling us about it."

Nathan's face fell. "That almost sounds like you're leaving."

"We are. I think Boomer's had enough for one day."

"But there's still so much to do." He looked around at the acres of corrals and buildings yet to be explored. "I thought this was what you were looking for."

"It was," she said. "And I really appreciate your bringing us here. But I want to go before he gets too tired."

They both glanced down at Boomer, who smiled up at them, still wearing the remains of his milky mustache.

"He doesn't look tired to me," Nathan said. "Can't you guys at least stay for the costume contest?"

Jennifer hesitated. She knew what he must think. After complaining that there was nothing exciting to do, she was leaving the best place they'd found so far. If Nathan knew how sick Boomer was, he'd probably understand, but she could barely stand to think about it herself, much less tell someone else. It was what she'd always done when bad things happened.

We aren't poor, I'm just not hungry. Dad isn't dead, he's just sleeping. Vic didn't hit me, it was just an accident.

Nathan looked at her quizzically, and Jennifer realized that he was still waiting for an answer. Maybe it was time to stop pretending, she thought. Maybe she could tell him about Boomer, and the world wouldn't end. For some reason she couldn't quite put her finger on, she thought he might just understand. She took a deep breath and forced herself to smile.

"How about lunch?"

They ordered hot dogs and chips at the concession stand and took a seat on a picnic bench. Boomer crawled under the table and started gnawing on one of the treats they'd bought him in the gift shop. Jennifer stared at her food, wanting to take a bite, but as she tried to find the words to talk about her dog's condition, her throat got tight and she was afraid she might choke. Nathan finished his first hot dog and started on another, apparently unfazed by her reticence. She licked her lips, absurdly grateful that he wasn't pressing her for details.

"We got some bad news before we left on our trip," she said. "In fact, it's pretty much the reason we're here."

He nodded and fished a potato chip out of his bag, saying nothing. It was as if he couldn't care less if she told him or not. Jennifer reminded herself that Nathan Koslow was used to interviewing reluctant subjects. No wonder he got people to talk to him, she thought. He was good at this.

"Anyway, the short story is, Boomer is dying. He has a heart condition that there's no cure for. The vet told me he had a month left and I thought—" Jennifer faltered, fighting to keep her voice steady. "I thought maybe if we could do some fun things in the time he has left, it would make up for all the times I left him alone while I was at work."

A tear spilled down her cheek, and she wiped it away.

"So, that's my story," she said. "What do you think?"

Nathan ate the last chip in the bag and crushed it between his hands, the savageness a stark contrast to his outward calm. He looked at her and shook his head.

"That sucks."

CHAPTER 13

Stacy sat at Derek Compton's computer, staring at the Facebook page that Jason and the social media team had created for Boomer. There was no question that the memorial page they'd come up with was way beyond anything she could have done herself; the graphics were amazing, and the pictures Jennifer had sent her had been cropped and edited professionally. But it looked more like one of the slick ad campaigns that Compton/Sellwood was famous for than the simple celebration of a dog's life that she'd envisioned. As the two men hovered, waiting to hear her reaction, she tried to think of something to say that wouldn't give offense.

"It's called *Boomer's Bucket List?*"

Jason nodded. "I think it pretty much says it all: Dying dog grabs for the brass ring one last time before he kicks it. My team worked on it all night. You like?"

"Yeah," she said, squirming in the oversized chair. "I guess so."

His eyes narrowed. "What do you mean, you guess so?"

"I don't know. It's just a little . . . different from what I thought it was going to be."

Stacy's hands felt clammy. The way Jason was glaring at her made her nervous. She glanced up at her boss, hoping he'd find the whole thing as over-the-top as she did. Instead, Derek Compton nodded approvingly.

"You and your team did a great job with this," he said. "I think she's just a little overwhelmed, aren't you, Stace?"

She swallowed, trying to ignore her misgivings. Criticizing something that someone else had made just for her would be really rude, she told herself. Without their help, the best she could have done would have been a bunch of photos with a few lame captions underneath, something she'd have been apologizing to Jennifer for the second she saw it. Just because *Boomer's Bucket List* wasn't exactly the way she'd imagined it, Stacy told herself, that didn't mean it had to change.

The two men were still waiting for a response.

"It's just so much better than I'd expected," she said. "I guess I don't know what to say."

With that, the tension in the room eased. Her okay had not only taken the edge off Jason's scowl, but it seemed to have given him carte blanche to expound on some of the site's more interesting features to the boss. Once again, Stacy found herself being forced into the background.

"There's a comment section for visitors who want to leave a message of support or share their own experiences, but for the time being we're limiting it to likes and shares on the content only."

"That's a good idea," Compton said. "We'll need to keep a tight rein on the content. I don't want anyone hijacking this thing."

"Agreed. As more pictures come in, Stacy can forward them to me and we'll get them cleaned up and published."

"Have we got a Twitter account set up yet?"

"I'm working on it."

While the two men talked over her, Stacy began scrolling down the page. It really was a cool Web site, and Boomer looked like he was having a good time. She hoped that when Jennifer looked back through all the photos, it would make losing him a little easier.

"Why is there an ad in here?"

Jason shot her an irritated look. "It's not an *ad*. Nobody's making any money off of this."

"It's just a way to remind people that our agency is the one managing the page," Derek Compton said. He gave Jason a significant look. "You know, maybe we could put a picture of Stacy somewhere on there, too. After all, the memorial page was her idea."

She gulped. Jennifer had never really given permission for anyone else to see her pictures. The only reason she'd even agreed to send them in the first place was because Stacy had convinced her that she'd be safer that way. Stacy was already feeling uneasy about the way this whole thing was turning out. If her name and face were on it, too, it'd look as if she'd been behind it 100 percent.

At least they hadn't made the page public yet, she told herself. Even if Jennifer was upset that her photos had been shared, once Stacy explained how inept she'd been and how much she'd wanted to do a really good memorial page for Boomer, she was sure that Jennifer would understand. You can't really blame a person for trying to do a good job, can you?

She shook her head. "That's okay. I don't really care if I get the credit."

"Are you sure?" Compton said. "We could get one of our photographers to take a nice glamour shot for you." He looked at Jason. "How hard would it be to add that?"

"It's doable," Jason said doubtfully. "But we'd have to take the page down while we did the update and it might scare off our followers. Changing a page isn't the same as just adding content."

"Wait a minute," Stacy said. "The page isn't live yet, is it?"

"Of course it is," Jason sneered. "You didn't think we were just going to sit on it, did you? This whole thing is going to have a very short shelf life."

"I suppose I should have mentioned it before." Compton gave her a guilty look. "I gave his team the okay last night."

Panic and remorse rose up in Stacy's throat, nearly choking her. Why had she ever shown them those pictures? All she'd wanted to do was to make something nice, something Jennifer could look back on when Boomer was gone and remember what a good time they'd had on their trip. Now all those private pictures were being used, not to memorialize Boomer, but to sell the Compton/Sellwood brand with the ads they were putting on his Web site. The two of them had used her idea as a tool to promote themselves. Did they even consider how it might impact either her or Jennifer?

She felt sick. What if Jennifer saw the page and hated it? What if she was angry with Stacy for showing her pictures to someone else? They'd always had a good relationship, almost like friends. How, Stacy asked herself, could she have put all that in jeopardy?

She had to get out of there. If she stayed in Compton's office for one more second, she was going to scream. She stood up abruptly and headed toward the door.

"I'd better get back to work. Thanks for showing this to me."

"Yeah," Jason said as he followed her out. "I need to go back to my office, too."

Stacy walked stiff legged back to her desk and started checking for phone messages, pointedly ignoring Jason. Now that they were out of Compton's office and the pressure to be accommodating was off, she was furious. How dare he? For someone who was so prickly about having his own ideas hijacked, he'd sure done his darnedest to hijack hers. As she reached for the phone, she wished that Jason would just go away. Hadn't he done enough to mess up her life already?

She looked up sharply. "Can I help you with something?"

Jason seemed oblivious to her hostile mood.

"Yeah, how soon can you forward the rest of those pictures to my team? We need to get our likes pumped up, pronto."

She felt her lips tighten. "I don't care how many likes the stupid page gets. You weren't supposed to make it public. I told you I just wanted it to be for Jennifer."

He looked abashed. "Then why did you want to build a Web page?"

"I didn't. I just wanted to, you know, do something . . ."

Stacy slumped a little in her chair. What *had* she been trying to do? Whatever it was, it seemed to have been lost somewhere along the way. She started out thinking she'd make a scrapbook, but that would have taken too much time, and she really wasn't a "crafty" sort of person. And after that, she'd figured, well, the pictures were already digitized, so why not make something that Jennifer could have on her computer, like a screen saver or something? But she'd had no idea how to do that, and besides, the GIFs were really funny and you couldn't really make those into a screen saver, could you?

So, yeah. Maybe she *had* been wanting to do a Web site. But it was supposed to be a gift, something personal that

Stacy could give to Jennifer as one friend to another, not a piece of clickbait on the Internet. Instead of memorializing Boomer's short life, Jason had exploited it. Stacy was ashamed that she'd ever told anyone else about it. She set her mouth in a firm line.

"I'm not giving you any more pictures," she said.

"What? Why not?"

"Because you already finished the Web page. You don't need any more."

"Are you kidding? People want to see something new when they come back. Content is king. A static page is a dead page."

"Fine," she snapped. "Boomer'll be dead soon, too. There's only so many more pictures that anyone will ever take of him. You might as well stop now."

Jason arched an eyebrow. "I'm not sure Mr. Compton's going to see it that way."

Maybe if he'd been nice, Stacy thought later, she might have backed down. Her job, after all, was to help make things at the agency work smoothly, taking care of the tedious details that the artists, designers, and ad executives didn't have time for. But if Jason Grant thought he could make her give him what he wanted by threatening to go to her boss, he had another thing coming. She knew how guys like Jason saw her. They thought she was a nobody—one of the little people who scurried around behind the scenes, as easy to hire as fire—someone of no importance. Well, that wasn't the way Jennifer saw her, and it wasn't the way Stacy was going to let herself be treated, either. She thrust out her chin and stood her ground.

"I. Don't. Care. I'm not giving you any more of *my* pictures. If you want some, you'll have to get them yourself."

She'd been braced for an outpouring of abuse. Instead, Jason stepped back and threw his hands up in surrender.

"You're right. Those pictures are yours." His smile was disarming. "Sorry. Guess I just lost my head. It's cool. No worries."

Stacy found herself groping for a response. This unexpected turnaround had thrown her off-balance. Had she misjudged the situation? she wondered. Maybe Jason wasn't such a bad guy after all.

"Thank you," she said. "I'm glad you understand. No hard feelings, right?"

"Absolutely," he said. "No hard feelings at all."

CHAPTER 14

The Ozarks are one of nature's most persistent optical illusions. As you drive west through Missouri, they seem to rise up around you, the small towns and modest cities along the route nestled in the rolling hills and valleys. But the Ozarks aren't mountains, and the road that carries you through them is actually at the bottom of a great rift that cuts through a high plateau. Unless you see it from the air, it's hard to reconcile the true nature of the phenomenon from the experience of being within it.

—"The Ozarks, Mother Nature's Op Art,"
by Nathan Koslow, staff reporter

Jennifer and Boomer spent the next day enjoying the sights as they made their way across Missouri. In the east, rivers crisscrossed the lowlands, some barely a trickle, others pockmarked with white water. Occasionally, they crossed one that was spanned by a covered wooden bridge, the humble, painted shelters harking back to a time when not only car travel, but life itself was slower, less hectic. Jennifer took a deep breath and loosened her grip on the steering wheel. With no e-mails to answer and no meetings to attend, the constant tension that she accepted as "normal" was finally easing. She'd needed this trip as much as Boomer had, she thought. She was glad she hadn't called it quits.

Telling Nathan about Boomer's diagnosis had been the right thing to do. Once he put away the quips and snappy comebacks, he was actually a thoughtful, sympathetic listener, and it was a relief to finally get it off her chest. He'd also helped ease her anxiety about trying to find fun things for Boomer to do by offering to use his own resources to put together a list of dog-friendly things along their route. They planned to meet up that night in Carthage and watch a double feature at the 66 Drive-In: *Beethoven* and *Beethoven's 2nd.* Not exactly highbrow entertainment, but she was tired of being stuck in her motel room every night, and Boomer might enjoy watching the dogs on the screen. Between now and then, Jennifer had promised to stop beating herself up and just enjoy having some low-key fun with her dog.

A few miles past Rolla, they stopped to play fetch and take a romp along the shore of the Gasconade River, where Boomer learned the difference between a Red-eared Slider and a snapping turtle. The painful lesson was short-lived, however, and it wasn't long before he was bounding through the water again, heedless of the wildlife that scuttled out of his way. Jennifer lay back on the riverbank and smiled. For the first time since leaving Dr. Samuels's office, she was enjoying the present instead of regretting the past. It was as if finally facing the truth had made it easier for her to accept it.

Boomer slogged up out of the water, dropped the stick beside her, and began shaking himself off. Jennifer squealed and turned away, raising her hands defensively as cold, silty river water went flying.

"No, Boomer! Stop!" she laughed.

Scrambling to her feet, Jennifer ran for the truck and grabbed one of the beach towels in back. When Boomer had finally finished shaking the water and slime from his coat, she threw the towel over him and rubbed him down.

When Boomer was as dry as a beach towel could make him, they got back in the truck and headed for Springfield. The softly rounded silhouettes of the Ozarks rose up on either side of them, blanketed in the reds and yellows of early autumn, and the crisp fall air was tinged with wood smoke. As the truck wended its way past still blue lakes and rushing streams, Jennifer turned on the heater. Boomer laid his head down on the seat and sighed contentedly. It wasn't long before he was sound asleep.

In Springfield, Jennifer stopped for gas and took Boomer for a walk at a nearby dog park. The days were getting noticeably shorter now, and the sun was nearing the horizon, but they were only about an hour away from Carthage, and for once they weren't in a rush to get to a motel. Knowing their destination ahead of time meant that Jennifer was able to call and make reservations, and it was a lucky thing she had. The woman on the phone told her she'd gotten the last room available that night.

As she pulled the truck back onto the highway, though, Jennifer felt a whisper of anxiety. Agreeing to see Nathan again had been a crazy impulse on her part, but was it really a good idea? Jennifer came from conservative Midwestern stock, and she prided herself on her levelheadedness; she wasn't the type to meet up with a stranger on a whim. Or at least, she told herself, she wasn't anymore. It had been a rash, impulsive action that led to her disastrous marriage to Vic, after all. She didn't want to make a mistake like that again.

But Nathan wasn't a total stranger; Jennifer knew him by reputation, and he'd been kind to her as well as to Boomer. In the end, his offer to help her find more dog-friendly places on their trip had simply been too good to pass up. Besides, she told herself, this wasn't a date. Nathan Koslow might be cute, but the teasing and smart comments got old quickly. If Jennifer had been looking at all, she'd want a man who was serious, someone mature. Nathan was more like an annoying kid brother than a potential boy-friend.

The Boots Court motel in Carthage was an authentic piece of Route 66 history. A white single-story building with a flat roof, rounded corners, and bright red awnings, it looked as if it had been made from giant Tic Tacs. As Jennifer got Boomer out of the truck, she took a quick survey of the parking lot. Nathan had told her he'd be there by mid-afternoon, and it was almost five thirty, but the blue Mustang was nowhere in sight.

At once, her good mood evaporated. She'd been counting on those dog-friendly tips to help get the two of them through the rest of their trip. What was she supposed to do now? She shouldn't have trusted him, Jennifer thought, as she grabbed their luggage. Hadn't living with Vic taught her anything? You give away your power to a man, and you end up helpless.

Boomer was still dozing on the backseat. She gave him a gentle shake and unlatched his harness.

"Come on, sleepy boy. You can finish your nap in the room."

Maybe it was a good thing that Nathan hadn't shown up, Jennifer told herself. She'd been having misgivings about meeting him there anyway. This way, she could just turn around and go home in the morning without having someone else try and talk her out of it. Nevertheless, as she walked through the door, she couldn't help feeling disappointed.

She gave her name at the front desk and signed the waiver promising to pay for any pet-related damage to the room. Jennifer wasn't worried. Boomer was fastidious about his elimination habits, and there'd been no chewing incidents since the Manolos. The only concern she had was keeping him from barking, but as long as she didn't leave him in the room by himself for too long, that wouldn't be a problem.

As the clerk stepped into the back room to get her motel key, Jennifer heard the front door open.

"Hey," Nathan said. "You made it!"

Torn between feelings of relief and aggravation, Jennifer said nothing. She was glad he'd made it there safely, glad, too, that she'd have help with her itinerary, but the revelation she'd had about misplaced trust still resonated. Was meeting him there asking for trouble?

Boomer, of course, had no such qualms. The second Nathan walked through the door, his bottom began wiggling and he chuffed happily in greeting. Nathan squatted down and grabbed his head, shaking it affectionately.

"How was the trip?"

"It was good," she said. "Where's your car?"

He threw a thumb over his shoulder and started scratching Boomer's belly.

"The shop. I figured it was time to check it out; it's been leaking oil since I left Joliet. I found a mechanic down the street who said he'd take a look and give me his verdict in the morning."

Nathan glanced up and his eyebrows drew together.

"What's wrong?"

"Nothing's wrong," she said. "I was just a little concerned when I didn't see your car."

"You were worried about me."

"I wasn't *worried*."

"Embarrassed about going to the movies alone, were you?"

"No. I just thought maybe you'd changed your mind."

"About our date? Never."

Jennifer pressed her lips together.

"We're taking my dog to a drive-in," she said. "It's not a *date*."

The desk clerk walked out of the back room and pulled

up short when she saw the two of them standing there. She glanced at the key in her hand.

"I thought you said you wanted a single room."

"A single plus a pet," Jennifer said.

The woman pointed. "No, I meant him."

Nathan put a hand on his chest and gave the woman a "who, me?" look.

"Oh, we're not together. She just followed me here."

Had Jennifer been thinking he wasn't so bad? She must have been crazy.

"I didn't *follow* you," she hissed.

"It's okay," he whispered. "I don't mind."

"Well, you can share a room if you want to," the clerk said. "But I can't give you a refund. The rooms are already paid for."

"I don't need a refund," Jennifer said, snatching her key out of the woman's hand. "And, we're *not* sharing a room."

Jennifer had never been to a drive-in theater. Her family had been too poor to take her when she was young, and by the time there was money to spare, there were more sophisticated forms of entertainment on offer. Vic had never been shy about cadging tickets to movie premieres in her name, and he always relished the opportunity to have people see him squiring his "discovery" in public. As she maneuvered her truck past the cars that were spread across the tiered rows of parking spaces facing the giant screen, it felt as if she were reaching back in time to capture a piece of childhood that she'd missed the first time around.

"If you back into a parking spot, the three of us can sit in the bed," Nathan said.

Jennifer drove slowly down the aisle, looking for an open spot, feeling uncertain. A truck bed wasn't the same neutral ground that a cab with bucket seats in front was, and being packed together like sardines while they watched a movie sounded an awful lot like a date. Nevertheless, if all three of them were going to see the screen, they'd have to find a better arrangement than the two-in-front, one-in-back they were currently using. She'd just have to make sure that Boomer got in the middle.

She found an area with several adjacent spots and stopped, pointing at the line of metal poles that cut across it like gates on a slalom course, their dented, thickly painted surfaces a testament to the perils of parking in the dark.

"How am I supposed to back in there with those things in the way?"

"Those 'things' are part of the charm. People like to come here and remember the way things were."

"Not everything's worth remembering," she grumbled. "If I'd ruined my paint job on one of those, I'd get rid of them."

"Yes, but you're a practical person. Nostalgia isn't practical." He opened his door. "Come on. I'll help you maneuver this behemoth in there."

When the truck had been safely docked, Nathan walked down to the refreshment stand and Jennifer started turning the truck bed into a makeshift movie theater. She laid Nathan's duffel and two cushions she'd taken from the room against the back of the cab, then spread out a tarp, congratulating herself for buying an insulating liner for the bed. Finally, she set out the pillows and blankets, trying to find some way of arranging them so that the truck didn't look like a bedroom on wheels.

"Okay," she told Boomer. "Remember our agreement. You're going to lie down here, in the middle, and we'll sit on either side of you."

She jumped down and patted the center of the truck bed encouragingly.

"Come on. Jump up and lie down. It's super comfy."

Boomer set his paws on the tailgate and inspected the makeshift boudoir. Jennifer glanced over her shoulder. Nathan was coming back.

"Hurry up, Boomster, don't mess around," she said. "Get in there and lie down."

He jumped up and started circling the bed. Nathan was only four cars away.

"Enough already," she whispered. "Down. Down. Lie *down.*"

At last, Boomer took the hint and stretched his body along the center of the truck bed, dividing it as neatly as the median line on a bell curve. The bed now had a "his" side and a "hers" side. Jennifer breathed a sigh of relief.

"Good dog."

"Who's a good dog?" Nathan set the drinks and popcorn down on the tailgate, admiring her handiwork. "Hey, this is great. Thanks."

She smiled. "Boomer helped. That's why I told him he was a good dog."

Nathan vaulted into the truck bed and patted Boomer's back, ruffling his fur playfully.

"Are you a good dog, Boomie? Are you? Are you?"

Boomer rolled onto his side, a none-too-subtle request for a tummy rub, and Jennifer frowned. Her perfect median was skewing dangerously toward the lower end of the curve.

"Oh, um, don't do that," she said. "I just got him settled."

"He's fine," Nathan said. "There's plenty of room back here."

As Boomer continued to roll, Jennifer started calculating how much room was left on the far side of the dividing line. It would be tight, but she didn't need a lot of space. It was getting cold, too; she wouldn't mind having a warm dog up close. She'd just have to stop him before he went all the way over. Putting her hands on the tailgate and pushing off, she boosted herself onto the pile of blankets and started crawling across the bed. There was still room, she thought, as long as Boomer didn't go . . . any . . . farther . . .

And then, like a tumbler on a mat, Boomer completed his barrel roll across the bed and finished with his body pressed firmly up against the wheel well. Jennifer ground her teeth.

A horn sounded and the lights flashed.

"What's that?" she said.

"The two-minute warning," Nathan said, lifting the blanket. "Hurry and get in before the movie starts."

Reluctantly, Jennifer crawled in next to Boomer. Nathan handed her a can of soda, then set the popcorn on her lap and crawled in beside her. As he settled in, she could feel the heat from his hip and thigh radiating into hers. Seconds later, the lights went out and the credits began to roll.

Jennifer leaned over and muttered in Boomer's ear.

"I hope you're happy."

CHAPTER 15

The mechanic wiped his hands on a rag as he emerged from his shop and greeted Nathan with the air of a doctor about to deliver an unfortunate diagnosis. Pale blue eyes stared out from the weather-beaten face, and the gray coveralls hung from a lean frame, but the man's fists were as fearsome as a bare-knuckle boxer's. He stuffed the tattered cloth into his back pocket and offered his hand. It was like gripping a vise.

"So," Nathan said. "What's the verdict?"

"Well, the good news is, it's just oil that's leaking. If it was power steering or transmission fluid, it'd be a whole lot worse."

"And the bad news?"

"The bad news is, it's coming from all over. Head gasket, cam seal, oil pan gasket are all leaking, some worse than others." He shrugged. "Rubber wears at the same rate so things tend to go all at once."

Nathan nodded. He wasn't surprised. This was pretty much what he'd expected.

"Can you fix it?"

The man scratched the back of his head thoughtfully.

"I've got most of the parts here in the shop, but the engine's not stock; I'd have to order the head gasket from Springfield. I'm pretty busy at the moment, but if I can get it by tonight, I'll have the car ready for you on Saturday."

Two days.

Nathan grimaced. "I'll have to talk it over with my brother. The car's his. Would you mind giving me an estimate so I can let him know what it's going to cost?"

The man walked into his office and took out a work order, filled it in, signed it, and handed it over.

"When you talk to your brother, tell him that the work's gotta be done soon. It'll be a lot easier to replace a couple of gaskets now than an entire engine block later."

"Thanks," Nathan said. "I'll do that."

He stepped out into the parking lot and dialed Rudy's work number.

"*Three grand for a couple of stinkin' gaskets?*" Rudy bellowed like a cow in heat. "Where'd you find this shyster?"

Nathan glanced back over his shoulder, hoping the mechanic hadn't heard.

"He's not a shyster. I got his name from Triple A. The guy's a certified mechanic."

"No. Absolutely not. No goober from Hicksville is touching my car. I've got a guy out here who'll do it right."

Nathan gritted his teeth. No one in the world could get under his skin quite like his big brother.

"Great. Wonderful. You've got a guy. Unfortunately, what you don't have is the car. So, what do you want me to do?"

Rudy huffed irritably; Nathan could almost see him pawing the ground in frustration.

"Okay, this is what I want you to do. You can still drive it, right? Get back on the road and hightail it out here. If you take the freeway like you should have in the first place, you can make it here in twenty-four hours."

"Sorry, no can do."

"What? Why not?"

"There's too much road with too little cell coverage between here and LA and the car is already running hot. I'm not going to risk getting stranded in the middle of nowhere just 'cause you don't trust this guy."

"Hey, you asked me what I wanted to do and I told you."

"Yeah, but that was when I thought you were going to come up with something reasonable."

"Like what?"

"Either I give this guy the go-ahead and finish the drive when he's done, or I find somebody who'll ship it the rest of the way for you."

A long moment of silence followed, during which Rudy was no doubt wishing he could reach out and strangle his kid brother. Nathan held his tongue. He'd been in enough negotiations to know that the first guy to speak was generally the loser.

"Fine. Ship it, then," Rudy said. "But if my car gets a single scratch, you're paying for it. You can tell inbred Jed he'll have to find another sucker to fleece."

"Okay. I'll give you a call when things are arranged."

Nathan shook his head in disgust and put the phone away.

Jennifer and Boomer were waiting in their motel room when Nathan got back from the mechanic's. The bags were packed and ready to be put in the truck, and Boomer had had a walk in the dog park down the street. After the successes of the last two days, she was looking forward to whatever Nathan had planned for them. It hadn't occurred to her that the news about the Mustang would be so bad.

"So, what are you supposed to do now?" Jennifer said.

Nathan sat down on a chair and hung his head.

"Do what Rudy said: Ship it. It's not my car. What choice do I have?"

"And then what?"

He shrugged. "Catch a bus back home, I guess."

She swallowed, trying to tamp down the panic that was simmering just below her breastbone. If Nathan left, she'd be on her own again, flailing around, desperately trying to find something for her and Boomer to do. And she'd have no one to talk to, either; no one to calm her down when it looked like Boomer was flagging, no one to distract her when she started blaming herself for all the things she hadn't done for him the past five years.

Irrationally, she felt herself growing angry—at Nathan and his brother. If Nathan had just written down his suggestions for her like he said he would, she'd at least have some things to do. And if Rudy hadn't insisted that Nathan ship the car right away, there'd still be time for him to make the list before he had to leave. But even then, Jennifer thought sadly, he'd still be gone and she'd still miss him.

"Maybe you could rent a car," she said. "That way, you could complete the drive and finish your travel articles like you promised your editor."

Nathan shook his head.

"Julia would never agree to that. Having me write those articles was just her way of keeping me from turning this trip into a vacation. Without Rudy's car to deliver, there's no reason for the assignment. Besides, you don't know Julia. She makes Mister Scrooge look like a spendthrift."

"Oh."

Jennifer stared at the floor and felt tears starting to well. Boomer was going to be really sad without Nathan around, she thought. He'd never had a man to play with before, someone who was up for more rough and tumble than she was. The two of them were like pals, head butting and pretend fighting with each other. With Nathan, Boomer had gotten to experience something he never knew existed. How could she let that be taken away from him?

"Why don't you come with us?" she said, her heart pounding.

Nathan's head came up. "What?"

"You heard me. Find somebody to ship Rudy's car and drive the rest of Route 66 with us. You can help me find places to take Boomer and I'll take you to the places you need to write about."

"I don't think so. Thanks anyway."

"Why not? It's perfect."

He gave her a skeptical look. "You sure your admin won't mind?"

Jennifer had told him about Stacy's warning regarding stranger danger on the road.

"What Stacy doesn't know won't hurt her," she said. "Besides, Boomer would never forgive me if we left here without you."

"Ah," he said. "So it's Boomer who wants me along."

Jennifer hesitated. She liked Nathan—more than she'd thought she would—but if they were going to be traveling together, she'd have to draw a line in the sand. Since her divorce, she'd worked hard to be independent. She wasn't going to give that up—even for Boomer—for a man she'd never have given the time of day to back in the "real" world.

"This isn't a proposition," she said. "We'd still be staying in separate rooms."

He nodded. "Okay, I'll think about it."

"You will?"

"Yeah," he said. "But let's eat first. I'm starving."

They found a coffee shop and parked outside the window so they could keep an eye on Boomer. While they waited for their meals to arrive, Nathan contacted a towing company about shipping Rudy's car to LA and arranged to meet the driver at their motel after breakfast. Nothing more was said about joining Jennifer and Boomer on their trip, but by the time breakfast arrived, it was clear that he'd made up his mind to say yes. As the two of them ate, Boomer sat in the truck bed, trying to follow both the food and their conversation and looking like a spectator at a tennis match.

"I'm sorry," she said. "But your brother sounds like kind of a jerk."

Nathan swallowed and shook his head.

"That's just Rudy. He's probably embarrassed that the great deal he thought he was getting turned out to be a lemon."

Jennifer bit off a piece of toast and chewed belligerently. Maybe Rudy wasn't a bad guy, but he was certainly an inconsiderate one. And the fact that he'd been willing to put Nathan's safety in jeopardy for his own convenience was galling.

The waitress came by, and Jennifer asked her for a to-go box.

"Look at that face," she said, pointing out the window. "How can I say no?"

Nathan glanced over his shoulder and laughed. Boomer was doing an excellent impression of a starving animal.

"So," she said. "Where to next?"

"I haven't exactly figured that out yet," he said.

"What? I thought you were going to be our guide on this trip."

"Oh, right. Like I've had time? Between researching my next article and chaperoning you at the movies—"

"Hey, that wasn't my idea."

"All right, all right. Don't get your knickers in a twist. I'll think of something. Just let me get rid of the car first."

"Okay," she said, tossing her head insouciantly. "You're off the hook—for now."

They settled their bill and rewarded Boomer for his patience, then headed back to the motel to meet the tow truck.

While Nathan talked to the driver, Jennifer got their luggage tied down in the truck and took Boomer out for a last-chance walk around the block. On the way back, she stopped by the front desk to check out and give their keys to the desk clerk.

The woman looked up from her computer screen and smiled.

"You guys checking out?"

"Yes," Jennifer said.

She set the key on the counter and waited for the woman to print out her receipt.

"Where you heading to?"

"I'm not sure. Got any suggestions?"

"Have you seen the Big Blue Whale yet?"

"The big blue—?"

"Whale, that's right. Over the border in Catoosa, about two hours southwest of here. It's quite a sight."

"Is it in an aquarium?"

"No," the woman said. "It's not a real whale, but it's still worth a visit. It's on the National Register of Historic Places, too. I think you and your dog would like it."

Jennifer bit her lip thoughtfully. Boomer might or might not like it, but a historic landmark would at least give Nathan something to write about. He could even include some pictures of Boomer so people could see how much fun it was.

"Thanks," she said. "I think we will."

"Great." The woman blushed. "Before you leave, though, could I ask you a favor?"

The Mustang was gone by the time Jennifer and Boomer returned. Nathan was waiting in the parking lot, leaning against the truck, his arms crossed over his T-shirt, blond hair tousled by the gentle breeze. When Jennifer saw him, her breath caught in her throat. How had she not noticed before what a good-looking guy he was?

He looked over and smiled as they approached.

"Well, it's gone," he said. "You're stuck with me now."

She nodded, still feeling a bit breathless.

"Great. Wonderful. Oh, and the desk clerk gave me a suggestion for a place we might go, if you're interested."

"What is it?"

"The Big Blue Whale. She said it's about a hundred and twenty miles southwest of here and it's on the Register of Historic Places, too. I thought maybe we could kill two birds with one stone. Boomer and I can check it out while you get the lowdown, and you'll have something to write about when we get to the motel."

"Sounds good."

Jennifer opened the truck and put Boomer in the back-seat.

"So, you're all checked out?" Nathan said, getting into the passenger seat.

"Yep." She slammed Boomer's door and opened her own. "The woman at the desk even took our picture."

"Really?" He glanced back at the motel. "I wonder why."

"Beats me." Jennifer said. "Maybe she thought we were somebody famous."

CHAPTER 16

It had been a crazy day at Compton/Sellwood. With Jennifer out of the office, people's nerves were frayed. Clients who'd been used to twenty-four-hour access were incensed when their calls weren't returned immediately, and account executives whose workloads had almost doubled overnight were frantic. Even the chairman, Mr. Sellwood, whose grace under fire was legendary, was snappish. The only one who'd had to keep a smile on her face was Stacy.

She stepped out onto the sidewalk, turning her coat collar up against the wind, and thrust her hands deep into her pockets. In spite of the chill, she'd decided to forgo the subway and walk to Jennifer's house. It wasn't a long way, and it would be good to stretch her legs and get some fresh air. She needed a chance to clear her head before catching the train home.

At least she hadn't gotten any more trouble from Jason over Boomer's Bucket List. After their run-in the day before, Stacy had fully expected him to complain to the boss, and she'd gone into work that morning ready for a fight. When nothing happened, she'd actually felt a little let down, but as the day wore on and the tension over Jennifer's absence grew, she was relieved that the whole thing had blown over so quickly. If she'd had to defend her position over the pictures on top of everything else that had been going on, she might have given in.

Jennifer's town house was on a quiet tree-lined street in the River East section of Chicago. The three-story brick building had a private entrance in front and windows that overlooked a quiet courtyard. With the kind of money she made, Jennifer could have afforded something in one of the steel-and-glass high-rises that loomed over downtown. That she'd chosen instead to live in a more modest building made Stacy feel proud to know Jennifer and prouder still to have been entrusted with its care. As she headed up the walkway, she imagined how it would feel to live in a place like that.

Someone had left a bouquet of flowers by the front door. Stacy scooped them up and hunted in vain for a tag, wondering if they were from a boyfriend. Jennifer never said anything about her love life—not that she would; it was unprofessional—but the thought that she might have someone special in her life made Stacy happy. At the office, it was generally assumed that Jennifer had no personal life, that a woman who looked like she did and worked that many hours was either frigid or gay. Stacy didn't care one way or the other, but she'd noticed that the people making those assumptions were generally men who'd flirted with Jennifer and gotten nowhere. It would serve them right, she thought, if she'd had a sweetheart all along.

The place smelled musty when she stepped inside. Stacy wrinkled her nose. She'd just been there on Tuesday, but even two days of sitting vacant could make a house feel stuffy. She slipped off her shoes and started looking for a vase to put the flowers in. It didn't seem right just to toss them out, and they'd make the place smell nice. Stacy didn't know how long Jennifer would be gone, but there was always a chance that they'd still be fresh when she got back.

In the meantime, she could enjoy them herself when she came by to check on the house. She put the flowers in a vase, set it on the kitchen counter, and went upstairs to open some windows and water the plants.

There were three bedrooms at the top of the landing: one for guests, one that had been converted into an office, and Jennifer's. Stacy opened the window in the guest room, gathered up the plants and then watered each one, setting them in the bathtub to drain. Then she grabbed a dust cloth, gave everything a quick wipe-down, and headed into the master suite.

It was her favorite room in the house. The coffered ceiling and pearl-gray walls were soothing, and the sea-foam green bedspread was made of a material that looked like ripples in a pond. Like Jennifer, the furnishings were timeless and elegant. Stacy crossed the room and opened the French doors to let in some air, then stepped out onto the balcony.

The river spread out before her. The sun had set, and the water sparkled with the reflection of city lights. Two men in overcoats were walking along the promenade, their heads lowered against the wind, and the rumble of an unseen motorboat faded in the distance as its wake slapped against the shore. Stacy sighed, thinking how nice it would be to sit there with a glass of wine at the end of the day, watching the world go by. She tried to imagine having a life like Jennifer's: a glamorous job, a beautiful home, money in the bank. Like being a princess in a fairy tale. She sighed again and stepped back inside.

Maybe someday.

With the plants back in their pots, Stacy went out to get the mail. When she came back, she found another flower arrangement and a teddy bear on Jennifer's doorstep. No name, no gift tag on either one. She looked around, wondering where the person who'd left them had gone. This had to be a mistake, she thought. No one who knew Jennifer would be leaving her another bunch of flowers, much less a teddy bear, while she was out of town. Stacy flushed with embarrassment. What if the other bouquet, too, had been delivered to the wrong address? Maybe she shouldn't have taken it inside without checking to see if it belonged to one of the neighbors first.

As she stood there on the stoop, trying to decide what to do, the next door opened and an older woman in a housecoat and slippers peered out.

"I thought I heard someone out here," she said. "Are you looking for Miss Westbrook?"

Stacy shook her head. "I'm taking care of the house for her while she's out of town."

The woman pointed at the things propped against Jennifer's door.

"Are those yours?" she said.

"No. I just went to get the mail and when I came back, someone had left them there."

"There was another bouquet of flowers out here a while ago. Someone must have taken it."

"Oh, no, that was me," Stacy said. "I found it when I let myself in. The flowers didn't have a card on them, so I assumed they were for Jennifer, but now I'm not so sure. Do you think they might have been delivered to the wrong address?"

The woman frowned thoughtfully.

"I doubt it. Not when there's more than one left at the same door. Is she all right?"

"Of course," Stacy said. "Last I heard, anyway. Why?"

"It just seems odd, strangers coming by and leaving all those things there like that. I thought there might have been a death in the family." She squinted at Stacy. "If you're taking care of her place, you might as well have the others, too."

"Others?" Stacy had a strange feeling, like a premonition, that made the hair stand up on the back of her neck. "You mean there's more?"

"Come see for yourself." The woman stepped back from the door and motioned for her to come inside. "My name's Millie, by the way."

"Hi, Millie. I'm Stacy."

They sat in a pile just inside the woman's front door: formal bouquets, bunches of flowers cut from home gardens, hearts, balloons, and stuffed animals. As Stacy stood there, staring at the offerings that took up most of Millie's foyer, the older woman disappeared into her kitchen and came back with a ten-gallon trash bag.

"You can put them in here," she said, shaking it open. "It'll be a relief to finally get rid of them. The darned things have tripped me up more than once today."

Stacy looked up. "Why would people be leaving these at Jennifer's door? I mean, what's the point?"

"I have no idea," Millie said, shoving a bouquet of tea roses and baby's breath into the bag. "I heard somebody drop the first one off around dinnertime last night, then this morning there were a few more. People have been coming by and dropping things off all day, but by the time I get to the door to ask them what's going on, they've already driven off. As soon as I realized that there was no one over there to pick them up, I went out and brought the lot of them in here, hoping someone would come by and take them off my hands before the whole place filled up."

She reached down and picked a little stuffed dog up off the pile.

"Look, this one's got a tag on it."

Millie reached into her pocket and took out a pair of reading glasses.

"Let's see . . . It says 'Boomer.'" She looked up. "That mean anything to you?"

"Yeah," Stacy said. "Boomer is Jennifer's dog."

She felt a stab of apprehension. Had Boomer died?

"Seems kind of strange." Millie handed her the stuffed

animal. "Why would someone leave all of these things for a dog?"

"I'm not sure," Stacy told her, glancing at the tag. "But I'm going to find out."

Stacy's hands shook as she sat down at her computer. She'd been a nervous wreck on the way home, wringing her hands and trying not to panic as the Metra made its way south. When it got to her stop, she hurried home, ignored the gnawing pain in her stomach, and ran to the desk in her bedroom. She had a hunch about what was happening, and it wasn't good.

Squeezing her eyes shut, Stacy prayed that whatever was going on had nothing to do with Boomer's Bucket List. After their argument about the pictures the day before, she and Jason hadn't seen much of each other, but he'd been pleasant enough when he stopped by her desk that morning, and she'd decided not to mention his not-so-subtle threat to Mr. Compton. As things got crazier at the office, it was just easier to convince herself that it was no big deal. Stacy typed in the URL and held her breath.

Tears of shame and embarrassment filled her eyes as Boomer's Bucket List came up on the screen. This time, Compton/ Sellwood's social media team had really gone all-out. Not only had Jason not backed down, she thought, he'd raised the stakes.

They'd started a contest called *Where's Boomer?* offering a prize for the best photo of Jennifer's dog submitted to the Web site each day. Followers were encouraged to travel along Route 66, looking for Jennifer and Boomer so they could take a picture and submit it to the contest in one of two categories: single photo and video. Contestants were encouraged to enter as many times as they wanted, the only restriction being that neither Jennifer nor Boomer could be tipped off. Violating the rule would immediately put an end to the contest, and with iPads, flat-screen TVs, and Apple watches being given as prizes, the chances were good that the contest would last as long as Boomer did.

But the worst part, as far as Stacy was concerned, was that the site was now covered with ads for Compton/Sellwood, shameless plugs for the agency that were so obtrusive they skirted the limits of good taste. If Jason had been capitalizing on Jennifer's misfortune before, he was wallowing in it now.

Stacy put a hand over her mouth and choked on a sob as hot tears ran down her face. Jennifer would never forgive her for this. Whatever good feeling there'd been between the two of them would be destroyed once she saw what had happened to her photos. She was heartsick. It was her fault—all of it. She hadn't meant to hurt anyone; she'd just wanted to do something nice, and it had all gone wrong. She ran to the bathroom and retched over the sink, then sank to the floor and covered her face.

"Oh, God," she whispered. "What have I done?"

CHAPTER 17

Another batch of *Where's Boomer?* entries had just been uploaded, and Jason Grant was over the moon. The contest was succeeding beyond even his own optimistic predictions, perfectly illustrating the power of social media to get people involved and generate buzz while promoting a client's product. He took out his phone and composed a tweet to his followers, alerting them that Jennifer and Boomer were approaching the Tulsa area and promising a bonus prize to the first one who uploaded a funny video to the Web site.

As he hit "send," Jason grinned. Once something like this caught fire, the dollars-to-eyeballs ratio diminished to practically nothing. He supposed he ought to thank Stacy for being such a pain about giving him the rest of Jennifer's pictures. If she'd just handed them over, he'd never have thought to do something like this. He couldn't wait to tell the boss.

His phone rang; Derek Compton wanted to see him.
Speak of the devil.

* * *

Stacy sat in Derek Compton's office, gripping the damp tissue in her hand as they waited for Jason to arrive. When she got to work that morning, she'd made a beeline for the CEO's office and tearfully poured her heart out. Jason's "upgrade" to Boomer's Bucket List was a disaster, she told him. Not only was the contest encouraging people to follow Jennifer and Boomer around, trying to take their picture, but the story of Boomer's diagnosis had prompted others to find Jennifer's home address and leave gifts and cards on her doorstep. Stacy had cleared them away last night, but when she'd stopped by the town house that morning, she found another dozen sitting on the stoop. If Jason didn't take down the Web site immediately, one of the neighbors was going to complain.

Compton had listened patiently as she filled him in on the details, shaking his head and grimacing occasionally to indicate how he felt about the situation. By the time Stacy had finished her story, it seemed clear to her that he was as upset by Jason's betrayal as she was. It felt as if a weight had been lifted from her shoulders. Thank goodness the boss had understood her predicament. The sooner that Web site was taken down, the happier she'd be.

Jason knocked on the door and stepped inside. His smile slipped for a moment when he saw Stacy sitting there, then quickly re-formed into a self-satisfied grin. She turned away, pretending to read one of the citations that hung on the wall. She knew she looked awful. She'd been crying most of the night, and her eyelids were as puffy as marshmallows, but she didn't want to give him the satisfaction of knowing he'd upset her.

"Have a seat," Compton said, motioning to the other visitor's chair. "We need to talk."

"Of course," Jason said, his voice oozing sincerity. "What's going on?"

"Stacy tells me that you've made some changes to Boomer's Bucket List. You want to tell me about that?"

"I'd love to. In fact, I was about to come talk to you when you called. Have you seen it?"

Stacy sniffed and shot him a dirty look. The guy had just destroyed her life, and now he was acting like it was something to be proud of. She hoped Compton would fire him.

"No, I haven't had a chance. Stacy just finished telling me about it." He typed in the URL and turned the screen around. "Why don't we all take a look and see what's going on so that Stacy can show you what she's concerned about."

"Great," Jason said, beaming. "I don't know what her problem is, but when you see it I think you'll be impressed."

As Jason pulled his chair closer to the desk, Stacy turned and stared. She'd already told Compton what the problem was. He should be ordering Jason to take it down, not giving the guy a chance to sell it. She glanced at the computer and took a sharp breath. Boomer's Bucket List was full of new pictures: Boomer beside something that looked like a whale and another of him going down a slide that projected from the whale's side like a flipper. There were several of him eating an ice cream cone and two with Jennifer and a man she didn't recognize taking Boomer on a walk. In spite of herself, she was overcome with curiosity.

"Who's that guy?" she said.

"Beats me," Jason told her. "But he shows up in a lot of the shots. Either he took off with her or she met him on the way."

He turned back to the computer screen.

"Who knows?" he said smugly. "Maybe I was wrong about her."

Compton was still scrolling through the pictures.

"These are good. A little amateurish, perhaps, but it lends authenticity to the product."

"My thoughts exactly." Jason nodded. "I had the team clean them up a little—correct the color, crop for balance—but nothing too slick. We wanted to keep this as serious and heartfelt as the subject."

Stacy's lips tightened. "How can you say that? You've covered the thing with ads. What's so serious and heartfelt about that?"

Jason glared at her.

"Stacy's got a point," Compton said. "When Jennifer started this trip, she wasn't thinking of its publicity value, and Boomer's diagnosis is serious. If anything posted here makes it look as if Compton/Sellwood is exploiting a tragedy, the whole thing could blow up in our faces."

Stacy frowned, no longer sure if the boss was on her side.

"How are we promoting this thing off-line?" he said.

Jason took a moment to consider. "I sent an e-mail blast to our customers"—Compton looked pained—"but we were careful to present it as just an update on Jennifer's situation."

"Good," he said. "Very smart. Reminds them they shouldn't be thinking only of the inconvenience her absence has caused."

"I've also been sending tweets to our followers, updating them on where Jennifer and Boomer are."

Compton scrolled back up the page. "Is that in connection to this contest?"

Jason's look was wary. "Yeah."

"That was an inspired move," he said. "I like it."

Now that he knew he was on firmer ground, Jason started warming to the subject.

"We've doubled the number of page likes since last night and the numbers just keep growing. Five of the videos have gone viral already and the YouTube crowd is going nuts, adding music and animation. Before I got your call, I'd been watching one in Japanese."

Compton glanced at Stacy. "Did you hear that? Boomer's famous in Japan."

Stacy gripped the arms of her chair. If he thought she was going to be impressed that somebody somewhere had overdubbed a video of Boomer, he had another thing coming. What did she care? And for that matter, what did he care? Ten minutes ago, Derek Compton had been as outraged as she was. Now he was trying to convince her that what Jason had done was the best thing that could have happened. Well, she wasn't buying it. Nothing either of them could say or do was going to change her mind. She wanted the Web site taken down, and she wanted it taken down *now*.

Of course, it was all well and good to get angry, she thought, but expressing that anger to the man who signed her paychecks was another matter. When she'd walked in there, it had been just the two of them, and she'd had all her objections on the tip of her tongue. Now she'd have to convince both of them, and she knew that Jason wouldn't be sympathetic to her cause. On the contrary, if he lost this argument, it would make both him and the social media team look bad. Was she really willing to do that, even to someone she didn't like? She swallowed hard. The boss was staring at her expectantly.

"I guess it's maybe not as bad as I thought," she said, ashamed of the hesitation in her voice. "But I'm still afraid that Jennifer will find out."

"She's not going to find out," Jason scoffed. "And even if she does, so what?"

"So, she'll be angry and hurt." Stacy's face felt hot. "You're exploiting her situation to get more customers for the agency."

"Oh, please. Jennifer's a big girl. You think she wouldn't do the same if she was in my shoes?"

Stacy felt as if she'd been slapped. "Jennifer's not like that."

"Of course she is," he sneered. "How do you think she got to where she is now? For God's sake, Stacy, grow up."

"That's enough," Compton said. "Let's not turn this into something personal."

Jason straightened up, visibly controlling himself, and Stacy smiled. She might not have won the argument, but knowing she'd rattled him gave her a small thrill of satisfaction.

"What you and your team have done is impressive," the boss continued. "But it doesn't resolve Stacy's problem."

She gave a start. Why was it *her* problem all of a sudden?

"I hope there might be some way we could keep the Web site running and still make you happy." Compton gave Stacy an indulgent look. "Maybe you could point out the things you still find objectionable and Jason could try to change them for you. Would that help?"

"Um, well," she said. "I guess so."

"Here," he said, motioning for her to bring her chair closer. "Let's just take a closer look."

As Compton scrolled back to the top, Stacy had to admit that Boomer's Bucket List was a great Web site, easy to navigate and interesting to look at. Once again, she was reminded of how lame her own effort would have been, something the men on either side of her understood as well as she did. As he handed her the mouse, she felt as if a rock had landed in her stomach. She stared at the screen.

Three new pictures had been added since she'd come in that morning. Stacy pointed.

"Where did those come from?"

Jason leaned forward to get a better look.

"My team must have just posted them. We curate all the submissions before they go up. Those look like they were taken yesterday."

"How can you tell?"

He pointed. "The Blue Whale. It's in Catoosa. They should be in Tulsa by now."

Compton nodded. "I suppose your followers clued you in to that."

Jason chuckled. "It's like having a network of spies."

Stacy gritted her teeth. "Right, and you've turned them loose on Jennifer and Boomer."

"Whose fault is that? If you'd just given me the pictures like I asked, I wouldn't have had to do it. You told me if I wanted more to get them myself."

She looked to Compton, hoping for support, and found him nonplussed.

"Is that true?" he said.

"I-I guess so. I'm not sure."

Stacy squinted, trying to remember exactly what she'd told Jason. Whatever it was, though, it had been in the heat of the moment. That didn't really count, did it?

"Well, if you did, then I'm afraid that changes things. You can hardly cry foul if Jason is just doing what you told him to."

She slumped in the chair, defeated. She never should have complained, Stacy told herself. Nothing was going to change.

"But she'll find out," she said weakly. "And then she'll be mad at me."

Compton gave Jason a sharp look. "How certain are you that we can keep Jennifer in the dark about all of this?"

Jason looked abashed. "It's hard to say. The contest rules say that they can't be tipped off, but I guess it depends on how discreet the public is."

Stacy snorted. "No chance of that."

"Maybe not," the boss said. "But it hasn't happened yet. I say we wait and see how things play out. If we get lucky and no one tips her off, great. If not, I'll tell Jennifer it was my call. That way, Jason and his team get to keep the changes they made and Stacy, you're off the hook."

She nodded, feeling somewhat better if also a bit guilty. Having Compton take the blame wasn't really fair, but it would ease her conscience, at least a little bit.

"That's settled, then," he said. "Jason, I want you and your team to make sure that everyone knows what the ground rules are for this game of yours. Believe me, I'm no more eager to be on Jennifer's bad side than Stacy is."

"Will do."

"And Stacy, let's keep the lines of communication open. If you still don't feel good about this in a couple of days, let me know and I'll see what we can do to make it better."

Jason stood up and walked out without a backward glance, but Stacy hung back. There was still one problem nagging at her.

"What about the stuff that people are leaving on Jennifer's doorstep?" she said. "Even if I go there every day, things still pile up."

Compton frowned thoughtfully.

"Tell you what," he said. "Why don't you go by her place before work and come in, say, an hour later? Or, if you'd rather, you could add an hour to your lunchtime and go pick up whatever's been left there then?"

She smiled. The thought of spending more time at Jennifer's apartment was enticing.

"Are you sure?"

"Of course. And maybe leave a little early at the end of the day, too, so you can swing by Jennifer's on your way home. I'll get a temp in here to cover for you until she gets back."

Stacy's eyes widened. With the extra time he was offering her, she could sit out on the balcony and have that glass of wine she'd been dreaming about and a cup of coffee in the morning, too! It would be almost like living there herself.

"Thank you," she said. "I'd like that."

CHAPTER 18

"Okay, you win," Nathan said. "It *is* hard to find places that accept dogs."

They were standing in the parking lot outside the Tulsa State Fair, their backs to the wind as they tried to decide what to do. Out on the main road, the line of cars waiting to park had backed up traffic for half a mile, and the crowd of expectant fairgoers heading for the front gate flowed around the three of them like water around a rock in a stream. If they weren't going to be allowed inside, Jennifer thought, they should just get back in the truck and go.

"Don't feel bad. I knew they wouldn't let us in."

Nathan shook his head, reluctant to admit defeat.

"There has to be someplace," he said. "I'm not giving up yet."

Having assured Jennifer that he could easily rescue her from the "boring" places she'd been taking Boomer, Nathan was discovering that most of the "fun" things out there didn't allow dogs on the premises. It was all well and good to know that there were things both memorable and exciting to be found along Route 66, but if they couldn't take her dog, she thought, what was the point? The urge to say, *I told you so,* was almost irresistible.

Jennifer looked down at Boomer and smiled. He was leaning against Nathan's leg again, panting happily as he looked from one of them to the other, apparently unfazed by this setback. While the two of them were knocking themselves out, trying to find things that he'd enjoy doing, he seemed perfectly happy just being there.

"We don't really have to 'do' a lot," she said. "Don't worry about it."

"Oh, no." Nathan shook his head. "I promised I'd come up with something and I will. You'll see."

A young couple and their son walked by, the boy lingering when he caught sight of Boomer. After a brief consultation with his mother, he sidled closer.

"Is your dog friendly?" he said.

Jennifer nodded. "He's very friendly. Would you like to pet him?"

The boy looked anxiously back at his parents, who nodded their approval.

"Yes, ma'am."

"All right." She bent down and motioned him closer. "He likes to be petted on his back. Just put your hand here, by his collar. . . . Yes, like that. Then you can stroke his fur."

The child grinned as his hand passed over the silky coat.

"He's real soft," he said, his voice barely more than a whisper.

Jennifer nodded proudly. "Yes, he is."

The boy gave another backward glance and nodded.

"What's his name?" he said.

"Boomer."

His eyes lit up, and he turned toward his parents.

"It's Boomer!"

Jennifer chuckled. Boomer might not be a common name for a dog, but it had never elicited a reaction quite like that one before. She looked over and saw the boy's father putting his phone away. He and his wife shared a brief, anxious glance, then the man stepped forward and took his son's hand.

"Come on, Zach. It's time to go."

As he tugged the boy away, the child was still marveling at the dog's name. Jennifer stood up and looked at Nathan.

"That was weird."

They started back toward the truck, Nathan staring straight ahead, his forehead creased in concentration. Jennifer could tell he was upset. He'd made a big deal about finding something fun for Boomer to do, and now they were right back at square one. She gave him a nudge with her shoulder.

"Hey, don't worry about it. We're still only halfway to the coast. We're bound to find something sooner or later."

He nodded reluctantly.

"Look, I know how you feel," she said, "but it's okay. It might even be a good thing that there isn't a lot of exciting stuff to do out here. The vet said Boomer needed his rest."

Nathan smirked. "You just want me to admit you were right."

"Of course."

The sound of footsteps approaching caught her attention. Jennifer turned and saw a heavy-set woman hurrying toward them, her boots kicking up a cloud of dust. A plaid shirt of red, white, and blue restrained the woman's ample bosom, and she had one hand firmly planted on her Stetson to keep it from flying away. The ribbon flapping on her chest said: *Fair Official*.

"Hold on!" she gasped. "Don't go!"

Jennifer and Nathan exchanged a look. What was this all about?

The woman came to a halt in front of them and put her hands on her knees, signaling for them to wait a moment while she caught her breath. When she straightened up a few seconds later, she was beaming.

"You're here for the dog show," she panted. "I'm Darlene. The gate's over yonder."

Jennifer was shaking her head, prepared to correct the woman's mistake, when Nathan cut her off.

"Thank you," he said. "We weren't sure which way to go."

Darlene turned and started toward the gate, motioning for them to follow. Jennifer grabbed Nathan's arm and held him back, shaking her head.

"This is a mistake," she hissed. "If we go in there, we'll all be thrown out."

"Why are you always worried about being thrown out? She invited us, didn't she?"

Boomer tugged at his leash, urging Jennifer forward; she was outnumbered, two to one. Nathan was right, she thought. Darlene had invited them. Still, that would be cold comfort when security showed up.

"All right," she said. "But just remember, I told you so."

The dog-show area was a hive of activity. Backstage, the day's contestants were up on tables, tethered to grooming arms, while their owners readied them for the ring. Hair dryers hummed, scissors snipped, and trimmers buzzed coats into perfection. Behind the tables, a double row of cages held the dogs that were waiting their turn. A sad-looking beagle was howling a complaint, but the rest were either sleeping or waiting in silence. As the three of them walked past, Jennifer kept a firm grip on Boomer's leash. No one had said anything, but she couldn't shake the feeling that they were being watched.

Meanwhile, Darlene was in her element: giving directions, admiring dogs, and greeting owners as she led the way toward the show ring. Jennifer's stomach churned; she could feel her armpits growing damp. It was like being in one of those dreams where you suddenly realize you've forgotten to put on your pants. How long would it be before someone noticed and started pointing?

At the end of the row hung a pair of curtains that separated the backstage area from the arena. The sign overhead said: *Show Dogs Only*. Darlene pushed the curtains aside and stepped through, motioning for them to follow. Jennifer stopped and looked at Nathan.

"Why does she want us to go out there? It says show dogs only."

"Beats me," he said. "Maybe she's got some VIP seats for us."

"Or maybe we'll be publicly humiliated when Darlene finds out we're not who she thinks we are."

"Will you cut it out?" he said, pushing her forward. "This wasn't our idea. Let's just keep going and see what happens."

She shook her head.

"Come on," Nathan whispered. "Do it for Boomer. Look how excited he is."

Jennifer grimaced. She had to admit it: Boomer did look like he was having a good time. If the point of this trip was to do things that he enjoyed, then maybe she should just go for it and forget about being embarrassed. Nathan was right; this hadn't been their idea. If anyone was going to be in trouble, it was Darlene.

She took a deep breath, loosened her grip on the leash, and let Boomer lead her through the curtains. As they stepped out into the spotlight, Jennifer saw Darlene waiting for them next to the judges' table. A man approached them from the left and touched Nathan's elbow.

"You can come on over this way, sir. We have a front-row seat picked out just for you."

A strangled protest escaped Jennifer's lips.

"Wait a minute. Isn't he coming with us?"

"It's okay," Nathan said. "Go!"

He gave her a thumbs-up sign and followed the man to his seat.

As Jennifer and Boomer approached the judges' table, Darlene picked up an official-looking name tag and pinned it on Jennifer's shirt, then took a judge's rosette and attached it to Boomer's collar. The dog's shoulder quivered under the red, white, and blue ribbons. Jennifer reached down and adjusted them so they didn't tickle.

"You two will be serving as alternate judges today," Darlene said. "In case of a tie, you'll cast the deciding votes."

Jennifer took a seat at the table and smiled bravely at the other judges. She had no idea what to look for in a show dog, and it was a relief when she noticed the clipboard in front of her. On it were several pages listing the dogs' names, the qualities they'd be judged on, and a box next to each in which to write her score. She unclipped the pen at the top, feeling like an impostor, and consoled herself that at least they weren't the only ones doing the judging.

The first dog was led out. Jennifer glanced back, searching for Nathan, but with the house lights dimmed and the show ring spotlighted, it was impossible to pick out one individual face in the crowd. It was his fault they were in this mess, she thought. They should have made him do the judging.

As out-of-place as Jennifer felt, though, Boomer seemed to be having a great time. Sitting by her side, watching the dog in the ring being put through its paces, he looked like a hunting dog waiting for a bird to fall. He might not know what was happening, she thought, but he knew it was important and he was giving it his full attention. The head judge—a thin-lipped man in a navy-blue blazer—leaned closer and gave her a condescending smile.

"This is just the amateur round. Household pets, pretty low quality contestants," he sniffed. "Awards are insignificant, but we do what we must. The real show is tonight."

Jennifer felt her jaw tighten. What a pompous ass. Those people backstage were working their hearts out, and if Boomer could take this job seriously, so could she. She snatched up her pen, clicked it firmly, and started marking boxes.

There were three classes being judged that day: Sporting, Non-Sporting, and Award of Merit. The judges' decisions for the first two were unanimous, and Jennifer was pleased to see that for the most part her own tally had agreed with theirs. Boomer, too, seemed to be in accord with the favorites; as the winners were announced, he thumped his tail in approval. When the time came to present the Award of Merit, however, the professional judges were deadlocked, their tallies a three-way tie. As all eyes turned toward her, Jennifer glanced at her tally sheet and squirmed. She, too, had scored all three dogs the same. How was she supposed to decide?

Darlene walked over and asked the judges for their decision. When the other four shook their heads, she turned toward Jennifer.

"All right, tiebreaker," she said. "What's the verdict?"

Jennifer showed the woman her tally sheet.

"I don't know," she said. "I gave the same score they did."

The woman nodded.

"Well," she said. "In that case, I guess it's up to Boomer."

Before Jennifer could stop her, Darlene had untied her dog's leash from the table leg and was walking him out into the ring. Applause rose up from the crowd as Boomer stepped out into the spotlight.

"Ladies and gentlemen." Darlene's voice reverberated in the open arena. "We have a three-way tie for the Award of Merit, and as you may know, the rules state that in case of a tie, an alternate judge will be asked to cast the final vote. I've asked Boomer here to be the tie breaker."

The crowd *oohed* and *aahed* their approval as Boomer was led around the ring. Jennifer was in shock, a smile frozen on her face. This could not be happening. Who asked a dog to judge a dog show? Nevertheless, there was Boomer, trotting around the ring like he'd been judging contests all his life. As unnerving as it was, she couldn't help feeling proud.

The three finalists and their owners stood at attention as Boomer approached. He and Darlene paused briefly in front of each one, then turned and repeated their inspection before returning to the starting point. Titters of expectation rose up from the crowd as Boomer looked carefully from each of the dogs to its handler and back.

"Take your time," Darlene said, winking at the audience. "This is an important decision."

Boomer took a step and tugged Darlene forward.

"Oops," she said, grinning. "Looks like he's gonna make another—Oh, hey boy. Where're you going?"

As Boomer led Darlene around behind the contestants, the head judge gasped and Jennifer smothered an embarrassed giggle. It was the ritual greeting, a dog's version of an exchange of business cards, but under the circumstances it seemed wildly inappropriate. As Boomer approached the first dog from behind, the audience realized what was happening and their titters of expectation turned to peals of laughter. Darlene, too, had figured out what was going on and was miming embarrassment even as her snorts of laughter were broadcast over the PA system.

Boomer, however, was taking his "inspection" very seriously. After giving each contestant's backside a thorough sniff, he led Darlene around and sat down in front of the winner. Cheers went up from the stands, and the camera flashes looked like the Fourth of July. The head judge glared and Jennifer turned away, sinking lower in her seat, hoping to become invisible.

Look on the bright side, she told herself. *At least no one here knows who I am.*

CHAPTER 19

They found a Mexican restaurant that night with a patio outside where Boomer could doze at their feet while they ate dinner. Jennifer sipped a margarita as Nathan described the dog show from his point of view, making what had felt like a minor disaster seem like something almost intentionally comical. She was grateful to him for helping her find the humor in the situation, especially since Boomer had had such a good time. By the time their food arrived, the pain of humiliation had faded to a dull ache.

"He's a natural born ham," Nathan said. "Did you see him shake hands with the runners-up? If Darlene was smart, she'd have asked Boomer to come back and judge next year's contest, too."

"Except that Boomer won't be here next year."

His face fell. "I'm sorry. I didn't mean—"

"No, it's okay," she said. "When he has a good day like this, it's hard to remember how sick he is."

"Do you ever wonder if the vet made a mistake? Boomer seems pretty healthy to me."

She shook her head, feeling the hot press of tears behind her eyes.

"I think I knew something was wrong even before Dr. Samuels did the tests. When we'd go to the park, Boomer didn't seem to want to run with the other dogs, but I told myself that it wasn't important. He goes to day care while I'm at work, and he seemed happy enough to stay inside when we got home, so I figured he was just tired from playing all day. Looking back, it seems obvious, but I guess I just didn't want to see it at the time."

She took out a tissue and blotted her eyes. It was hard to admit how selfish she'd been, even to herself. Having Nathan question her about it only made her feel worse. He must think she was an awful person, ignoring Boomer in favor of her work, letting him waste away while she played superwoman at Compton/Sellwood. If she had to do it over again, she'd make every second count, but it was too late now. She put the tissue away and picked up her fork.

"I must sound like some sort of monster."

"Hardly that," he said. "Nobody sees what they don't want to."

"I suppose you're right," she said, stabbing at a piece of lettuce. "Must be a habit of mine."

Nathan chewed thoughtfully.

"Is that what happened with Vic Ott?"

She shrugged, keeping her eyes on the food in front of her.

"Someone's been reading Wikipedia."

"Hey, we're not *all* off the Internet."

Jennifer set her fork down and gave him a frank look.

"Okay, Mr. Newspaper Reporter, what do you want to know? Did I love him? Yes. Did he hit me? Several times. Did I blame myself? Of course; we all do. But it has nothing to do with how I feel about losing Boomer."

"Really? 'Cause that sounds a lot like what you said before. You didn't want to think about losing your dog so you ignored the problem and now that the evidence is overwhelming, you're blaming yourself for not doing something about it sooner."

She narrowed her eyes. "You're a pain in the ass, you know that?"

"Hey, the truth hurts, Sweetie."

Suddenly, the urge to cry overwhelmed her, and Jennifer sobbed.

"Hey, look, I'm sorry," Nathan said, glancing nervously at the other tables. "I didn't mean it. Don't cry."

"No. No, it's all right," she said, taking the tissue out again. "I guess I just never put two and two together before. You're right; I do the same damned thing every time there's a problem. I pretend that everything is fine until it's so bad that I can't stand it and then I explode, run away, and berate myself for getting involved in the first place. I'm just as dumb as I was when I let Vic talk me into leaving school."

"I think you're being a little too hard on yourself. I mean, I read that entire Wikipedia entry and there's no way you could have been as successful as you are if you ran away every time your clients had a problem."

Jennifer sniffed and blew her nose.

"That's just the point. I can fix other people's problems, just not my own."

"Listen to me. Not facing an uncomfortable truth is perfectly normal. I think everybody's done it at one time or another."

"But I feel so helpless, and Boomie's not the only one I've ignored in favor of work, either. At this point, he's pretty much my only friend." She laughed ruefully and pressed the tissue against her eyelids. "Sorry. I don't expect you to understand."

"Actually, I do," he said, taking her hand. "More than you know."

She lowered the tissue and gave him a hard look. If this was just some I'll-say-anything-to-get-into-your-pants move, he was going to regret it.

"I know how it feels to lose a dog," he said.

Nathan glanced down at Boomer, and the corner of his mouth lifted.

"His name was Dobry and he looked a lot like this guy."

The tension in Jennifer's face eased. When she'd asked before about his dog's name, Nathan had brushed her off.

"When was that?"

"I was eight when we got him, almost ten when Mom took him back to the shelter."

"Oh. So, he didn't *die.*"

"Does it matter? He was my best friend and he wasn't coming back."

"You're right," she said. "I'm sorry. Gone is gone. So, what happened?"

"Dad was in the Army, so we moved around a lot. I was always the weird kid who didn't have any friends. Losing Dobry was like losing a part of myself."

"Why did your mom give him away?"

"Divorce. No pets allowed at the new place."

"Your poor mom. Sounds like she didn't have much choice."

"Adults always have a choice. She just didn't bother." He picked up his bottle of Dos Equis. "Still bitter, I guess. Sorry."

"And you never knew what happened to him?"

Nathan swallowed, shaking his head.

"Mom said another family would probably adopt him, but who knows? The shelters are always crowded and it was Dobry's second time around. I'm not sure I've ever really forgiven her."

"I suppose I should be grateful, then," she said. "At least Boomer and I still have some time left."

"No, don't do that. Not now, anyway. Let yourself feel

angry and sad and whatever else you need to. There'll be plenty of time later to be grateful."

Jennifer nodded, and the two of them finished their meal in silence. She appreciated the advice, and it was good to hear from someone who'd been through the same thing. When this whole thing was over, though, she just hoped she wouldn't feel as bitter about it as Nathan did.

When the bill came, Jennifer paid it and the three of them started walking back to the motel. It was her treat, she told him, payment in advance for helping her out on the trip. After all, if it hadn't been for Nathan, she'd have given up and gone home a long time ago.

They were sixty miles west of Tulsa now, far enough from big city lights to see the Milky Way, spread across the sky like a banner. The last few days had been warm for late October, a phenomenon Jennifer remembered her father telling her about when she was a child. She took a deep breath and exhaled a sigh.

"Feels like Indian summer."

"We called it 'Grandmother's summer' in my house." Nathan grinned. "Different neighborhood."

"Koslow." She raised an eyebrow. "Polish?"

"Got it in one. And Westbrook is . . . English?"

"Dutch," she said. "But it's just one name among many in the family."

His smile broadened. "American, then."

"Yes, definitely. I'm a mutt."

Nathan pointed at Boomer. "Unlike our friend here."

"Oh, no," Jennifer said. "Boomie's not a purebred; his mother was a yellow Lab. He just takes after his dad."

"And who do you take after?"

Jennifer had to think about that for a moment. She'd never given a lot of thought to which one of her parents she was most like. If she had a choice, she supposed she'd pick "none of the above."

"Most people say I look like my mother, but I think my

personality is more like my father's. You know: serious on the outside, goofy on the inside. What about you?"

"The same: Mom's looks, Dad's personality—unfortunately."

"Why unfortunately?"

He smirked. "My, you're a curious little thing, aren't you?"

She looked down at the long legs that had gotten her a modeling contract at sixteen and laughed.

"Curious, yes, but *little?*"

He rolled his eyes. "It's just an expression."

A gust of cold wind came up suddenly and ruffled her hair. Jennifer looked up and saw clouds gathering on the horizon.

"Looks like the weather's changing." She shivered. "I should have worn something warmer."

Nathan offered his arm, and without thinking, Jennifer hugged it to her chest, feeling the warmth of his body penetrate her summer-weight jacket. *If I'm not careful,* she thought, *I might fall in love with this man.* She handed Nathan the leash. Boomer glanced back briefly and kept walking.

As they got closer to their motel, Jennifer felt a heightened tension between them. The two of them had gotten separate rooms, but after the intimacy they'd shared at dinner, it seemed prudish to just shake hands at the door and say good-night. They were adults, after all. She smiled, considering the possibilities.

Gravel crunched beneath their shoes as they headed across the parking lot. Jennifer's truck was parked under the marquee, its windshield offering a distorted reflection of the neon *Vacancy* sign. She remembered driving to the gas station back in Atlanta and seeing Nathan, how excited she'd been to have a chance to thank him for helping her out at the speedway. Then she remembered his comment when he saw her truck: *You don't seem like the type.*

Jennifer could feel herself retreating from an emotional

precipice, the distance between the two of them widening to a chasm. How much did she really know about Nathan Koslow? He seemed nice enough, and his story about losing Dobry had touched her, but that was no reason to drop her defenses and jump into bed with him. Hadn't she made that mistake before, with Vic, seeing only what she wanted to and running headlong into a disastrous relationship? Feeling sorry for someone wasn't a substitute for love and mutual respect. If she and Nathan had a future together, there had to be more there than just a superficial attraction.

As they stepped into the lobby, Jennifer took out her key card and headed for her room. As Nathan followed her down the hallway, she felt her heart pounding. She might have made her decision, but that didn't mean she wasn't conflicted about it. When she turned her back to open the door for Boomer, she could almost feel Nathan's disappointment. Every atom in her body was telling her that this was real, something worth taking a risk for. Even Boomer, who'd never taken to another man in her life, seemed to have been egging her on since they met. Gritting her teeth, determined to keep her resolve, she turned back to say goodnight.

Nathan smiled, waiting for her to make the first move, and Jennifer hesitated. All right, she told herself. Maybe one kiss, on the cheek, but that's it. Something to show him that she was interested, but not ready to take the next step.

Then suddenly, she felt her knees give way as Boomer butted her from behind. Jennifer fell into Nathan's arms and planted her carefully calculated kiss directly on his mouth, feeling the warmth of his eager response. Reeling back, stuttering an apology, she darted back across the threshold and slammed the door. Boomer was sitting by the bed, thumping his tail proudly.

"What was that all about?"

He lowered his head, gazing upward in a counterfeit show of contrition.

"I know you like him," she said. "But you've got to let me do this my own way."

Jennifer threw her shoes in the closet and stomped into the bathroom. What must Nathan be thinking? she wondered. That she was drunk? Too clumsy to stand upright for a few seconds? She'd had everything under control until Boomer came along and made a mess of things.

She scrubbed her teeth and raked a comb through her hair before heading back out to get her pj's. Boomer was still sitting where she'd left him, his head hanging, looking crestfallen. Jennifer sighed. How could she stay mad when he looked like that? She held out her hand, and he inched toward her. "It's okay, Boomie, I know you meant well." She bent down and gave him a hug. "Who knows? Maybe you were right."

CHAPTER 20

"Good morning," Jennifer chirped, as she sat down at the table. "I see you got my message."

She'd left it at the front desk, asking Nathan to meet her for breakfast at the Denny's down the road at eight o'clock. He'd gotten there early. She was five minutes late.

Nathan squinted at her through bleary eyes.

"You're awfully chipper this morning."

He hadn't slept well. Their kiss last night had been a shocker, as surprising as it was enjoyable. For the first half an hour after he'd gotten back to his room, he was expecting her to show up for an encore; the next was spent wondering if she wanted him to go back to hers. Finally, he'd just broken into the minibar and tried to forget the whole thing. Jennifer Westbrook would not be the first woman he couldn't figure out.

The waitress came over and set a Bloody Mary down in front of him. Nathan swirled the ice cubes around a second and took a sip. Jennifer regarded him with lips pursed.

"It's a little early, don't you think?"

What did she care? He was just the tour guide on this trip. He could guide a tour just as well drunk as sober.

"It's five o'clock somewhere," he grumbled. "Besides, I had a bad night."

She didn't even flinch. It was as if she was determined to forget what she'd done. Nathan regarded her with something akin to hatred. She was toying with him, he thought, punishing him for pointing out the obvious last night: that she was just like everyone else, capable of making the same mistakes over and over. Oh, but that couldn't be right, could it? Because Jennifer Westbrook was strong and independent and oh so perfect. He wanted to reach out and mess up her perfect hair.

She shook out her napkin and spread it on her lap.

"We need to talk."

Okay, here it comes.

"So talk already."

"I know I said I needed help finding fun things for Boomer to do, but it's important that he not get too tired."

Nathan took another sip of his drink.

"Go on."

"I thought maybe it would be better if we trade off. You know, you can pick exciting things to do one day and I'll pick quieter things the next."

"So . . . one day fun, the next day boring."

"That's not what I meant. I just want Boomer to be able to rest. Take breaks. Like that."

"Sure. Fine. Whatever."

The waitress returned, set down his two fried eggs with ham steak, and took Jennifer's order.

"The slower days will be good for you, too," Jennifer said. "They'll give you time to do interviews and research for your articles."

Nathan's stomach lurched. It had been days since he'd sent anything to Julia. He reached for the Tabasco sauce and started dousing his eggs.

"Anyway," she continued. "I don't want you to think that I'm just being overprotective."

Nathan took a bite of fried egg, and his mouth began to burn. He dropped his fork and reached for a glass of water.

"You *are* overprotective," he croaked.

She pressed her lips together.

"Please don't trivialize this; it's important."

"Believe me," he said. "I'm giving the subject all the seriousness it deserves."

Jennifer looked down and ran a fingernail along the faux wood grain.

"You know, I never realized before how much Boomer needed to have someone like you around—a man, I mean. He always acted like he didn't like the men I met, but the truth is, I don't think I liked any of them all that much, either. Maybe he just didn't want to get attached to someone who wasn't going to stick around."

Nathan squinted, trying to focus on her words through the hangover.

"If this is about last night," he said. "I haven't forgiven you."

She rolled her eyes. "Believe me, I haven't forgiven myself. Though in fairness, it was Boomer's fault, not mine."

He smirked. "Oh, that's right. Blame the dog."

"The thing is, Nate, I'm scared—about a lot of things. I need to get past this thing with Boomer before I can think about what might happen with us. Assuming, of course, that you're interested."

Nathan was staggered, fully awake now, all senses on high alert. The most beautiful woman he'd ever met had just said—well, almost said; she'd definitely implied it—that she was falling in love with him. This was about as close to a hangover cure as he was ever going to get. He pushed the Bloody Mary aside.

"Look," he said. "I know you're scared about Boomer and I get why you're trying to protect him, but if the point of your trip is for him to enjoy himself, then you've got to find a way to let him do that."

"But what if it makes him worse? The vet said that if he got too tired it could kill him."

"Are you sure that's what he said? Because when you mentioned it before, you said he told you what to do if Boomer got too tired. That's not the same as saying you'd be hastening his death if you let him have a good time."

Jennifer's breakfast arrived. As the waitress walked away, she picked up her fork and pursed her lips thoughtfully.

"I don't know," she said. "Maybe you're right."

"Will wonders never cease."

"Okay, then, smart guy. What fabulous fun place are we going to today?"

Nathan gaped. He'd been so busy getting plastered the night before that he hadn't had a chance to find a destination for them.

"Uh . . . well . . ."

Jennifer gave him a sassy smile.

"So," she said. "A boring day it is."

"The Round Barn? Seriously? That's the best you could do?"

They'd taken the turnoff for Arcadia and were following the signs to one of Oklahoma's most distinctive landmarks, an enormous round red barn.

"What are you talking about?" Jennifer said. "This place is perfect. While Boomer and I poke around, you can pick up a few brochures, interview a docent or two, and take some photos."

Nathan closed his eyes against the still-throbbing headache.

"Just kill me now."

"Hey, don't blame me," she said, pulling into the parking lot. "You gave up your right to complain when you got drunk last night and didn't find something better to do."

"Point taken."

"Anyway, the barn is on the National Registry of Historic Places. You can probably find plenty to write about."

Boomer was sitting up in the backseat, looking around and panting happily. Nathan got out and attached his lead while Jennifer put on her jacket.

"That warm weather sure didn't last long," she said, taking Boomer's leash. "It's really starting to feel like fall all of a sudden."

Nathan scrubbed a hand over his face and squinted up at the enormous structure in front of them. The barn was, indeed, very red and very round—even the roof was round. It looked like a big red muffin. Contrary to his previous assumption, the place was also quite busy. He might even be able to glean enough interesting tidbits to build an article around it. He just wasn't sure he wanted to.

"I don't know," he said. "I'm not feeling it."

The look she gave him was pitiless.

"Since when does a professional writer need to be able to 'feel' his subject?"

Nathan had never enjoyed being pushed, and this newfound bossiness on her part was particularly annoying.

"I can't write a good story if I don't like the subject."

"That's because you're a man," she said sweetly. "Any woman will tell you, you don't have to *like* something to be *good* at it."

There was a moment of hesitation before Nathan burst out laughing. Once again, Jennifer Westbrook had astonished him. The second he thought he had her pegged, she said or did something that reshuffled the deck.

"Okay," he said. "I get your point. I'll go see what I can find out about this place."

"Good. You can find us when you're done. Ta-ta."

While Jennifer wandered off with Boomer, Nathan did

as she'd suggested. He walked the outside perimeter to get a feel for just how big the barn was, then stepped inside to take a look around. The individual strips of lumber underpinning the domed roof were exposed, making it seem as if he were standing under an enormous upturned basket, and the acoustics were intriguing. Even with several dozen people talking at once, he would occasionally hear a conversation from the opposite side of the barn as clearly as if the person were standing next to him.

Next to the barn was a museum/gift shop where Nathan found an entire room filled with maps and displays about the Round Barn and its place in the history of Route 66. There was even a replica of the barn that had won a blue ribbon, which the museum kept under a giant plastic bubble—an excellent idea, judging by the hundreds of sticky-looking fingerprints that covered it. Nathan bought a pack of postcards from "Butch the barn man," the colorful septuagenarian who ran the gift shop, then grabbed a map of the grounds and a couple of brochures before heading back to the barn to take a few pictures and talk to the docent.

Jennifer and Boomer were standing right outside the door.

"How's it going?" she said. "You feeling it yet?"

"Alas, yes, in spite of myself." He looked around. "What have you two been up to?"

"Oh, lots of good stuff," she said. "We saw the outhouse—a one-holer. It was pretty cool."

"Gosh," he said. "I must have missed that."

She pointed. "It's right over there—"

"Sorry. No time. What else?"

"Well, Boomie saw a"—she mouthed "squirrel"—"and that was exciting."

"I'll bet."

"A couple more kids asked about Boomer, too, and some guy wanted to know if he could take his picture. You'd think the people around here had never seen a dog." She glanced at his notepad. "So, are you ready to go?"

"Not quite," he said. "The docent said he'd be free in a few minutes; I was just killing time in the gift shop. It shouldn't take too long, though."

"Okay. We'll make a pit stop and get back in the truck. I'm getting pretty cold."

Nathan headed back up the steps toward the barn, wondering about the man who'd asked to take Boomer's picture. Probably just wanted a photo of Jennifer, he thought. Some guys were pathetic.

Phil, the docent, was waiting for him just inside the front door. A burly man in a CAT hat and overalls, he looked like he'd just stepped out of a cornfield.

"Thank you for meeting with me," Nathan said as they shook hands.

"No problem," Phil said. "You want the full tour today, or you just need a few questions answered?"

"Probably just the latter. I've got someone with me," Nathan said, flipping open the notepad. "She and her dog are waiting outside in the truck."

"Well, bring her in."

"No, thanks." He shrugged and took out a pen. "Boomer's a good dog, but I don't think you want him scratching up these floors."

Phil nodded sagely. "You've got that right. Most of these boards were put down when the barn was built in 1898. You can't find old wood like that now. No more old trees around to get it from."

"I can imagine."

"Do you mind if I ask where you three are headed after you leave here?"

"Hmm? Oh, well, I'm not sure," Nathan said. "We're driving Route 66 to the coast, so somewhere west of here. Why? Do you have a recommendation?"

"As a matter of fact I do," the man said, grinning. "You all looking for a good steak?"

Boomer was sound asleep when Nathan got back to the truck. Jennifer had pushed her seat back and was watching the clouds bunch up and then break apart as they floated across the sky. It was so peaceful out there, she thought. No cars, no sirens blaring or horns honking, no phones ringing incessantly, no clients complaining and complaining and complaining.

The passenger door opened and Nathan got in.

"That was quick," she said.

"I told you it wouldn't take long."

She put her seat back up and started the engine.

"Did you get all the information you needed to write your article?"

"Yep. And I got something else, too."

"Really? What?"

"A special place for the three of us to eat dinner."

CHAPTER 21

Nathan took over driving duty after lunch. His headache was gone, he assured Jennifer, and any alcohol he'd consumed the night before had long since left his system. Besides, it was a long way to Amarillo and she needed a break. Boomer was snoring softly on the backseat, his head resting on his paws, and the steady hum of the engine was soothing. As they crossed the Texas panhandle, Jennifer nestled back into her seat and felt a sort of Zen-like calm come over her.

The countryside there was different from what they'd driven through farther east. The trees and rolling hills had been replaced by a vast plane of sun-bleached grasses that stretched for miles in every direction. They passed a building that looked like a stack of wooden blocks, then two rusting silos and a lone windmill that stood out like beacons on the featureless plane. A dirt road branched off to the right, with no indication as to where it might lead. Jennifer felt as if she was sailing on the open ocean with no land in sight.

"Your dog's name—Dobry—what sort of name is that?"

Nathan kept his eyes on the road. "Polish. It means 'good,' or 'kind.'"

"I like that."

"My *babcia,* Dad's mother, wanted my folks to name me Dobry, but Mom thought it sounded too ethnic. These days, parents seem to be looking for unique names, but back then? Nuh-uh."

She smiled dreamily. "Maybe there are a lot of Dobrys running around out there now."

"I've never heard of any."

"No, me neither," she said, as her eyelids closed. "But it's a nice thought."

Jennifer woke with a start. Someone was calling her name.

"What? What is it?"

She sat up and looked around, feeling disoriented. There was a town up ahead. Boomer was awake, and Nathan was still at the wheel. Both of them were staring at her.

"Hey, Sleeping Beauty, time to rise and shine."

"Where are we?" she said, rubbing her eyes.

"Just coming into Amarillo. I thought you'd like to do a little sightseeing on the way to the motel."

Jennifer yawned and smacked her lips. Sightseeing was fine, she supposed, but a few more minutes of sleep wouldn't have been so bad, either.

"How far away is it?"

"About five miles and twenty-seven stop lights."

They checked in at the front desk, and Jennifer took Boomer out for a walk while Nathan headed to his room—to work, he told her, but that wasn't the real reason. He tossed his duffel on the floor and dialed Rudy's number.

"Hey, big brother of mine. How's it going?"

"It would be better if I had my Mustang. Are you back in Chicago?"

"No, actually, that's why I'm calling. I'm in Amarillo, Texas."

"What? Why?"

Nathan stretched out on the bed and kicked off his shoes.

"It's a long story. I'll fill you in on the details when I get there."

"You change your mind about dumping the *Trib*? I still need that rewrite."

"I need a favor."

"So did I, but what have I got to show for it?"

"Come on, Rude, I need to borrow some money."

"Uh-huh."

"See, I met this girl—"

"A hooker? Geez, Nate, you should have told me you were that hard up. I coulda set you up with one of the so-called actresses out here."

"Will you shut up a second? Jennifer's not a hooker."

"But she wants money."

"No. She's got a ton of money. It's me who wants it."

"Why not borrow it from her, then, if she's got so much?"

Nathan sat up. "Look, I'm not asking for a lot. Just enough to pay for a couple nights in a decent motel and maybe a dinner or two."

"I thought your editor was picking up the tab."

"On the per diem she's given me? I'd be eating bread and water the rest of the way and sleeping at the Y. Come on," he wheedled. "You know I'm good for it. I just need a few bucks until payday."

There was a long silence on the line while Rudy contemplated his request. Nathan forced himself to keep breath-

ing. If Rudy refused to loan him the money, his only choices
would be telling Jennifer what his situation was or getting
on a bus and going home. At last, he heard his brother let out
a pained sigh.

"Okay, I can give you six hundred, but that's all. If it
doesn't get you into her pants, you're on your own."

"Thanks, Rude. You're the best."

"And don't I know it."

Nathan hung up and took out the piece of paper that
Phil the docent had given him back at the Round Barn.
There was a phone number on it and the name of a steak
house that the guy had sworn could accommodate the three
of them. All he had to do was tell them he wanted the BBL
special when he made their reservation. Jennifer was going
to love this, he thought, as he dialed. Taking Boomer out for
a steak dinner was about as special as it got.

"I can't believe you got the two of us *and* Boomer into
an honest-to-God steak house," Jennifer said as he drove to
the restaurant that evening. "How on earth did you do it?"

Nathan gave her a smug smile. "I have my ways."

The truth was, he was as surprised as she was. When
he'd called and asked for the BBL special—whatever that
was—the manager himself had gotten on the phone to make
the arrangements.

"Seven o'clock sharp," the man said. "Use the north entrance with the door marked 'Banquet Rooms.'"

Jennifer had insisted upon wearing a dress, and Nathan
was able to find a one-hour dry cleaner for his sport coat, so
at least the two of them didn't look too mismatched. He reminded himself that this was Texas, after all, the spawning
ground of beauty pageant winners; nobody really paid any
attention to the men. He drove into the restaurant's parking
lot and headed to the north entrance.

"Oh, my gosh," Jennifer said, pointing. "Look, Boomie! There's a sign up there with your name on it."

Nathan stopped the truck and stared at the banner hanging above the north entrance:

Welcome Boomer!

"Oh, Nate. That's so sweet. Thank you." She leaned across the console and kissed his cheek. "Come on, Boomer, let's go inside."

Nathan sat there, staring at the banner—the balloons, the huge block letters—feeling unnerved. Had he mentioned Boomer's name to the manager? He couldn't remember. He didn't think so, but how else could the guy have known? Maybe it was Phil the docent, he thought. Yeah, that had to be it. Phil must have called and told them that Nathan would be calling and that he was bringing a dog named Boomer.

Jennifer tapped on his window and Nathan jumped.

"Are you coming?"

"Yeah, sorry," he said, opening his door.

"Is something wrong?"

"No, not at all."

Nathan got out and shook off the lingering weirdness. He was having dinner with a beautiful woman, he told himself. He needed to just go with it. He offered her his arm.

"Shall we?"

They were seated at a table for three in the middle of an empty banquet room. It felt a little awkward at first, having all that room to themselves, but it didn't take long to get used to. How else, they asked themselves, could a restaurant accommodate a dog?

Nathan opened his menu and looked at the prices, silently totaling up the cost and hoping that the money Rudy was wiring to him had hit his bank account already. His credit card might still have enough on it to pay for his own meal, but if Jennifer was expecting him to cover hers, too, he'd need some backup.

She reached across the table and set her hand on his.

"Why don't you let me get this?"

He shook his head. "No, it's fine. Really. I'm okay."

"I mean it," she said, tightening her grip. "This is exactly the kind of special thing I wanted for Boomer and we could never have done it without you. Please?"

Nathan could feel himself wavering. He hated the thought of letting a woman pay his way, but it would certainly be a big relief.

"I don't know . . ."

"What if I told you I was charging it to those clients of mine who you torpedoed? Would that make it easier to say yes?"

He laughed. "You can't do that."

"I could. I'd just tell them I was trying to persuade you to issue a retraction."

Nathan sobered. "There's just one hitch. I don't have a column anymore, remember?"

"That really bothers you, doesn't it?"

"You're darned right it does. It was like watching my dreams die. My self-esteem went into the dumper, I started drinking, my girlfriend left me . . .

"You've still got a job," she said, withdrawing her hand. "And frankly, I think the stuff you're writing now is much better than your old column was. You have a beautiful way with words, Nate."

He shook out the napkin and placed it on his lap.

"I didn't know you'd read my other stuff."

Jennifer reached for her water glass and took a sip.

"There are a lot of things you don't know about me."

A bottle of sparkling wine arrived "on the house" and a parade of waiters began marching through the room, refilling glasses, giving status reports on their dinner, and constantly checking to see if there was anything else the three of them needed. Even before their steaks arrived, Nathan had counted eight different people who'd come into the room.

"Must be a slow night," he said, as the latest one walked out.

Jennifer nodded. "It's like eating in Grand Central Station."

Then the door flew open, and the manager himself wheeled in a serving cart, followed by a member of his waitstaff. Boomer licked his chops as he watched first Jennifer's and then Nathan's plates being set down before them. Finally, the waiter flourished a linen towel, tied it around Boomer's neck, and picked up the third plate.

"I had the chef cut Boomer's porterhouse into small pieces," the manager told them. "He should have no trouble eating it."

"Thank you," Jennifer said.

"And, um, would you mind . . . ?" He took out his cell phone. "As a memento."

She looked at Nathan.

"It's fine with me, if you don't mind," he said. "Boomer'll probably be finished way before we will."

"All right," she told the manager. "But then we'd like to eat on our own after that."

"Of course," the man said.

He turned on his phone and signaled to the waiter. The man set Boomer's steak down, stepped back, and for just a moment, Boomer hesitated, staring at the plate like a man in the desert might stare at an oasis, wondering if it was a mirage. Then he placed his paws on either side of the plate and set to. As the steak began to fly, Jennifer and Nathan shielded their dinners and laughed out loud.

"Ha-ha, very good!" the manager said as he caught the action for posterity.

It seemed like only seconds later, the show was over. The manager put his phone away, and he and the waiter bowed out graciously.

"That was great," Jennifer said. "I wish I'd thought to take a picture."

"Why don't I see if I can get the guy to send us a copy before we leave?"

They ate their dinner in companionable silence. Boomer jumped down and searched the floor for any steak bits he might have missed, and Nathan and Jennifer toasted each other with the sparkling wine. Boomer was given some, too—a splash that Nathan poured onto a bread dish—but the bubbles bothered him, and after a single slurp, he stomped on the side of the dish, turning it upside down.

"Everyone's a critic," Nathan said, as he mopped up the spill.

Jennifer smiled. "This has been lovely, Nate. Thank you."

"My pleasure."

She looked down at the table. "I feel like I should ask you back to the room, but . . ."

"It's okay," he said, taking her hand. "You need this time to concentrate on Boomer. There'll be time for us later."

"Thank you."

"Unless," he said, smiling. "You've changed your mind."

She shook her head.

"No, actually. I haven't. I just thought I should say something after you set all this up."

They put Boomer back on his lead and headed out to the truck.

"Oops, I almost forgot," Nathan said as Jennifer put Boomer inside. "Hold on, I'll be right back."

He ran back across the parking lot and ducked into the restaurant to talk to the manager.

"We had a great time," he said. "Thank you all again."

The man nodded graciously. "Of course. It was our pleasure."

"I was wondering," Nathan said. "If I give you my e-mail address, would you mind sending me a copy of that video? We didn't think to take one of our own."

"Nice try, buddy," the manager snapped. "Go take your own damned video."

CHAPTER 22

When Jennifer got up the next morning, Boomer was still asleep on the bed—something that hadn't happened since that first morning in Joliet. Seeing him lying motionless on the bed brought on a fresh flood of anxiety, something that was never far away in spite of Nathan's advice not to worry. Was Boomer just sleeping off last night's meal, or was something more serious going on?

She crept quietly out of bed and started getting dressed. After their visit to the Round Barn yesterday, this was supposed to be a "fun" day with Nathan in charge, but perhaps it'd be better if the three of them just took it easy. Last night's dinner had been pretty special, after all, and Nathan was the one who'd convinced her not to try and squeeze excitement out of every second of the trip. Two low-key days in a row would be no big deal.

By the time she was ready, Boomer had roused himself and jumped down from the bed.

"Good morning, sleepyhead," she said, watching him

saunter toward the bathroom. "I certainly hope you're not thinking of drinking from that toilet."

He made a quick course correction and headed for his water bowl. Jennifer smiled.

"No, I didn't think you were."

There was a knock at the door.

"That must be Nate."

Jennifer opened the door and her breath caught in her throat. Standing there in jeans and a body-hugging T-shirt, his hair still damp from a morning shower, Nathan looked good enough to eat. Impulsively, she leaned forward and kissed him.

"Wow. Can I go away and come back again?"

"Don't be greedy," she said, stepping back from the door.

Boomer had finished his drink and was coming toward Nathan, his tail sweeping side to side, his entire body signaling a warm, if somewhat subdued welcome. Nathan bent over and started beating a firm tattoo on his side.

"You guys ready to have some fun today? I found a great place for us to go."

"I don't know," Jennifer said. "Boomer seems kind of tired. I was thinking maybe we'd just take it easy."

"Oh, Mom," Nathan whined. "Don't be a buzzkill."

She smiled, looked away, and thought about what he'd said. Was she being a buzzkill? Back in Illinois, she'd been ready to go home, thinking that she and Boomer would never be able to do anything that was special on their trip. If it had been up to her, the two of them would be back at home now, and she'd be sitting the deathwatch. Instead, Boomer had visited farm animals in Missouri, judged a dog show in Oklahoma, and even had dinner at a Texas steak house. If Nathan had been right about those things, maybe he was right about this, too.

"All right," she said. "Let's go have some more fun."

* * *

"A squeaky-toy factory?" Jennifer said when they were finally on the road. "How on earth did you find out about that?"

Nathan was in the passenger seat, looking at the brochure he'd been given at the motel.

"The desk clerk told me about it. They give tours every day at eleven and two. I figure if we stop in Tucumcari for lunch, we'll get to Santa Rosa just in time for the second tour."

"And you're sure Boomer can go in with us?"

"That's what the man said."

She looked at Boomer in the rearview mirror. He wasn't sitting up with his nose out the window like usual, just lying quietly on the seat with his head hanging over the edge. The same uneasiness she'd felt when she woke up began to creep over her again.

"Does he look okay to you?" she said.

Nathan took a quick glance over his shoulder and shrugged.

"Sure, why?"

"I don't know. I just hope that steak wasn't too rich for him."

"He's fine, Jen. I promise you. Can't a guy take a break without everybody freaking out?"

She nodded. "I'm sure you're right. Sorry. How's the writing coming along?"

"Hmm? Oh, fine. Just, you know, knocking out the words."

He seemed distracted, and Jennifer decided not to say any more. God knows, she didn't like having people ask her how things were going when she was in the middle of a project at work.

"The scenery out here is so beautiful," she said. "The plateaus in the distance are really interesting."

Nathan folded up the map.

"High plains," he said. "Most of New Mexico is dry and high."

She nodded. "I used to travel a lot when I was modeling and I thought I knew what the country looked like. Taking this trip, though, I realize what a small part of it I'd actually seen. It's just . . . vast."

He looked at her.

"Can I ask you something? If you don't want to tell me, it's okay."

"Oh, boy. Here it comes." She laughed. "All right, what is it?"

"Why is it that beautiful women always act as if they don't know how good-looking they are?"

Jennifer threw him a sidelong glance.

"Are we talking about me?"

"See there? You just proved my point. How about a serious answer?"

She sighed and pretended to think about the question, but she was stalling for time. The fact was, Jennifer had asked herself the same question many times over the years. Why did a compliment always trigger an automatic denial? She'd seen other women do it and had done it herself so many times it was almost a physical reflex.

"It's not as easy to be a good-looking woman as you might think." She rolled her eyes. "I know, 'Waa, waa, poor me,' but it's true. Other women don't like you, for one thing, so you get a lot of nastiness for something you can't really help. Plus, there's this pressure not to do anything else with your life because then you're taking something away from a not-so-great-looking woman. Somehow, just winning the good looks lottery is supposed to be enough."

"You've already gotten more than your fair share."

"Exactly. The only thing you're allowed to do is be

beautiful. The problem is, if you play along then once that's gone, you lose everything."

Nathan considered that.

"Yeah, but at least you're never lonely. Not many gorgeous women sitting home alone on Saturday nights."

"You'd be surprised," she said. "Most of the men I meet are too intimidated to ask me out, and the ones who do are generally looking for someone to make them look important to other men. God help you if you get tired of being someone's arm candy."

He gave that some thought.

"Did you always know you were beautiful?"

"God, no. When I was fourteen, I was the ugliest girl on the planet. Five foot nine and not much over a hundred pounds with buck teeth and a rat's nest for hair. I was so skinny that if I put my ankles together a weaner piglet could run between my thighs."

Nathan made a face. "I don't believe that."

"It's true," she said. "Luckily, we couldn't afford a lot of mirrors or I'd have had terrible self-esteem."

"What saved you? Besides the lack of mirrors, that is."

"My dad," she said. "He told me I was the prettiest girl in the world, and even though I didn't really believe him, I knew he wasn't a liar, either."

"So, what turned the ugly duckling into a beautiful swan?"

"Victor Otchenko—Vic Ott to you. I was looking for a summer job and he'd put an ad in the local paper for people to give out handbills. He said I had potential."

"What did your father think of that?"

"Not much, but he died a few months later and we were desperate for money. Vic convinced my mother to sign a contract making him my manager and started grooming me—literally—for a modeling career. The hair, the teeth . . .

he fixed everything. In many ways, I'm still grateful to him for that. Which is a good thing, since it made it easier to pay him all that alimony when we divorced."

"Yikes."

"He's remarried now." She smiled. "I was tempted to send his wife a thank-you card on their anniversary."

They arrived in Santa Rosa with ten minutes to spare. As they drove through the town, Jennifer marveled at the number of lakes there were in the area.

"It's like an oasis in the desert."

"That's exactly what it is," Nathan told her. "The ground underneath us is limestone, which is essentially sand that's been packed together into rock. When water trickles through it, the rock starts to break down, leaving gaps that fill with water. If the ground above gets thin enough, you get a sinkhole and the water fills it up. Voilà, you have a lake."

"Too bad the weather isn't better," she said. "I'll bet Boomer would love to get out and play in the water."

"Maybe, if we'd been here in the summer, but it's too cold now. Besides, we have something even better to do." He pointed. "And there it is."

The toy factory was in a nondescript building on the outskirts of town. Other than a small hand-lettered sign, there was nothing to indicate that it was a manufacturing facility at all. Jennifer parked her truck near the front door, and the three of them got out.

"Are you sure this is the right place?" she said.

"According to the brochure, it is."

They opened the front door and stepped into a room not much larger than Jennifer's closet at home. Inside were two chairs upholstered in pea-green Naugahyde, a plastic Parsons table, and a water cooler. On the left was another door and what looked like a fast-food drive-up window. As the door closed behind them, a buzzer sounded. A few seconds later, a teenaged girl appeared at the window.

"Can I help you?"

"Yes," Nathan said. "We're here to take the tour."

Her eyes widened.

"Really? Oh, hey. That's cool. Hold on a second, I'll get one of the guys to show you around."

Jennifer turned and gave Nathan a skeptical look.

"Two tours a day?"

"I'm just going by what the brochure says. I can't be held responsible for false advertising."

She heard a key in the lock, and the door on their left swung open. A small Hispanic man stood there, looking as pleased and surprised to see them as the girl had. The embroidered patch on his shirt said *Isidro*.

"You come for the tour?" he said.

Jennifer nodded. "Yes, if it's not too much trouble."

"Oh, no trouble. Come in, come in. Welcome."

As he turned and led the way inside, Jennifer looked back at Nathan.

"I don't know about this."

"Oh, go on," he said, giving her a push. "It's a fun day, remember?"

They proceeded into a large metal building with high ceilings, concrete floors, and little or no insulation. Small dark-haired women sat at long rows of wooden tables, bundled against the cold. Some were sewing pieces of brightly colored cloth together; others stuffed the sewn-together pieces with foam and the plastic squeakers that would make noise when chewed or shaken. It wasn't a sweatshop, exactly, but Jennifer couldn't help thinking how tedious it must be to sit at those tables day after day.

Isidro, however, didn't seem the least bit troubled, and as they walked past, he proudly pointed out the design area, the cutting tables, and the bolts of material that would be made into items shipped to happy dogs all over the world. Thinking of the pile of toys that Boomer had stashed away at home made Jennifer smile. Maybe the women here thought of the dogs that would be receiving their handiwork, she thought. If they did, perhaps the work itself didn't seem so bad.

As they passed from the assembly room to the packing and shipping area, the teenage girl they'd seen up front joined them. She seemed keen on inserting herself into the tour and interrupted Isidro several times to ask them where they'd been and where they were planning to go next. Jennifer found the girl's questions annoying, but Nathan seemed to have an infinite supply of patience and Boomer was enjoying the pats and compliments the girl lavished on him. She decided that the best thing to do was to just keep her answers short and get through the tour as quickly as possible. Unless something spectacular happened soon, though, this was not going to qualify as a "fun" tour.

Isidro was pointing out the huge bins of finished toys waiting to be packed into boxes, when the girl asked if she could give Boomer a toy. Jennifer nodded curtly.

"What kind's his favorite?" she asked.

Seeing that Jennifer was weary of the girl's incessant badgering, Nathan stepped into the breach.

"He likes cars," he said. "I think he has a Lightning McQueen at home."

"Oh, we make a car that looks just like Lightning McQueen," she said. "Here, I'll get one for you."

Before Jennifer could object, the girl had grabbed Boomer's leash from Nathan and ran with him toward a bin full of thousands of red race cars.

"Hey!"

"No worries," the girl said. "I'll bring him right back."

Nathan placed a hand on Jennifer's shoulder.

"It's okay, we're inside. They're not going anywhere."

Isidro frowned as the girl got on tiptoe and reached for a toy.

"*Cuidado!*" he warned. *Be careful!*

"You want a car, Boomer?" the girl said. "I'll get you one."

Grabbing the side of the bin, she leaped up to get a toy car.

"Oops!"

The bin overturned, sending a tsunami of toy cars tumbling onto the packing-room floor. Boomer dove into the pile, grabbing the toy cars one by one and shaking them violently.

"Look at him go!" Nathan yelled. "He's in dog toy heaven."

The sound of squeaky toys being stepped on, shaken, and dropped echoed through the metal building, increasing Boomer's frenzy. Nathan was howling with laughter, as were several of the other employees, but Jennifer could only titter nervously. It wasn't like Boomer to attack his toys so violently. He might be having a good time, but he was making a mess, and the toys he was savaging would be too damaged to sell. They needed to get him out of there before he ruined the whole batch. She hurried forward, hoping to get things under control.

The overturned bin had been righted and Isidro was waving his arms, trying to keep Boomer away from the undamaged toys as the other workers scooped them up. Jennifer waded into the sea of red cars and retrieved the dog's leash, then tugged him out of the fray. Boomer's sides were heaving; he seemed to be gasping for breath. She checked his mouth and felt a shock when she saw the blue tinge on his gums. As she lifted her head to tell Nathan, Jennifer caught a glimpse of the girl who'd overturned the bin, sliding a cell phone into her pocket.

What the hell is going on?

"Let's get out of here," she said.

Nathan sobered quickly.

"Why? What's the matter?"

"I'm not sure, but Boomer looks bad. I'll put him back in the truck while you ask Isidro what the damage is. After that, we're out of here."

CHAPTER 23

Black clouds hung like funeral bunting overhead, the bleak gray sky reflecting Nathan's inner turmoil as he drove determinedly to Albuquerque. A storm that had been brewing in the west, dumping a foot of snow in the Sierras and torrential rains across northern Arizona, was about to overtake New Mexico. The sooner the three of them got to their motel, he thought, the better.

Jennifer had her face turned away from him, staring out her window. The two of them hadn't said much since stopping for dinner, but Nathan knew she hadn't forgiven him for the disaster at the toy factory. He'd resisted the idea for the better part of an hour, but finally admitted to himself that it had been his fault. He might not have known that things would get out of hand, but when they did, he'd done nothing to intervene. He should have kept a tighter hand on Boomer's leash; he should have stopped the girl when he saw her trying to climb up into the bin; and most of all, he shouldn't have laughed. If he hadn't, he thought, Jennifer might not be so angry.

He still wasn't convinced, however, that Boomer had been in any danger.

In spite of Jennifer's insistence that there was a blue tinge to the dog's gums, no one else had seen it, and Nathan suspected that it was fear that had caused her to imagine she had. She'd taken only the briefest of glances before declaring that Boomer's gums were blue, after all, and it wasn't easy seeing into a dog's mouth without a flashlight. Given that Boomer had been breathing hard and that Jennifer was always thinking about the vet's warning, it would have been easy for her to see something that wasn't there.

Even if Jennifer was right, though, and Boomer had been cyanotic, by the time they got him back to the truck, he clearly was not. If he'd recovered that quickly, Nathan argued, then whatever the problem was, it couldn't have been very serious. Furthermore, Boomer seemed to be suffering no lingering aftereffects. He was tired, sure, but that was to be expected after all the excitement he'd had. Nevertheless, there was no denying that the tour had not been the fun experience Nathan had promised, and the damage done to the factory's toys had cost him almost a quarter of the money Rudy had loaned him, so calling it a disaster wasn't much of a stretch.

A spiderweb of lightning crackled across the sky, followed by a low roll of thunder that sounded like a warning from a dangerous dog. As the truck pulled into the motel parking lot, enormous drops of rain started hammering the windshield. Nathan jumped out and wrestled their luggage out of the back while Jennifer and Boomer ran inside.

At the front desk, there were no coy looks, no intimate discussions about how many rooms they'd be needing. Jennifer gave her name to the clerk and handed over her credit card without consulting Nathan, then picked up her suitcase and headed off to her room with only the briefest of thanks.

As she hurried down the hall with Boomer in tow, the dog gave him a sad, backward glance.

The motel room was modest—a single queen bed, a nightstand, a wooden desk, and chair—with pictures of livestock and Stetson-wearing cowboys on the walls. Nathan stepped inside and put his sodden duffel in the bath to dry, then grabbed a towel and started drying his face and hair. It was as if the heavens had opened up out there, he thought, the rain coming down in sheets. In the time it had taken him to haul the bags into the lobby, he'd been soaked to his skin. He stripped off his T-shirt, hung it over the shower rod, and kicked off his shoes.

Why was Jennifer so mad at him? Nathan wondered. Did she really think that he'd suggested the toy factory so that Boomer could exhaust himself? He'd thought she was putting the paranoia aside and letting the poor dog have a good time. Instead, she'd started blaming him for Boomer's poor health. Well, forget it. If that was the way things were going to be from now on, he was going to have to take a step back and rethink this whole relationship.

Nathan was wiping down his backpack when his phone rang. He felt a jolt when he saw the caller ID.

Julia.

It had been four days since he'd sent her a story, four days without a single word of explanation. Not that any excuse would absolve him. She'd just say they'd made a deal and that any deviation on his part was a betrayal. His only hope was to distract her long enough for her ire to cool. Nathan took a deep breath and tried not to panic.

"Hey, Julia. What's up?"

His editor was in the middle of one of her nicotine-fueled coughing fits.

"Ooh," he said. "That sounds bad."

"Just a cold," she gasped.

"Maybe you should take some time off."

"I *did* . . . three days"—she hacked again—"in the hospital."

"For a *cold?*"

"It was a bad cold."

He heard paper ripping and the distinctive snick of a cigarette lighter followed by a wheezing inhale.

"And yet, you're still smoking."

Julia cleared her throat. "I got the kind with menthol. They're good for you."

Nathan shook his head. If the woman wanted to kill herself, there was nothing he could do about it.

"I don't see your articles in my in-box," she said.

"I'm working on them."

"Of course you are."

Julia's sarcasm was irksome. Nathan felt his lips tighten.

"Look, we both know you're not going to run them anytime soon. What's the rush?"

"You're right," she said. "If I run them at all, it'll be next summer."

"So why the call? And don't tell me you miss me."

There was a long pause while she took another drag on her cigarette. The smoke coarsened Julia's voice, but she sounded more avid than annoyed.

"How'd you like your old column back?"

Nathan's heart began to race. Was she kidding? After his ignominious demotion the year before, his entire world had gone to pieces. He felt like a starving man being offered a five-course meal.

"If this is a joke—"

"It's not. I've already cleared it with the powers that be."

His eyes narrowed. A column was a plum position at a newspaper. Nobody just gave it to you without expecting something in return.

"Okay, you've got my attention. What do I have to do?"

"Have you got Wi-Fi out there in the hinterlands?"

"Supposed to, yeah."

Nathan pulled the laptop out of his backpack and started groping around for the username and password the clerk had handed him when he checked in.

"Good," she said. "I want you to get online and take a look at something."

He signed on to the motel's system and grimaced at the hundreds of unanswered e-mails that filled his in-box. It wasn't just work he'd been avoiding the last few days, Nathan thought guiltily, it was the entire world.

"Okay, I'm on. Now what?"

"There's a page I want you to check out that's generating a lot of buzz. It's called Boomer's Bucket List."

He hesitated, his fingers poised over the keyboard.

"Boomer's . . ."

"Bucket List, three words. It's about a woman who's taking her sick dog on a trip across the country to do things she thinks he'd enjoy before he dies."

Nathan typed in the name and hit "return," feeling as if a cold hand had seized his heart. Sure enough, a Web page full of pictures of Jennifer and her dog filled the screen. It was quite a production, too, with funny memes, GIFs, and a place for comments. Visitors to the page could even play a game called *Where's Boomer?* by uploading pictures they'd taken of Boomer and Jennifer. As he scrolled down the page, he saw himself in one of them, sitting in the audience at the dog show, and felt a shock. If Julia had seen it, too, that might explain the phone call.

"Okay, I see it."

"What do you think? Pretty slick, isn't it?"

"Yeah, so?"

"So, it's grabbed a lot of eyeballs and generated a lot of interest in a story that was practically tailor-made to do just that."

He blinked. "Are you telling me it's a fake?"

"I don't know if it is or it isn't. What I do know is that the PR firm managing it has a reputation for, let's say, playing fast and loose with the truth where generating business is concerned. That, and the fact that its ads are all over the page make me very, very suspicious."

Nathan sat back and ran a hand through his hair. Was Jennifer's story about Boomer's illness a publicity stunt? He'd wondered himself just how sick her dog was, but the way she'd choked up when she told him about the vet's diagnosis had been pretty convincing. He walked over to the window and parted the curtains, peering out at the black Toyota truck sitting in the motel's parking lot not twenty yards away. The thought that he might have been duped put a bitter taste in his mouth.

"So, what is it you want me to do?"

"See if you can find out what's really going on. The Web site says the two of them are following Route 66 west to the coast. It's a long shot, but if you can find them, the *Trib* is willing to resurrect your column so you can tell the world about it."

"An exposé?"

"That depends on what you find. Right now people are going crazy over Boomer and this Westbrook woman. If you can nail their story down before the competition does, it'll mean a ton of exposure—for you *and* for us."

Could he do it? Nathan wondered. If Julia was wrong and Boomer's condition was as bad as he'd been told, he could put the rumors to rest, but if she was right, he'd not only have his column back, he'd be scooping the competition on a big juicy scandal. Either way, though, he didn't think Jennifer would ever forgive him.

He pushed the thought away. This wasn't personal, it was his job, and Jennifer was a big girl. If she was telling the truth, then she should understand. If she wasn't . . . He shook his head. Well, if she wasn't telling the truth, then it didn't matter because she wasn't the woman he'd thought she was. The only important question was, Did he want his column back or not?

"So, what do you think?" Julia said. "Can you find them?"

Nathan closed the curtains.

"I think I already have."

CHAPTER 24

"Oh, my God, Stacy. This place is gorgeous."

Stacy and her best friend, Madison, were standing on the sidewalk, admiring Jennifer's town house. The tree-lined street, tasteful exterior, and lush landscaping were a far cry from the South Side apartment building the two of them called home.

"I come here every day now," Stacy said. "Jennifer told me to just make myself at home while she's gone."

Ever since Boomer's Bucket List had taken off, Stacy had become something of a celebrity to her friends. The notoriety had not only helped to dispel her lingering unease about the Web site, but she'd found that she enjoyed their envy and newfound respect. It seemed only fair that she should share it with her BFF.

As they started up the walkway, Madison spotted the accumulated offerings on the front stoop.

"Look at all the flowers! You were right; this place is like a memorial or something." Madison glanced at the stuffed animal in her hands and bit her lip. "Would you mind if I just put it down here for a second so I can take a selfie?"

"Go ahead."

Stacy smiled indulgently. She'd told her friend not to bring anything, that too many gifts had been left there already, but Madison said that it would be practically sacrilegious to show up empty-handed, and in the end she'd given in. As long as it wasn't another bunch of flowers, she could bring whatever she liked.

Madison stepped forward and set the miniature Rottweiler—a Beanie Baby she'd had since the second grade—down on the pile, then took out her phone and snapped a couple of selfies, checking after each one to make sure that both she and the toy were clearly visible. As she scooped the Rottweiler back up, Stacy opened the door, leaving the flowers behind.

"Aren't you going to get those?"

Stacy shook her head. "There are already tons of them inside. I've been donating the new ones to a nursing home."

Madison was eyeing them covetously.

"You can take a couple if you want."

"Really? Thanks."

They stepped inside and slipped off their shoes. The bouquet in the foyer had started to wilt; Stacy put it in the trash and poured the water out in the powder room sink, then checked on the plants downstairs to make sure they were still moist. Madison stepped into the living room and set the Rottweiler down reverently on the pile of stuffed animals.

"You think she'll like it? I put a note on it to tell her how sorry I am about Boomer."

"Sure," Stacy said. "Jennifer's really nice."

She opened the curtains, turned off the porch light, and started slapping incipient dust bunnies off the furniture while Madison surveyed the room.

"It's like a picture in a magazine."

Stacy looked around, seeing the place anew through her friend's eyes. It did look like something out of a magazine.

The colors Jennifer had chosen were soothing, and the style was classic, neither extravagant nor too trendy.

Perfect, she thought. Everything about Jennifer was perfect. She might be beautiful and rich, but she wasn't bitchy or stuck-up and she didn't act like she was better than anybody else, either. Stacy smiled. It was like Jennifer was what she wanted to be when she grew up.

"When can we eat?" Madison said. "I'm starved."

"In a minute. I have to check upstairs first."

"Can I come?"

"Of course," Stacy said, grinning.

Madison was as impressed with the second floor as Stacy had been the first time she'd been there.

"Look at all this space," she said, throwing her arms wide. "And she doesn't even have a roommate."

"She doesn't need one," Stacy said. "The place is hers."

Madison huffed. "Yeah, well. You're born on third base, you don't have to run too far to score a homer."

Stacy was checking the moisture in the office plants.

"That's the thing, though. She came up from nothing— worse than us, even. Her dad died when she was in high school and her mom was too depressed to work so Jennifer had to get a job and support her."

"In high school?"

"Right after. She got married, too, and the guy used to beat her up."

Madison's look was skeptical. "Did she tell you that?"

Stacy blushed. "No, but I read her Wikipedia page and you can pretty much tell by what it says."

"Oh, well, I guess she's earned it, then." Madison grimaced. "Can we eat now? I'm dying here."

They walked into the kitchen, and Stacy set the Dunkin' Donuts bag on the counter, then turned on the Keurig and checked the K-Cup supply. She bit her lip; the drawer was almost empty. Had she really used that many? She'd have to remember to buy some soon. Jennifer probably wouldn't mind that she'd been using her stuff, but she didn't want her to come back and find everything gone, either.

"Ooh, this is real granite." Madison ran her hand over the countertop. "Feel how cold it is? When I win the lottery, I'm getting a kitchen just like this."

There was a tray next to the sink that Stacy used when she ate outside. In the three days since Derek Compton had given her permission to spend more time at Jennifer's, breakfast on the balcony had become her morning ritual. She set two plates, plus napkins and spoons, on the tray, then took out a third plate and started arranging the donuts on it.

"I brought the paper from home. You want to read it while we eat?"

"Sure." Madison walked over and peered at the Keurig. "What's that thing?"

"It's a fancy coffeemaker. What kind do you want? There's Green Mountain, Tully's, and Starbucks."

"Is the Starbucks light or dark roast?"

Stacy checked. "Dark."

"I'll take the Tully's."

"Latte?"

Madison giggled. "Of course."

When the coffee was ready, they set their mugs on the tray and went out to the balcony. The air was chilly that close to the river, but the fog had broken up, and there was very little breeze. The promenade was busy. Joggers and bicyclists passed by in neon-bright outfits, and a teenager on a hoverboard slalomed through the fallen leaves. A young woman walked by, pushing a stroller while she talked on her phone, and a man in a gray tweed suit sat on a bench, holding a large orange cat in his lap. The two friends watched it all in companionable silence while they shared the donuts and hugged their coffee mugs for warmth.

"This is so civilized," Madison said. "Must make it hard to go to work some days, huh?"

"You can say that again."

Stacy sighed. Sitting there, she could almost forget the town house wasn't hers and that as soon as she left she'd be going back to a thankless job for which she was paid less than the janitors.

"How are things at work with that Jason guy?"

"Better, I guess." She made a face. "Mostly, he just leaves me alone."

"You ask me, he sounds like a jerk." Madison reached for the newspaper. "You want sports, local, or headlines? I've got dibs on the comics."

"Sports, I guess. Everything else is too depressing."

Madison parceled out the paper and handed her the sports section. Stacy pursed her lips as she scanned the first page. The Bears had lost every one of their first three games, and basketball season wouldn't start for another month. Except for a few rivalries she remembered from high school, there was nothing else on the sports pages that held any interest for her. Maybe she should have taken the headlines.

"Ooh, this is interesting," Madison said. "Looks like they're bringing back Nathan Koslow's column."

"I thought they fired him after that lawsuit."

"I guess not."

Stacy was glad the *Trib* had reconsidered; she'd missed the guy's take on Chicago's movers and shakers. Some people, she thought, just needed to be taken down a notch.

"So, who's in his crosshairs this time?"

Madison was skimming the article, looking troubled.

"Maddy, what's wrong?"

"I'm not sure," she said carefully. "I mean, it almost sounds like it's about your friend and her dog."

"What?" Stacy snatched the paper out of Madison's hands and started to read.

The title was "Heartaches, Headaches, and Hoaxes," and the first two paragraphs were about a bookkeeper who'd been caught embezzling from a local charity.

Stacy scowled. "What's embezzling got to do with Jennifer?"

"Keep going. It's near the end."

She skimmed the next couple of paragraphs—something about a fight between the mayor and advocates for the homeless—still wondering what Madison was talking about. Then Stacy reached the final paragraph, and the hair rose up on the back of her neck.

> No one who's ever read a quote from "Abraham Lincoln" about the dangers of the Internet believes that the World Wide Web is a purveyor of unvarnished truth. Nevertheless, one hopes that there are some lines even the most cynical among us won't cross; lies about kids and animals happen to be at the top of my list. So when rumors about a popular Web site featuring a local woman and her "dying" dog reached my ears, discovering the truth became my top priority. No answers for you yet, dear readers, but rest assured that this reporter is on the case. Stay tuned for more and better particulars.

"What do you think?" Madison said. "Is he talking about Boomer's Bucket List?"

Of course he was, Stacy thought. How many popular Web sites featuring a local woman and her dying dog were there? Except that it wasn't a hoax. She felt like calling up the paper and giving Nathan Koslow a piece of her mind.

Furious, Stacy shoved the paper aside, knocking over her coffee cup. Madison shrieked, and the two of them jumped, but it was too late. As the cup hit the ground, it spattered caramel-colored liquid over both of them.

"What did you do that for?" Madison wailed, trying to wipe away the rapidly spreading stain with her napkin. "These are my best pants."

"I'm sorry, Maddy, I didn't think."

The two women dashed inside to see what they could do to salvage their clothing. Stacy's pants legs had been doused, and warm, milky coffee was running into her shoes.

"Does she have any seltzer?" Madison screamed, tearing off a length of paper towels.

Stacy checked the pantry.

"It looks like I drank the last one," she said. "See if regular cold water helps."

As Madison administered first aid to her slacks, Stacy grabbed a sponge and ran back out to clean up the mess on the balcony. Lucky for her, she was wearing black pants that day. If she stayed behind her desk at work, maybe no one would notice. She sopped up as much of the spill as she could, and then brought everything back inside so she could reread Koslow's column.

Madison was blotting the last of the water out of her pants.

"What Koslow said, it isn't true, is it?"

"Of course not," Stacy snapped. "Jennifer was completely torn up about Boomer's diagnosis, and she'd never have taken a month off if he wasn't really sick. She's super dedicated to her job."

She set the paper on the counter and smoothed out the wrinkles. She'd been so shocked when she read the part about Boomer's Bucket List that she couldn't remember exactly what it said.

Madison looked around. "I need to dry my pants. Is there a hair dryer?"

Stacy pointed absently. "Check the guest bath upstairs."

On the second reading, the column didn't seem quite so bad. Saying that there were rumors wasn't the same as saying they were true, after all, and Koslow admitted that he was still investigating. Still, writing something like this was irresponsible without checking the facts first, and he couldn't do that until he'd spoken to Jennifer. How did Koslow think he was going to find out the truth if he couldn't even find her?

The Web site, of course. Jason's stupid *Where's Boomer?* contest had enough clues on it to lead Koslow straight to her. Well, maybe that was a good thing, she thought. Jennifer's reputation was on the line. If clients thought she couldn't be trusted, they'd go running like scared cats. The sooner Koslow found out the truth, the sooner the *Trib* could issue a retraction and apologize for their mistake. In the meantime, though, she had to give Jennifer a heads-up.

Stacy went to the foyer and grabbed her purse off the floor, pawing through its contents to find her phone. If Koslow was looking for her, Jennifer would need to be ready for him. The guy was like a shark; if he smelled blood in the water, it would be hard to come away from the encounter in one piece. She turned on the phone and started flipping through her contacts. Jennifer had said no calls unless it was an emergency, but she was pretty sure this qualified.

"Stace?" Madison was coming down the stairs. "People are staring at the house."

"Hold on a sec. I'm trying to make a call."

"No, I'm serious. Look."

Stacy glanced out the window. Two women were standing at the end of Jennifer's walkway, each holding a bunch of flowers as they looked uncertainly at the front door.

"They're just leaving more flowers for Boomer," she said. "Don't worry about it."

"Are you sure? They look kind of mad."

She looked out again and saw a man walk by. The women stopped him and pointed at the town house. He nodded, spoke to them briefly, and continued down the street. The women stood there a moment longer, shaking their heads, then turned and left, taking their bouquets with them.

Stacy licked her lips. Why hadn't they left the flowers? This wasn't about Koslow's column, was it?

Madison walked down the stairs and crossed to the front door, keeping her eyes averted. She slipped her shoes on.

"I'd better go," she said. She grabbed her purse. "I thought you were making a call."

Stacy looked down at the phone, her finger hovering over the "call" button. What would she tell Jennifer when she asked how Koslow could find her? Would she be angry when she found out about Boomer's Bucket List? If Stacy did call her, she'd probably come rushing back home, too. Stacy wouldn't be able to come to the town house anymore, and Mr. Compton would expect her to be at her desk early again. There'd be no more breakfasts on the balcony or glasses of wine while she watched the sun go down.

There were supplies she'd have to replace, too, and some of them were pretty expensive. Jennifer might not be very happy if she found out that Stacy had been practically living in her house for the last few days, eating her food and pretending she was something other than the caretaker. She'd probably never trust her again.

"Um, hello?" Madison said. "Earth to Stacy. Are you going to make the call or what?"

Maybe she'd just wait awhile, she thought. There was no guarantee that Nathan Koslow would even find Jennifer, and if he did, well, Stacy would deal with that later. She turned the phone off.

"It wasn't important," she said, tucking it back into her purse. "I can do it later."

CHAPTER 25

The storm had passed, but the damage it caused was everywhere, and the weather bureau was warning that more of the same was on the way. Roads were flooded—some of them washed out entirely—and the saturated, unstable ground was making travel through the mountains treacherous. As they got closer to the Arizona border, Jennifer was thankful that Nathan had agreed to join them. Knowing there was someone else to help out in case of an emergency was a big relief, even if things between them were still strained.

He hadn't said much at breakfast, but she could hardly blame him. The way Jennifer had acted when they checked into the motel had been rude and immature. She'd passed a restless night in her room, angry with Nathan about the toy factory incident and angry with herself for blaming him. She was even angry with Boomer for forgetting himself and tearing so many of the squeaky toys apart. It was embarrassing to see him acting so savagely. He knew better than that.

Jennifer glanced over at Nathan, sitting quietly in the passenger's seat, and felt her heart warm. He'd tried so hard to find something fun for them to do. Who knew that things could go wrong at a squeaky-toy factory, for heaven's sake? It was silly to let this quarrel continue, she thought. If they were going to have a future together, there'd be other arguments; she didn't want a pattern of letting things fester become a habit. Better to clear the air now and get it over with.

"I'm sorry I gave you such a hard time about the toy factory," she said. "It really was a good idea and I know Boomer enjoyed it."

"No, I'm the one who should be sorry," Nathan said. "I let things get out of hand."

She smiled. "And I'm the one who begged you to think of something fun to do. Besides, it wasn't your fault the bin turned over. If that stupid girl hadn't launched herself over the edge, it would have been fine. Did you see her taking Boomer's picture while the whole thing was going on? It was like she thought it was funny."

Nathan frowned. "No, I didn't see that."

"I did, and it's not the first time it's happened, either. Remember those people at the fair with the little boy who kept making such a fuss about Boomer's name? They were taking pictures, too."

"So? People always take pictures of their kids."

Jennifer sighed and studied the road ahead. She knew she hadn't been seeing things. Ever since that desk clerk had taken their picture back in Carthage, people seemed to be watching them. She didn't expect Nathan to agree, necessarily, but it felt as if he was deliberately dismissing her concerns.

Give him time, she told herself. *You were pretty awful to him last night.*

"It still seems strange the way they did it, too," she said. "Like they were trying to hide what they were doing."

He shrugged. "Who knows? You can never tell what someone else is thinking."

"I guess. Anyway, I shouldn't have gotten so upset about what happened at the factory. I'm sorry."

Nathan nodded and went back to staring out the window. It didn't feel quite the same between them as it had before, Jennifer thought, but at least they were talking again.

They stopped in Gallup for lunch and ate at the Route 66 Drive-In where they stayed in the truck and had their lunch brought out to the car. Boomer sniffed his burger and made a halfhearted attempt to eat, but he left most of it in the basket. Jennifer watched him anxiously.

"He still doesn't look good to me," she said. "I'm glad we're not having a fun day today."

"Look, I *said* I was sorry," Nathan snapped. "Can we just drop it?"

She drew back. "I didn't say that to make you feel—" She pursed her lips. "Oh, forget it."

They finished their lunch in silence and switched drivers. While Nathan adjusted his seat and mirrors, Jennifer gathered up the remains of Boomer's hamburger and surreptitiously checked his gums. They looked a little pale to her, but she didn't see any blue and she wasn't about to ask Nathan for his opinion. She was trying not to be upset with him—it was obvious he was still upset about the night before—but it was hard not to feel that this attitude of his boded ill for their having a more permanent relationship. She'd just have to have faith that things would work out, Jennifer told herself. Nathan wasn't like Vic. She might not know him well, but she knew that much.

Nathan felt his teeth clench as he drove down the highway. Everything—the road signs, the other cars, even the road itself—made him feel irritable. Why should life go on the same as always when his own life had been turned upside down? Julia wanted him to find out the truth about Boomer as soon as possible, and he still had no idea how he was going to do it. He could come right out and ask, he supposed. It would certainly save time, if it worked, but there was no guarantee that Jennifer would tell him the truth. If she'd been lying all along, what were the chances she'd suddenly drop the pretense and fess up? Trying to trick her into making an admission wouldn't be easy, though. The longer things went on like this, the more likely it was that she'd figure out what was going on.

When Jennifer had shared Boomer's diagnosis with him, Nathan thought that she was revealing a confidence; he felt honored that she'd trust him with something so personal. Now he wasn't sure what to think. It was clear that she'd been reluctant to talk about it, but had it been because she was telling him a painful truth, or was Jennifer's revelation meant to throw him off the scent of a potential scandal? She'd known by then who Nathan was. Maybe she figured that playing on his sympathies would make it less likely that he'd check into her story.

I should have known better.

Now that he'd been tipped off, however, his reporter's instincts were starting to kick in. Suddenly, everything she'd said to him since they met had taken on a sinister meaning. Telling him she preferred his other pieces to the stuff he'd written for his column? False flattery, a way to throw him off her scent. And what about that comment the other night about his not knowing everything about her? Maybe she'd been telling him something important that he was too blind to see.

It was time to go back to basics. Was Jennifer's trip just about driving business to her agency? If Boomer wasn't really dying, why make such a blatant appeal to the public's sympathy? The percentage of people following Boomer's Bucket List who would ever be in the market for a PR firm's services had to be miniscule. Surely there were better ways for Compton/Sellwood to increase their market share than by abusing people's trust. If Julia was right and the whole thing was a hoax, the backlash when it was finally discovered was going to be intense.

On the other hand, a person like Jennifer didn't just drop everything and take off across the country without a good reason. She held a key position at her agency; having her gone for even a short while would cause serious difficulties for them and their clients. He'd even looked up HCM and found that her description of Boomer's alleged ailment was correct. It might be unlikely that he was suffering from it, but it wasn't impossible, either. The problem, Nathan realized, wasn't that her story couldn't be true, it was that he wanted it to be true, and that made him less confident in his own judgment. If he was going to do this job, he needed to weigh the evidence like someone who was seeing it for the first time. If he couldn't do that, then he might as well call Julia and have her give the story to someone else.

"I'm glad you're not writing your column anymore," Jennifer said.

The comment, coming out of left field as it did, struck Nathan like a blow. He flinched, jerking the wheel hard enough that the truck veered briefly onto the shoulder.

Jennifer grabbed her door handle.

"What was that? What happened?"

"Sorry," he said. "I saw something in the road."

She turned and looked through the back window.

"Are you sure? I don't see anything."

"It probably ran off," Nathan said. "Don't worry about it."

She reached over and put her hand on his shoulder.

"Are you tired? You want me to drive?"

"No, I'm fine." He shrugged his shoulder, and Jennifer removed her hand. "What made you say that?"

"Say what?"

"That you're glad I'm not writing my column anymore."

"Oh. I was just thinking that you should write a book, something about this trip, maybe. You're a really good writer, but your column was always so nasty. It just didn't seem like you."

He hooted. "Write a book? Are you kidding?"

"Why not? Wouldn't you like to?"

"Sure. Me and every other guy out there."

"But you're good, Nate. Why not use your talent to elevate the conversation?"

"You mean use my power for good, instead of evil?"

She scowled. "No. Give people something joyful and uplifting to read instead of making them and yourself cynical and unhappy."

"That wasn't part of my job description," he said. "I'll leave the joyful noise stuff to the saints."

Jennifer shrugged and turned back to the window.

"Anyway," she said. "I'm glad you're not like I thought you were from reading your column. I don't think I'd have liked you very much."

It was the last thing either of them said until they got to their motel.

CHAPTER 26

Jennifer was signing the motel register when Nathan walked in with their luggage. As the door closed behind him, the acrid smell of ozone wafted into the small lobby. She wrinkled her nose.

"What is that?"

"Lightning," the desk clerk said, handing her the key. "No more rain just yet, but there's plenty on the way."

They were staying in Holbrook that night, just west of Petrified Forest National Park. Jennifer was disappointed that they hadn't been able to stop and take a look, but the road leading into the park had still been partially underwater, and with more rain expected soon, the rangers had advised them not to chance it. Between that and the lack of conversation coming from Nathan, the hours had dragged by. It wasn't so much that it was a not a "fun" day that bothered her; it was that it had turned out to be exactly what Nathan had said it would be: boring.

Jennifer reached for her suitcase and looked over at Nathan. When she first stepped into the lobby, she'd been entertaining the idea of sharing a room, but he'd taken so long getting their things out of the truck that she'd decided to just continue with the way things were. His gaze met hers briefly and slid away in a gesture that could mean anything from guilt to resentment, and Jennifer felt a prick of annoyance. Was he still angry about last night, or was something else going on? She wished he'd just tell her so they could clear the air.

"I've got work to catch up on," he said. "I'll probably just eat in my room."

So much for clearing the air.

"Yeah, we'll probably do the same," she said. "See you in the morning."

Jennifer led Boomer down the hall toward their room. Thank God she hadn't asked Nathan to join them, she thought, or she'd be regretting it now. If he wanted time to himself, he was welcome to it. After the silent treatment he'd been giving her all day, she wasn't exactly dying to fall into bed with him.

Being cooped up in the truck had apparently taken its toll on Boomer, too. He seemed crankier than usual, impatiently scratching at the door when Jennifer didn't open it fast enough. There hadn't been much opportunity for him to walk around during their bathroom breaks, and Jennifer had no doubt that he'd picked up on the tense atmosphere in the truck, as well. When she finally shoved the door open, he dragged himself across the threshold and collapsed in a heap, not even bothering to get up on the bed.

Jennifer started putting her clothes away, keeping a close eye on her dog as she did. Was this was a normal reaction to a long day on the road or something more ominous? She wished she could ask Nathan what he thought, but he'd made it clear that he wasn't in the mood to talk. Anyway, she thought, he'd probably just tell her she was imagining things. She fished the novel she was reading out of her purse and lay down on the bed, reassured by the sound of her dog's deep, unlabored breathing. It had just been a hard day, she told herself. Things were going to be all right.

Hours had passed by the time a gnawing ache in Jennifer's stomach woke her. She opened her eyes and looked around the darkened room, disoriented by the unfamiliar surroundings. At some point, Boomer must have roused himself; he was sleeping peacefully beside her. She set a gentle hand on his side and felt his heart beating. Was it faster than usual? she wondered. No, Dr. Samuels had said he still had a month left. It was probably just her overactive imagination.

The pain in her stomach intensified, and she heard a protracted growl. Jennifer looked at the time. *No wonder,* she thought. She should have eaten hours ago. She walked into the bathroom and splashed cold water on her face, wishing she'd bought a sandwich somewhere before checking in; there was no room service at the motel and she hated to leave Boomer on his own. Then again, she thought, glancing back at the bed, it didn't look like he'd be getting up any time soon. There was probably time for her to go and get some dinner before he needed to be taken for a walk.

Gathering up her purse and keys, she opened the door and glanced down the hall. There was a light on in Nathan's room. Should she ask him to join her for dinner? No. He'd said he was going to eat in his room, which meant that he'd probably already gone out and gotten something. Chances were, he was hard at work on the next article for his editor. Preventing him from doing his work wouldn't make whatever was bothering him go away.

The Tee-Pee Restaurant and Lizard Lounge was only about a block away—walking distance, really—but she didn't want to risk getting caught in a downpour on the way back. In spite of its odd name, the place had been given high marks by the motel manager, and Jennifer was too hungry to quibble. After all, wasn't part of the point of taking Route 66 to find places with names like that? As she got out of the truck and headed toward the front door, she felt the first drops of rain on her face.

Stepping inside the restaurant was a shock. She'd assumed it would be quiet at that time of night, but the place was almost full. The crowd was pretty noisy, too, split between a multigenerational birthday party that had taken up most of the tables and two groups of rowdy teens who'd commandeered the booths. She was about to go looking for a quieter place to eat, when the hostess appeared. Seeing the look on Jennifer's face, she pointed toward the entrance to the lounge.

"Anything on the menu, you can get in there. Probably quieter, too."

"Thanks," Jennifer said. "I'll do that."

She stepped into the darkened room and gave her order at the bar. There was a stage on the right that was not much bigger than her truck, but this being Monday, there was no live music, only Waylon Jennings coming through the PA system singing about Luckenbach, Texas, and "getting back to the basics of love." As she waited for her Bud Light, Jennifer wondered if she and Nathan were ever going to get to "the basics." It seemed as if they were always working at cross-purposes to each other. Whenever one of them made a move, the other one seemed to back off.

The bartender slid her drink across the bar, and she handed him a ten, told him to keep the change, and started searching the room for a table. Her eyes had adjusted to the low light by then, and she hoped to find an empty spot near the back. She'd been in enough bars to know that the drunker a man got, the more likely he was to approach her—and she wasn't in the mood to socialize. She'd just spotted a nice secluded table across the room, when a man sitting in the corner caught her eye.

*   *   *

Nathan couldn't remember how many drinks he'd had since walking into the Tee-Pee Lizard Lounge. Enough that he'd felt compelled to tell the waitress that he wasn't driving, but not enough yet to stop feeling guilty about agreeing to Julia's proposal. Having his column restored was the answer to a prayer, but having it at the cost of losing Jennifer Westbrook had made it a devil's bargain. He'd told himself it would serve her right to be humiliated, that Boomer's Bucket List was nothing but a cheap ploy to gain market share, and that taking advantage of people, playing on their sympathy, and having them worry themselves sick over a dog's fate just to prove how good her agency was at manipulating public opinion was disgusting. But what if . . . ?

What if Julia was wrong? What if Boomer was really dying, and Nathan had called Jennifer's private pain into question? He wasn't infallible; he'd been wrong about things he'd written in his column before; he'd just never considered it a big deal. After all, that's what retractions were for. So, why now? What was it about this situation that was making him drink himself into oblivion instead of finding the answer to a very simple question. Was Jennifer Westbrook a liar or not?

He saw someone coming toward him and looked up, squinting at the blurred image of a tall, dark-haired woman with a drink in her hand. He looked down at his glass. Was it time for a refill? He didn't think so. The last time he'd ordered one, the waitress had seemed pretty reluctant. His mind was so sluggish that the woman was standing next to the table before he realized it was Jennifer.

Her mouth was pinched in an unattractive expression that had all but eliminated the outline of her full lips. Staring at it made Nathan feel sad. Jennifer had such soft, warm lips; it seemed a shame to bunch them up like that. Was she just going to keep standing there all night, looking at him like that? He curled his lip and blurted a favorite childhood taunt.

"Didn't your mother ever tell you your face would stay that way if you didn't stop?"

The corner of her mouth quirked, but the expression didn't change. Jennifer motioned toward the chair across from him.

"Mind if I sit down?"

"Be my guest," he said, waving his arm in an expansive gesture that came perilously close to toppling his drink.

She sat down and set her glass on the table.

"I thought you had work to do."

"I did. I do," he said. He lifted his glass. "I'm taking a break."

Jennifer looked at the half-empty scotch in his hand.

"I've got dinner coming. Mind if I eat it here?"

"Not at all." Nathan smiled magnanimously. "Maybe I'll have something, too."

She looked at him sharply. "You haven't eaten yet? How long have you been in here?"

He frowned. How long had he been in there? He remembered he'd left the motel just after they checked in, and now it was . . . Nathan looked at his watch, and the dial swam, something that struck him as incredibly funny for some reason. He started to laugh.

"You're drunk," she said.

The edge in Jennifer's voice spoiled the mood. Nathan scowled at her.

"What are you doing here, anyway? I thought Boomer couldn't be left alone."

"He's been sleeping ever since we got to our room," she said. "I thought I could risk it."

His eyes narrowed. *Maybe she's telling the truth,* Nathan thought. *Or maybe she just didn't think I'd be here to catch her.*

"That's very convenient," he said.

Jennifer set her glass down hard enough to slosh beer onto the table.

"What's that supposed to mean?"

Nathan's heart was racing. This was it, he thought. The perfect opportunity. He was tired of dancing around the subject, looking for some way to catch her out, trying to come up with a scheme to get her to tell him the truth so he could give Julia the scoop she wanted and go back to the life he loved and was no longer sure he wanted. Why prevaricate?

Go ahead. Ask her.

A plate swooped down between them, and a cheeseburger and fries landed on the table.

"Cheddar cheese, medium well, hold the mayo," the waitress said as she set it down. "Ketchup's at the bar."

Jennifer paid the check and cut the burger in half.

"Here," she said, shoving it toward him. "Eat this. You'll feel better."

The adrenaline rush that had been fueling his courage vanished, leaving Nathan feeling weak and disoriented. Unable to remember what he was going to say and too addled to argue, he took a bite and started to chew. He'd had no idea he was so hungry. The cheeseburger was delicious.

Jennifer gave him a wary smile.

"You looked like you were going to say something."

He swallowed. "I was."

"I'm glad," she said. "I think we need to talk."

Nathan nodded, reminding himself that he was a journalist, and attempted to regain the impersonal mien he'd used over the years when conducting interviews of both the famous and infamous. This wasn't about his feelings for Jennifer Westbrook, he told himself. He had a job to do, one that he was good at. It wasn't personal, it was just business. But as he opened his mouth, Jennifer held up a finger to stop him.

"Hold on a sec."

She took the phone from her back pocket and blanched when she saw the number.

"It's my mother," she said. "I'm sorry, I have to take this."

As she hurried away, Nathan felt an odd mixture of frustration and relief.

CHAPTER 27

Jennifer's hands shook as she answered the phone. It had been two years since she'd moved her mother to a full-time care facility. Two years of worry and guilt, of temper tantrums and late-night calls from a woman whose mind had been twisted out of true by the twin demons of depression and dementia. Only in the last few months had the situation begun to improve, and then only because her mother rarely remembered she even had a daughter. Whatever the reason for this call, Jennifer thought, it could not be good.

"Jenny, is that you?"

Her mother sounded frightened, breathless, as if she'd been chased to the phone by her own demons.

"Yes, Mom, it's me. What's wrong? Are you okay?"

"Promise me you're all right, dear. I've been so worried."

This was the curse of motherhood, Jennifer thought. Even when she couldn't remember much else about her only child, Ida Westbrook knew she should be worried about her.

"Yes, I'm fine. I promise."

"Oh, thank the Lord. I was afraid . . . so afraid for you."

This concern for her daughter's welfare was new, and for a moment Jennifer allowed herself to think it might be a hopeful sign, that the medications were finally starting to work. Then she reminded herself that this had happened before with no noticeable improvement. Like an amputee feeling the pain of a phantom limb, her mother was simply responding to a need that no longer existed. "Jenny" had grown up and left home years ago.

"Everything's okay," she said, doing her best to sound reassuring. "There's nothing to be afraid of."

"But he's trying to hurt you. I heard them talking; they all said so. Even Vera."

Jennifer frowned. Why would her mother's private nurse be talking about her?

"No one's trying to hurt me, Mom. Boomer and I are on vacation, remember?"

Before her mother could answer, Jennifer heard Vera's voice in the background. Poor woman was probably wondering how her charge had gotten hold of the telephone. The sound of her mother's feeble protests died away as the phone was taken from her, then the authoritative voice of Vera Brown boomed in Jennifer's ear.

"I'm sorry, Miss Westbrook. I stepped out for a pee break and when I come back, here she is, calling you on the phone."

"Is everything okay, Vera? Mom seems to think I'm in some sort of trouble."

"Oh, yes. Everything's fine. Your mother's just got her knickers in a twist over that story in the newspaper."

Jennifer breathed a sigh of relief. As the dementia worsened, her mother was having difficulty separating what was going on in her own life with the things she read about in the news. Considering the state of the world, it wasn't surprising the woman would feel alarmed about something.

"Of course, I know you," Vera continued. "But there've been a few tongues wagging around here since that story came out. I wouldn't be surprised if that's what set her off."

"I'm sorry, Vera. You lost me. What are we talking about?"

"Oh, just that silly column in the *Trib.* Don't you worry. Anybody who knows you knows it's not true."

Jennifer looked at the phone, wondering if Vera, too, was becoming delusional.

"'Course, we've all been following Boomer's Bucket List," the woman added, "so when that fella made it out like you were lying about your dog, well, it just set all our teeth on edge. No doubt, that's what your mama was calling about."

Jennifer's mind reeled as she tried to make sense of what she'd been told. *Someone was trying to hurt her . . . there'd been a story . . . a column in the* Trib *. . . a reporter who said she was lying. . . .* She shook her head. Why would the *Trib* be interested in Boomer? She didn't even know anyone who worked there. Except . . .

She took a step backward and peered into the darkened lounge. Nathan was hunkered over the table, munching on the burger she'd given him. Jennifer still had no idea what was going on, but she had a feeling she knew which reporter Vera was talking about, and unless she was mistaken, he knew exactly what was going on.

"I'm sure you're right," she said. "Thanks, Vera. I'll give you a call in the morning to check on Mom."

Nathan was polishing off the last of the French fries when Jennifer returned to the table. He looked up and gave her a wan smile.

"Everything okay?"

"Everything's fine," she said. "Come on, I'll give you a lift."

He shook his head. "I can walk."

"No, you can't. You're drunk and it's pouring outside. Let's go."

Neither one said a word on the drive back to the motel. Rain pelted the windshield, and the steady beat of the wipers felt like the inexorable ticking of a time bomb. Jennifer kept a death grip on the wheel, trying to keep the rage that was growing inside her from bursting forth. She was still in the dark about most of what was going on, but in the end what it came down to was this: Nathan had lied to her and about her. Why he'd done it didn't matter.

She pulled into the parking lot and turned off the engine. Nathan was staring out the windshield, acting as if nothing was wrong. It made her heart ache to realize how much she cared about him, and how hard it was going to be to rebuild the wall she'd so carefully constructed as protection against this kind of hurt. Then she thought about how hurt Boomer was going to be when the man he adored left him, and Jennifer felt a rush of anger.

Damn you, Nathan Koslow. How could you?

"My mother was pretty upset," she said. "Apparently, a columnist at the *Trib* accused me of lying. You know anything about that?"

He hesitated only a second before turning toward her.

"What do you want to know?"

"For starters, why are you writing about me?"

"I got a tip from my editor that Boomer's story might make an interesting article."

Of course, she thought. Of course.

"I'll admit I'm surprised," she said, "but maybe I shouldn't be. After all, what are the chances we'd keep running into each other on the road? I must have been crazy to think it was just a coincidence."

His face reddened. "Okay, first of all, Boomer ran out to me at the speedway, and as I recall you were the one who approached me at the gas station, too, so don't make it sound as if I made the first move. And when I ran into you at the bridge, you were the one who was all, 'Boo-hoo, I can't find anything to do with my dog.' I was just trying to help you out."

"By using me."

"Me using *you?*" Nathan sputtered. "How about the other way around?"

"What are you talking about?"

He shook his head. "God, you are so good at this. I should have known you'd stonewall once the cat was out of the bag."

She stared at him, still completely at sea. First her mother calls, saying she's in danger, then Vera tells her someone's been telling tales about her in the newspaper, and now Nathan was saying it was all part of a plan that Jennifer herself had hatched. She felt like she was in a house of mirrors. Had the entire world gone mad?

"What cat? What bag?" she said. "You are making absolutely no sense right now."

Nathan leaned closer. Jennifer could smell the booze on his breath.

"Why do you think Boomer was chosen as a judge at the dog show? Or that he was given a special tour of that toy factory? I mean, you didn't really think we could have gotten into that steak house if the owner hadn't wanted to host the famous Boomer in his restaurant, did you?"

Jennifer was at a loss for words. The *famous* Boomer?

"You've lost me. I really don't know what to say."

His look was pitying. "Please don't pretend you don't know that you and your dog are all over the Internet. Last time I checked, there were hundreds of pictures of you two on Boomer's Bucket List. It's got over a million followers." He shook his head. "I'll admit it seemed pretty crass, using your dog's illness to generate business for Compton/ Sellwood, but it looks like it's worked out for me, too."

Suddenly, things that had seemed strange to Jennifer the

last week began to make sense: the desk clerk wanting to take their picture at the motel; the boy at the fair; the people at the Round Barn asking if they could take Boomer's photo. But how could strangers know anything about her and Boomer? How would they even know what she and Boomer looked like? No one knew where they were . . . unless . . .

Stacy!

Stacy, her biggest fan, the girl who just wanted a few pictures so she could track Jennifer and Boomer while they were on their trip. Had she built the Web site herself, or had Derek Compton just talked her into passing the pictures along to him? Probably the latter, she thought. As much as she liked her admin, the poor girl had neither the ambition nor the talent to create the kind of Web site that would attract hundreds of thousands of followers.

She looked at Nathan. "So, instead of coming right out and asking me what was going on, you made a public accusation."

Nathan glanced down, his face coloring. At least he had the decency to look shamefaced, she thought.

"For what it's worth," he said. "I didn't mean to hurt you."

"Of course you did," she said. "Just like you hurt every other woman in your life: so you could get back at dear old Mom."

"What?"

"'Guess I'm still bitter,'" she said, mocking his own words. "'I haven't forgiven Mom for getting rid of my dog.'"

Nathan's lips thinned. "You're crazy."

"Am I? What other reason would you have to ridicule me in public?"

"Julia said they'd give me my column back if I did an exposé on you and Boomer. I figured you'd lie if I came right out and asked you about it."

"Oh, please. This isn't about doing what your editor

wants, it's about proving that any woman who'd love you can't be trusted."

"Wrong. I was doing my job, period. Julia said there were rumors that Boomer wasn't really sick. It was my duty to check it out."

"No, Nate. When you lost Dobry, you decided to show the world that you didn't need anyone, and to prove it you used the one talent that sets you apart to tear other people down. You can't stand the thought that Boomer is really sick because that would mean that I'm getting the chance to say good-bye—a chance *you* never had." She put a trembling hand over her mouth. "When you said I shouldn't coddle him, I listened to you. I've been tiring him out when I should have gone back home and let him spend his last days around the things he loved."

"That's a terrible thing to say."

"Oh? Well, I suppose you'd know since you're the master of saying terrible things."

Jennifer pointed to the door.

"Get out," she said. "We can figure out how to get you to LA in the morning. Assuming, of course, that that's where you're really going."

Nathan set his hand on the door and contemplated the rain outside.

"There's a bus station a few blocks from here. I'm sure I can find a way there."

Jennifer watched impassively as he zipped up his jacket and opened the door. There'd be time for tears later, she told herself. Right now she just wanted Nathan Koslow out of her sight.

CHAPTER 28

There were no bouquets or stuffed animals on Jennifer's doorstep that morning, no letters of support tucked into her mailbox. Now that Nathan Koslow's column had cast doubt upon the truth of Boomer's illness, the only thing Stacy got when she stopped by the town house were dirty looks from the neighbors. She decided to skip having coffee on the balcony and go straight to work.

The mood in the office was subdued. Mr. Sellwood was at his desk, quietly fuming, and clients were being ushered in and out like visitors to a funeral home. Derek Compton was meeting with Jason behind closed doors, no doubt working on a plan for damage control. Everyone knew that the burst of interest the agency had gotten from potential clients when Boomer's Bucket List took off might very well turn ugly if something wasn't done soon. Stacy had spent an hour the night before trying to contact Boomer's veterinarian and have him confirm the dog's condition, but without Jennifer's okay, there was nothing he could do. Once this meeting was over, she had no doubt that the boss would have her call Jennifer and ask her to call the man's office.

Stacy just wished she knew how she was going to break the news.

The thought of what would happen after that made Stacy's stomach churn. What would Jennifer do when she found out about Boomer's Bucket List? Would she see it, as Stacy did, as a tribute to her dog, or as a way for Compton/Sellwood to cash in on her private agony? Either way, she knew, it would be Stacy that Jennifer would blame. Without the photos she'd shared, the Web site could never have been created. Any good feelings there'd been between the two of them would be lost.

The phone rang, and Stacy pulled her thoughts back to the present. For now, at least, she still had a job to do, and fretting about what might or might not happen in the future wouldn't make things any easier. She adjusted her headset, put a smile on her face, and answered the call.

"Compton/Sellwood, this is Stacy. How may I direct your call?"

Jennifer's voice hit her like a slap in the face.

"Stacy, this is Jennifer. What the hell is going on out there?"

Tears sprang into Stacy's eyes. She'd thought she could face whatever happened, but the cold fury coming through her headset was worse than anything she'd imagined.

The door to Derek Compton's office opened, and Jason stepped out, giving her a questioning look. She pointed at the phone and mouthed the word "Jennifer." He nodded, stepped back inside, and shut the door.

"Hello? Stacy, are you still there?"

Stacy swallowed the lump in her throat, fighting to keep her voice under control.

"Please hold for Mr. Compton." She reached for her console to transfer the call, then paused. "I'm sorry," she said, and pushed the button.

The three of them—Stacy, Jason, and Derek Compton—

stood around the speakerphone in the CEO's office. As soon as Stacy had transferred the call, Jason came back out and told her the boss was insisting she take part in the conversation. Jennifer's voice sounded calm, almost bloodless, as she vented her frustration, devoid of the kind of animation that made her such an inspiring person to work for. Stacy felt like crawling under the desk.

"I want it taken down, Derek—now. You had no right to use those pictures."

Jason shook his head and looked pleadingly at Compton. Of the three of them, he had the most to lose if Boomer's Bucket List went away. The response they'd gotten from the Web page had been a coup for his social media team. If it ended in humiliation for the agency, there was no doubt that heads would roll, the first one being his.

Derek Compton scowled, waving off the other man's concern. From the way the conversation was going, Stacy could tell that the boss had already made up his mind. Jason was expendable; Jennifer Westbrook was not.

"Sure, Jen, sure," he said. "I completely understand where you're coming from; that column was a shock to all of us. But believe me, the Web site was created with the best of intentions. Don't you think you ought to at least take a look at it before we pull the plug?"

"You don't honestly think I'm going to change my mind, do you? Derek, Nathan Koslow accused me of perpetrating a hoax; my reputation is on the line."

"And I've already demanded an apology from his editor. As soon as your vet's office calls and confirms Boomer's diagnosis, the *Trib* will issue a retraction—"

"Which almost no one will see. And the ones who do will still suspect that something fishy is going on. Damn it, you know how these things work!"

As Derek Compton's face darkened, Stacy backed away, remembering the screaming match they'd had when

Jennifer told him she was taking a month off. She closed her eyes, praying that the two of them would take a step back before things were said that couldn't be unsaid.

"I think you're being unfair," he said, his voice tightly controlled. "There was no way that any of us could have known what Koslow was planning, and in spite of what you think, this wasn't just about attracting business. Boomer's story has touched a lot of people, and frankly I don't think it's fair to leave them hanging."

"And whose fault is that?"

There was a long pause as options were considered. Jason shook his head, mouthing the words, "No way," but Compton raised a hand to stop him.

"All right," the boss said. "I'll have it taken it down today."

At that, Jason turned on his heel and stomped out of the office. Stacy watched him go, her relief mixed with unease. If heads rolled after this, chances were that one of them would be her own. Where was she going to find another job in this economy?

Jennifer was still on the line. Derek Compton sat down behind his desk and picked up a pen, staring glumly at the speakerphone.

"If you could give Dr. Samuels's office a call and have them release Boomer's records, we'll get that retraction in the works."

"I'll do that. Anything else?"

"I'm thinking of having the agency put a full-page ad in the *Trib,* telling people the truth about Boomer's illness. It may not satisfy everyone, but at least our clients will see it. No one would be doubting your honesty."

"Thank you. I appreciate it. Do you need anything else from me?"

Compton sighed, rubbing his temples. He glanced at Stacy; she shook her head.

"No, I guess that's it."

"Good," Jennifer said. "Then do me a favor and transfer me to the front desk. I have a few things I need to say to Stacy."

Stacy's eyes widened. She shook her head, silently pleading for him to say no. Instead, Compton gave her an admonishing look and pointed toward the door.

"Hold on a minute," he told Jennifer. "I'll get her for you."

Stacy felt sick as she returned to her desk. There was nothing she could say to make things better, only that she was sorry for what had happened. As tempting as it was, blaming the other two wouldn't be fair. The fact was, it had been her idea to make a memorial page for Boomer, and if it hadn't been for her own incompetence, she'd have been the only one in trouble now. Better to just face the music and get it over with. She stiffened her resolve and answered the phone.

"You want to tell me how this happened?"

The tightly controlled quality of Jennifer's voice had changed to one of injured pleading. Stacy felt her chin pucker.

"It's my fault," she said, unsure exactly how the whole thing had gotten started. "I thought it would be fun to do a memorial page—a private one, just for you—but I couldn't figure out how to do it, and I guess I was watching the GIF of Boomer eating his breakfast when Mr. Compton walked by and asked what I was looking at and I felt like I had to show it to him. . . ." Her voice trailed off as she stifled a sob.

"Is that why you asked me to send you those pictures? Was that your plan all along?"

"No!" Stacy shook her head. "That wasn't it at all. Honest, I wasn't lying about that. I was just really concerned about your safety."

"I believe you." Jennifer sounded weary. "I just don't know what to do now. Things out here have gotten . . . complicated."

"Because of that reporter?"

"Pretty much."

"But Mr. Compton's going to take care of that. As soon as your vet tells his editor that Boomer's really sick, they'll print a retraction."

Jennifer's sigh was painful to hear. Stacy closed her eyes, wishing that she could turn the clock back so that none of this had happened.

"Why not at least check out the Web site?" she said. "Mr. Compton is right. You might really like it."

"No," Jennifer snapped. "I've wasted too much of Boomer's life being 'connected.' I promised I'd be spending this time with him and that's what I'm doing."

"I know. I just thought maybe, if you could see what a good job they did—"

"That what? All would be forgiven?"

Tears flooded Stacy's eyes. It was no use trying to make amends. The best thing for her to do now was to apologize again and let Jennifer decide what to do about their relationship. They both knew she'd been in the wrong. Only time would tell if what she'd done could be forgiven. She wiped away a tear.

"Any idea when you'll be back?"

"I'm not sure," Jennifer said evenly. "I guess it all depends on when my dog dies."

Jennifer put the phone down and stalked across the motel room, muttering to herself as she packed her bags. She didn't know what she'd been expecting from the phone call, but it certainly wasn't that. Derek Compton acted as if he and Jason had been doing her a favor, not holding her pain up to public ridicule. Did he have any idea what she'd been going through the last week and a half, waking up in a cold sweat to check on her dog, terrified that every day would be Boomer's last? That her own employer had been capitalizing on the prospect of Boomer's death hurt almost as badly as what Nathan had done.

She heard a whimper and saw Boomer cowering in the corner. Jennifer had a vague recollection of her dog darting off the bed when she and Derek Compton started to argue. No doubt, he'd picked up on the tension in her voice and body language in spite of what she'd thought of as her admirable self-restraint. She put down the shirt she was folding and held out her hand.

"It's okay, Boomie. Nobody's mad at you. It's all right."

Boomer got hesitantly to his feet, his head down, his tail hugging his hindquarters, and Jennifer felt a stab of guilt. Between her fury at Nathan the night before and the quiet fuming she'd been doing that morning, the poor dog must have thought he'd done something wrong.

"I'm sorry," she cooed. "I didn't mean to scare you."

Boomer's tail came up, and he started toward her, relief evident in the happy wiggle of his body. His pace quickened, he was stretching out his neck, poised to receive her reassuring pat. Then he fell forward and collapsed at her feet.

Jennifer screamed.

CHAPTER 29

The trip to the animal hospital went by in a blur. After her first horrified reaction, Jennifer was relieved to find that Boomer, though unconscious, was still alive. Her screams had yielded one unintended benefit, though, as two strong men showed up at her motel room door to offer their help. As they placed Boomer gently into the back of her truck, the assistant manager called an emergency vet service, told them they had a patient on the way, and drove them there. Jennifer sat in back, stroking Boomer's head and whispering assurances. Once Boomer was with the vet, she forced a twenty into the man's reluctant hand and paid for a taxi to take him back to the motel with her heartfelt thanks. Now there was nothing for her to do but wait.

The waiting room was cramped, about the size and shape of a galley kitchen, with two rows of straight-backed chairs that faced each other across a narrow coffee table. A few ancient copies of *Dog Fancy* magazine and a stack of brochures for heartworm pills were all there was to read. Jennifer picked up one of the magazines, flipped through it for a few minutes, and set it back down with no recollection of what she'd read. Her thoughts were too scattered, her emotions too raw, to make sense of what was happening. First Nathan and now Boomer. Trying to imagine a future without either of them was like staring into a bottomless pit.

She shifted in her seat, trying to ignore the furtive glances coming from the receptionist's desk. The woman had been conducting her clandestine surveillance ever since Jennifer and Boomer arrived, and it was becoming increasingly uncomfortable. Whatever was on this woman's mind, she'd rather hear it straight out than sit there and imagine the worst. She walked over to the reception window and found the woman engaged in a whispered conversation with one of the veterinary assistants.

"Excuse me," Jennifer said. "I don't mean to be rude, but do we know each other?"

The women shook their heads, wide-eyed.

"No, ma'am," the receptionist said. "But we know you."

"We love Boomer's Bucket List," the assistant blurted. "So do our patients."

Jennifer bit back a retort. Wasn't it bad enough that she had a life-or-death situation on her hands? Did she really need to be dealing with more fallout from that stupid Web site? Look at them, sitting on the sidelines like a couple of ghouls, waiting for Boomer to die. She'd have expected better from people like that.

No, she thought, that wasn't fair. She had no right to be judging these women. After all, they weren't the only ones who'd been caught up in the frenzy caused by her agency's misadventure. She forced herself to smile.

"I'm glad you're enjoying it," she said. "To be honest, I've never seen it."

The two women stared.

"Never?" the assistant said.

"Nope."

"Would you like to?" the one at the desk asked. "I can show it to you on my computer."

Jennifer hesitated. She had to admit she was curious. She'd even been tempted to check it out on her iPhone, but had refused out of sheer stubbornness, unwilling to cede even an inch of ground to Derek Compton. With Boomer behind closed doors, though, and nothing else to do but fret, she figured she might as well take the plunge.

"Sure," she said. "Why not?"

The two women hovered at her shoulders as Jennifer started scrolling through the Web site. She was speechless. Perfect strangers had sent in hundreds of pictures and videos of Boomer in only a few days! There he was at the motel, the Blue Whale, the Round Barn, and—Jennifer cringed—judging the dog show at the fair. From the steak house alone there were multiple shots: a waiter tying on his "bib"; Boomer licking the butter off a roll, snarfing down his steak. She laughed. There was even one of Boomer wrinkling his nose at the sparkling wine. No wonder they'd had so many waiters that evening, she thought. Every one of them must have been vying for a prize in Jason's *Where's Boomer?* contest.

And as she scrolled farther down the page, Jennifer started noticing a pattern. The photos where Boomer looked the happiest were the ones where both she and Nathan were with him. She felt a lump in her throat and swallowed, trying not to think about how hard it was going to be on Boomer without Nathan around. His heart, already so weak, would be broken. It almost made her glad he wouldn't have long to suffer.

The receptionist was pointing at the screen.

"Did you see the comments? Some of them are real heartbreakers."

Jennifer scrolled to the comment section and started to read:

". . . thank you for letting me share Oscar's story. . . ."

"Puggles was my best friend. . . ."

"Rusty never left Mom's side. . . ."

She leaned back. So, Boomer's Bucket List wasn't the ghoulish spectacle she'd thought it was. Far from being a public flaunting of her personal agony, the Web site had become a celebration—not only of Boomer's life, but of the lives of other dogs whose owners had finally found a way to express their appreciation for the joy their animals had given them. That she'd been unwilling to even consider that her colleagues had meant well made her feel small. Derek Compton was right. The people who'd been following Boomer's Bucket List deserved to see him through to the end.

"Would you excuse me a second?" she said. "I have to make a phone call."

Derek Compton sounded wary—not surprising considering how contentious their last conversation had been.

"Are you sure?"

"I'm sure," Jennifer said.

She was sitting in her truck, looking out at the rain-scoured landscape. The storm that had passed through might have flooded a few streets, but it had also washed away the accumulated dirt and dust of a long, hot summer. The sun's reflection on the wet pavement was dazzling.

"Tell Stacy that all is forgiven, too, will you? The Web site was a good idea. I'm sorry I didn't realize it before."

She hung up and took a deep breath, preparing herself for the next call. She owed Nathan an apology. Even if he had implied that Boomer's Bucket List was an advertising ploy, it was no worse than she'd suspected herself once she heard about the Web site. After all he'd done for the two of them, she felt bad for throwing him out like she had. She'd enjoyed his company on the road, and it had been good for Boomer to have him along. Whatever happened now, at least her dog had had some fun days on their trip, not just boring ones. She dialed Nathan's number and held her breath, hoping he'd pick up.

There was a tap on her window. The receptionist was standing outside. Jennifer hung up; she'd call again later. As she opened her door, the woman gave her a tentative smile.

"You can come back now. Boomer would like to see you."

Dr. Padilla was a petite woman with chin-length salt-and-pepper hair and piercing brown eyes that looked out from a softly rounded face. When Jennifer walked into the examination room, she set Boomer's chart aside and the two women shook hands.

"Where is he?" Jennifer said.

"Still receiving treatment," the woman said. "My assistant will take you back to see him in a moment, but I wanted a chance to talk to you first."

Jennifer's heart was pounding. "Is he going to live?"

"For a while yet, yes," she said. "But I'm afraid he's not out of the woods. Acute Mountain Sickness can strike very quickly and an animal with HCM is at much higher risk for complications."

"Acute Mountain Sickness?" Jennifer frowned. "You mean it's not his heart?"

"Not primarily," Dr. Padilla said. "Not in this instance, at least."

She glanced at the chart.

"I see you're from Chicago. When did you and Boomer arrive here, in Holbrook?"

"Yesterday. We've been taking a road trip."

"Yes, I know," the vet said, glancing toward the door. "You have many fans in this area."

"So, you're saying that there's something about being in Arizona that caused Boomer's symptoms?"

"Not just Arizona. I should think he's been showing signs—lethargy, nausea, irritability—since shortly after you left Oklahoma. The difference in elevation between Chicago and where we are here is over five thousand feet. Boomer's heart has had to work much harder to supply his body with oxygen now than it did when you began your trip."

Jennifer started to shake. "Oh, my God. I've killed him."

"Oh, no," Dr. Padilla said. "Boomer still has some time left. I've administered dexamethasone and acetazolamide, which are the standard of care for both mild and moderate altitude sickness, and he's receiving oxygen now. Once he's released, though, you'll need to get him back down to sea level as quickly as possible."

Jennifer nodded. "I will," she said, wiping away a tear.

"It's a bit costly, but I could also send a pressure bag and supplemental oxygen with you, if you'd like."

"That would be great. Whatever it costs, it's fine."

"Very good. I'd advise you, though, to have someone with you to monitor Boomer's condition while you're on the road. Trying to drive and keep an eye on him at the same time could be disastrous for you both."

Jennifer nodded. Nathan would do it, she thought. He might be angry with her, but he loved Boomer. There was no way he'd turn down a chance to help him.

"All right," she said. "How soon can we leave?"

"Let's give him another hour, at least," the vet said. "Boomer had a small amount of fluid in his lungs when you arrived; I'd like to make sure that that's been cleared up before we let him go."

"That sounds good," Jennifer said. "It'll give me a chance to check out of our motel room and find my copilot."

There was a knock on the door, and the vet's assistant came in.

"You can come see Boomer now."

He was strapped down on a padded table, an oxygen mask over his muzzle and an IV line in his right foreleg. For a large dog, he looked terribly small and frail lying there. Jennifer was fighting back tears.

"Hey, Boomie. How ya doing?"

His tail thumped once and stopped as his gaze slid away.

She glanced up at the assistant. "I didn't think he'd been sedated."

"He wasn't. He's just tired."

"But is this normal? He almost seems depressed."

"Could be. Animals have feelings, too. Once the meds finish working and his oxygen level is back up, we think he'll be fine."

Jennifer bent down and kissed the top of his head.

"You stay here and be good," she whispered. "I'll be back soon. I'm going to go get Nathan."

CHAPTER 30

George, the assistant manager, looked worried as Jennifer came charging through the motel's front door.

"What happened? How's Boomer?"

"He's okay," she said. "They've given him some medication and he's getting oxygen now. I just need to pack up and get out of here so I can get him down to sea level."

"He's got altitude sickness?"

She started. "Yeah. How did you know?"

"Not a week goes by that we don't get somebody in here with it. Too bad you can't just tell him to breathe faster. That clears it right up for a lot of folks."

"Thanks," she said. "I'll remember that."

Jennifer started down the hallway, thinking about all the things she'd need to do before they hit the road: pack, fill the truck with gas, get some sandwiches and maybe some water for them to drink on the way. Not too much, though. She wanted to keep the pit stops to a minimum. First, however, she'd have to convince Nathan to come, too.

"Do you know if Mr. Koslow is in his room?" she said.

"Oh, no, he's already checked out."

She jerked to a halt, her heart racing.

"What? When was that?"

George's eyes darted around the room. He looked like a cornered rat.

"I don't know. Not long after I got back from taking you, I guess. One of the other guests gave him a ride to the bus station."

The bus station! He'd told her last night that he might catch a bus, but she didn't think he'd leave so soon.

"Did he tell you where he was going?"

"No, ma'am. Just that you'd decided to drive the rest of the way alone and that he had some things of his own to take care of."

She looked back down the hallway. The door to Nathan's room was open, a maid's cart sitting outside. If he'd left for the bus station that long ago, he might be on his way out of town by now. There wasn't time to pack her things and check out. She had to get down there and see if she could stop him.

"Could you write down the bus station's address for me?"

"Sure. No problem."

He took out a piece of paper and a pen.

"I'm afraid I'm not going to be able to get out of here before checkout time," she said. "Would it be possible for you to hold my room and just charge me for a second night?"

George handed her the address and smiled.

"Don't worry, Miss Westbrook, I'll hold it for you," he said. "No charge."

Jennifer grabbed the piece of paper and ran back out to her truck. As she started the engine, she dialed Nathan's number again. This time, it kicked her straight into his voice mail.

"Nate, it's Jen," she said, when she heard the beep. "Listen, Boomer's had an emergency and I need your help.

I'm heading to the bus station right now. If you haven't left yet, please don't go before I get there."

As she hung up, she saw the light in the upcoming intersection turn yellow. Jennifer stepped on the accelerator and nipped through just as it turned red. A quick glance in the mirror said she was in the clear. She smiled and kept going. The bus station was only a block away.

Nathan wasn't there.

"I'm sorry, ma'am. I'm not allowed to give out the names of our passengers to the public."

The middle-aged woman in the blue shirt looked genuinely sorry, but that didn't make the bad news any easier to take. Jennifer had checked the schedule for buses going east and buses going west, hoping to at least narrow down which direction Nathan had taken, but one of each had left in the last hour and a half. Her only chance was to persuade someone in authority to tell her which bus he was on. She took a deep breath and felt her lips tremble as she explained her situation again. Couldn't the woman at the counter bend the rules, just this once?

"I wish I could help you," the woman said. "Honestly. But the only person I could release that information to would be a member of the family. And even then, I'd still need a picture ID."

Jennifer's eyes widened. A member of the family! Why hadn't she thought of that before? Nathan's brother Rudy might know which way he'd gone. She felt like kissing the woman.

"Thank you," she said. "You've been a big help."

Rudy Koslow sounded pretty much like one would expect the director of *Hollywood Zombie Hookers* to sound. As Jennifer explained the situation to him, she could almost hear him panting on the other end of the line. She told herself not to let him get to her. The fact was, she'd dealt with much scummier guys than him in the past.

"I don't know where the little twerp's going," he told her. "I just know he's not coming here."

And if he wasn't going to LA to see his brother, she thought, the chances were that Nathan was heading back home. Which meant she was after the eastbound bus.

"He was pretty broken up when he called," Rudy said. "Even worse than when Sophie left him. You must be some kinda looker."

Jennifer's lip curled. How could it be possible that Nathan was related to this moron?

"He's probably going to Chicago, then," she said. "So I'll need to get back on the road. Thanks. I appreciate the help."

"Whoa, whoa, whoa. You're going after him?"

She took a deep breath and tried to stay calm in spite of the time pressure. This was Nathan's brother, after all.

"I plan to, yes."

He laughed. "Okay, but when you get tired of my nerdy little brother, give me a call. I can show you what real excitement is all about."

There were times, Jennifer thought—not many—when having a checkered past paid off in spades. This was one of them.

"Rudy, dear," she drawled. "Keith Richards once drank champagne out of my bedroom slipper. Believe me, I've had more excitement than you could handle."

There was a different clerk at the counter when Jennifer walked back into the terminal, a younger woman with a stud in her nose and tattoos laddered up her left arm. When Jennifer told her that she was hoping to intercept the last bus that had left for Chicago, and why, the girl was eager to help. Perhaps she was less of a stickler about the rules, Jennifer thought, or maybe she was just hoping to add her own sighting to the *Where's Boomer?* page, but whatever the reason, Jennifer was grateful for the assistance.

"He must have taken the thirteen sixty bus," the girl said. "It left here about seventy minutes ago."

"Where's the first stop?"

"Gallup, New Mexico."

Jennifer groaned. Gallup was almost a hundred miles away. With the rains they'd had, parts of the freeway might still be flooded. She'd never be able to get there in time.

"Oh," she said. "So he's long gone."

"Not necessarily." The clerk pointed to a laminated map on the counter. "The thirteen sixty isn't due to arrive in Gallup for another hour and a half and it's scheduled for a half hour layover at the station. If you hurry, you can probably catch him before the bus leaves for Albuquerque."

Jennifer's heart leaped. "That's great! Thank you."

As she ran for the truck, she called Dr. Padilla's office and told them she'd be picking Boomer up a little later than she'd planned. Then she dialed Nathan's number. Once again, the call went immediately to his voice mail. Who the hell was he gabbing with for so long? she wondered. Jennifer left another message, telling him she was on her way, and took off.

"It sounds like you've got another call coming in," Sophie said. "You going to get it?"

Nathan shook his head. "No. The first time she called, she hung up as soon as I answered. I'm not in the mood to play games."

"Mmm," she purred. "Good old Nate. Why fix a problem when you can ignore it?"

CHAPTER 31

Now that she didn't have to stick to Route 66, Jennifer found that the miles were going by much more quickly than before. As enjoyable as the trip had been, the constraints imposed by having to follow the Mother Road had been a hindrance to forward progress. After a quick stop for gas, she was on the freeway and making good time. The rain was gone and the traffic was light. For the first time that morning, it felt as if things were going her way.

She wished that Nathan would hurry and call her back. Jennifer knew he must still be angry about their fight the night before, but she hoped he'd put it aside for Boomer's sake. No matter how he felt about her, she didn't think he'd turn his back on her dog. If he would just listen to his messages—or better yet, if he'd get off the phone—she was sure they could find a way to call a truce long enough to get Boomer down to a safer altitude. She dialed his number again, heard his voice mail message, and screamed.

"Nathan Koslow, get off the damned phone!"

There were flares up ahead in the distance and cones narrowing the freeway down to a single lane. She eased up on the gas. A lighted sign on the right warned about mud and water on the freeway for the next ten miles, reducing the speed limit to forty-five. Jennifer bit her lip and did a quick calculation. She could still make it to Gallup in time, but it was going to be close. She'd just have to make it up once the roadway was clear.

The next ten miles were excruciating as Jennifer found herself behind a line of cars that was moving at much less than the recommended speed. More than once, she considered pulling off the roadway and blowing past the slowpokes ahead of her, but she couldn't afford to get a ticket and they didn't have much farther to go. Finally, just as the freeway opened up again, her phone rang. Jennifer snatched it up.

"Hello?"

"Jen, it's Derek. Are you all right?"

She stared at the phone.

"Of course I'm all right. Why are you calling me?"

"Someone just posted a picture of Boomer at an emergency animal hospital. Did something happen to him?"

Jennifer howled with ironic laughter. Boomer's Bucket List had struck again! It was like having a thousand stalkers on her tail.

"I'm fine, Derek. I'm sorry I didn't tell you when I called before. Boomer got altitude sickness and he needed to be treated at the vet's. He's still there and I'm on the road trying to find someone who can help me get him back down to sea level."

"Is there anything we can do from here?"

"No," she said. "But thanks. I'll let you know once we're out of the woods."

Jennifer hung up and glanced down at her speedometer. Without realizing it, she'd sped up and was doing almost ninety-five. She took her foot off the gas, hoping there were no highway patrolmen around.

No such luck.

The man in the Smokey the Bear hat stayed in his patrol car for what seemed like hours. Running her plates, Jennifer thought. Making sure she wasn't listed somewhere as armed and dangerous. As the minutes ticked by, she could feel her chance to catch Nathan slowly fade. The stopover in Gallup was too short, and leaving Boomer overnight at Dr. Padilla's wasn't an option. As soon as this guy finished writing her a ticket, she'd have to turn around and go back. In spite of her determination not to, she began to cry.

The patrolman got out of his car and walked slowly toward the truck, watching her through the back window, then in her side mirror, before coming to a stop outside her door. Jennifer rolled down the window, still sobbing her heart out. She knew how foolish she must look, knew he must think she was just another weepy female angling to get out of a ticket, but she couldn't help herself. It had all been too much. She was tired of trying to put up a brave front.

"License and registration, please." His voice was cool, emotionless.

Jennifer took them out, handed them over. He glanced at the picture on the license, looked back up at her, and the corner of his mouth turned up. What did he want? she wondered. For her to bat her eyelashes at him? Try to flirt her way out of a citation?

"I know you," he said. "You're Boomer's owner."

Jennifer's mouth fell open. She couldn't have been more shocked if he'd punched her in the face.

"That's right," she said. "How did you—?"

"My wife and I are big fans. We lost our Bubba to cancer last month and it's been a huge help to be able to share his story with your followers."

"I'm glad," she said, trying to wipe the tears from her face. "That's really nice."

He leaned forward and looked into the backseat.

"But . . . Where's Boomer?" he blanched. "He hasn't—"

"No," she said, a fresh flood of tears overwhelming her.

"He got altitude sickness and he's in the emergency clinic. I'm sorry I was speeding, but I was trying to catch my friend's bus so he could help me get Boomer back down to sea level. I don't think I can get there in time, though, now. I don't know what I'm going to do."

The patrolman stepped back.

"I'm afraid you're going to have to step out of your vehicle, Miss." He grinned. "We're going for a little ride."

The thirteen sixty bus out of Holbrook was five miles from the New Mexico border when Nathan took out his laptop and started composing the last column he'd ever write. It was ironic, he thought. After a year of making bargains with the universe, pleading with Julia, and offering to do anything to recover the one thing that had given his life meaning, once it was within his grasp, he'd found that he no longer wanted it. What was the point of publicly humiliating people for the enjoyment of others? He'd told himself he was performing a public service, that the folks he shamed were deserving of their fates, but what he'd really been doing was inflicting pain in the hope that it would make his own go away. Instead of maturing, of gaining perspective and appreciating that life throws everyone a curve ball now and then, he'd stubbornly remained the smart, friendless kid who'd lost his dog and wanted everyone else to suffer for it. The problem was, being the smartest guy in the room doesn't mean much once you've driven everyone else away.

He never should have accepted Julia's assignment; he knew that now. Nathan had let the prospect of getting his column back override his own instincts. Of course Boomer was ill. What possible reason could Jennifer Westbrook have had to lie about it? Even if her agency prospered from the popularity of Boomer's Bucket List, it would have been a negligible gain compared to the backlash once they were found out. The more he thought about it, the more convinced

he was that Julia's suspicions were based on her own pre-
conceived notions about Compton/Sellwood, not the truth
behind Jennifer's claim. He'd ask her about it when he got
back to work, he thought. It would give them something to
talk about while he cleaned out his desk.

Giving up his column had made quitting the *Trib* easy,
too. Without that carrot hanging in front of his face, Nathan
could see how ill-suited he was to the life of a staff reporter.
The time he'd spent with Jennifer and Boomer had shown
him that his heart wasn't in it anymore—hadn't been for
some time, in fact. The column he'd been so proud of might
have played to all his worst traits, but it had sharpened his
chops as a writer, forcing him to dig deep for the perfect turn
of phrase, the just-right word, and the poetry in the otherwise mundane that were both a literary gift and the bane of
tight deadlines and limited word counts.

He could freelance, he thought, maybe start on the book
about Boomer that Jennifer had suggested. In a pinch, he
might even fix Rudy's screenplay for him. Nathan felt as if
he was standing on the precipice of a new adventure, ready
to take a fateful leap. There was no turning back. He would
either spread his wings and be airborne or tumble ignomin-
iously to the rocks below. As clichéd as it was, he felt as if
love had set him free.

And he'd thrown it away.

Nathan set his fingers on the keyboard. He would start
with an apology, he thought. A mea culpa that would cover a
multitude of sins. He closed his eyes, trying to conjure up
the right words, the best ones, to say what was in his heart.
As his concentration deepened, it felt as if the world itself
was slowing down.

He opened his eyes. It *was* slowing down.

Brakes hissed as the bus changed lanes and jounced
onto the shoulder. Necks craned and passengers murmured
in the aisles. What had happened? Was the driver ill? Did
they have a flat? Nathan looked out his window and saw the

flash of blue lights. Maybe the driver had been speeding, he thought. At any rate, this problem—whatever it was—had nothing to do with him. He returned to his contemplation.

The bus came to a halt, and the doors sighed opened. From the corner of his eye, Nathan saw a patrolman walk purposefully by his window, the firm jaw, mirrored sunglasses, and fearsome shoulders more than compensating for the ridiculous hat. Even knowing this had nothing to do with him, he found himself sinking lower in his seat, like a student trying to avoid being called on in class.

The man stepped onto the bus and said a few words to the driver, who nodded his head nervously. Then he stepped into the aisle, arms akimbo, and made his announcement.

"Is Nathan Koslow on this bus?"

Nathan's first reaction was to look around, as if some other Nathan Koslow might be sitting nearby. Then, realizing the infinitesimally small chance that it was true, he raised his hand.

"I'm Nathan Koslow," he said, watching every other face on board turn toward him.

Questions were flying through his brain. Why was he being singled out? What had he done? Was this about the library book he hadn't returned back in the fifth grade?

Then another person stepped onto the bus, and every other thought he had departed.

Jen?

"Grab your gear, son," the patrolman said. "There's a dog back in Holbrook who needs your help."

CHAPTER 32

Their reunion was necessarily brief. After Jen explained what Boomer's situation was, Nathan had quickly agreed to drive the two of them to California that night. Nothing was said about the argument that had precipitated their estrangement, but then sitting in the back of a patrol car wasn't exactly conducive to having a personal conversation. When Nathan reached for Jennifer's hand, however, she did not withdraw it. He smiled. For the time being, at least, that was good enough.

Jennifer gasped when she saw Boomer. He looked thinner than he had only a few hours before, and he was too weak to walk to the truck. As Nathan carried him out and placed him into the backseat, she asked Dr. Padilla about the dog's prognosis.

"I wish I knew," the veterinarian said. "These things are hard to predict. His oxygen saturation is good, but his heart sounds are bad—worse even than when you brought him here this morning. It may be that the altitude sickness did more damage to the heart muscle than I thought. Without more tests, however, there's really no way to know how bad off he is and in the end, it would only make the little time he has left uncomfortable. My advice to you is the same as I'm sure Dr. Samuels's was. Keep him comfortable, enjoy him while you can, and prepare yourself for the inevitable."

"Thank you," Jennifer said as they hugged. "For everything."

"*Ve con Dios,*" Dr. Padilla said. Go with God.

Jennifer got into the backseat with Boomer and gently lifted his head onto her lap before putting on her seat belt.

"Hiya, Boomie. You ready to go to Cali? Play in the waves in Santa Monica like I promised?"

Boomer thumped his tail weakly and licked her hand. Jennifer took his ear and rubbed it between her fingers, feeling the silky fur, hoping they would still have time. Nathan started the engine, and she caught his eye in the rearview mirror.

"Thank you. I couldn't have done this without you."

"Thanks for asking me. I wouldn't have missed it for the world."

He pulled the truck out onto the road and headed for the freeway entrance.

"How long will it take, do you think?" she said.

"To get to Santa Monica? About eleven hours, plus stops."

Jennifer frowned. A lot could happen in eleven hours.

"How long 'til we're no longer at elevation, then?"

"Dr. Padilla suggested we go through Phoenix. That'll put us at about a thousand feet in three hours. Boomer should be feeling better by then."

She nodded and looked out the window. They were on the freeway now, the world flying by. After riding in a patrol car, though, even seventy-five felt slow.

"I'm sorry I said that stuff about Dobry."

"Why? You were right. I think I've been trying to hurt everyone since I lost him. Stupid, really. Like making other people miserable was going to help me feel better."

"Feelings aren't logical, especially when you're a kid."

"Yeah, but I'm not a kid anymore."

Jennifer sighed, looking at nothing in particular, and stroked Boomer's head. She thought about the day she got him, an energetic bundle of golden fur with brown eyes that turned downward at the outer edges, creased in a perpetual smile. He'd been a good puppy—easy to paper train, mortified by the occasional accident, not too many shoes destroyed—but he had his faults. Heeling never made much sense to him—he was either jerking her forward or yanking her back—and even friendly cats were an abomination, fit only to be barked at or chased up trees. There were neighbors, she knew, who would not miss him.

"Did I tell you I called Sophie?" Nathan said.

She felt her stomach lurch. *Sophie—the love of his life until last year.*

"Oh?" she said. "When was that?"

"This morning, while I was on the bus."

Jennifer thought of all the times her phone calls had been sent to his voice mail, how she'd been praying that he'd get off the phone, and felt her lips tighten.

"How is she?"

"Doing well. I wanted to apologize to her for the way I'd treated her. At the end, you know, I was pretty awful. She'd wanted to talk about things back then and I just pretty much checked out. It was over as far as I was concerned, but I was too much of a coward to say so. I wanted to tell her I was sorry. I thought I owed her that."

Of course he did, Jennifer thought. It was a decent thing to do. So, why was it making her unhappy?

"I suppose you two will be getting together again?"

"Yeah, I think so. Not for a few months, though. At least not until she has the baby."

The baby?

Nathan looked back at her and grinned.

"Sophie got married six months ago. Didn't I mention that?"

He started to laugh, and Jennifer kicked the back of his seat, careful not to disturb Boomer.

"No wonder I couldn't get you on the phone."

"I called my mother, too," he said. "I wanted to ask her about Dobry."

Jennifer sobered. "How did that go?"

"Better than I thought it would. It'd been pretty much the third rail of our relationship ever since it happened. Something you said made me think it was time for us to get past it."

"Oh? What was that?"

"You told me she probably hadn't wanted to give him away, either, but that she'd had no choice. I never really thought of it like that, that she might have been suffering as much as I was. I figured it was time to clear the air."

"And did you?"

"Oh, yeah. Turns out that after we took him to the shelter, she kept bugging the landlord to let us have him, offered to babysit his kids or clean the other apartments for free when folks moved out, anything so we could get Dobry back."

"That was nice of her. It's too bad it didn't work."

Nathan shook his head.

"That's just the thing. It did work. The problem was, when she went back to claim Dobry, he'd already been adopted by another family. She told me she'd cried for days afterward. I remember her crying, but I always thought it was because of the divorce."

"And you never guessed?"

"Nope."

"Oh, Nate. That's so sad."

"Yeah, the two of us had a good cry about it. It's over now, though. Thanks for helping me see that I wasn't the only one who'd been hurt."

Jennifer swiped at a tear. "Thanks for telling me."

He looked at her in the mirror. "You weren't really jealous about Sophie, were you?"

She shrugged. "Maybe a little."

"Well, don't be. I told her my heart was taken. I said I wasn't sure, though, if you wanted me back."

Jennifer felt her heart warm. She smiled.

"What did she say to that?"

"She said it served me right."

They got dinner at a Subway in Phoenix and ate in the truck. Boomer turned his nose up at the kibble Jennifer offered him, but he sat up and drank some bottled water from his bowl. She watched him with concern.

"He should be over the altitude sickness by now," she said. "Why isn't he eating?"

Nathan shrugged. "Who knows? Maybe he's just tired."

"Oh, Nate. What if he doesn't get any better? What if this is it?"

"I don't know, Jen. You're asking me a question I don't have the answer to."

She nodded. "We should go."

Back on the road now, they had six hours to go—three hundred eighty-seven miles. As the sun set, Jennifer stared at Boomer, silently urging him to hang on. He had to make it, didn't he? He wouldn't quit so close to the end. She took a deep breath and tried to calm down. She remembered her father's death. Sitting by the bedside, watching his chest rise and fall, slower and slower, faltering, then one more breath and then . . . nothing.

Everyone dies. We all do. It's what we do with the time we have that matters.

"Nate?"

"Uh-huh?"

"Do you think that all dogs go to heaven?"

"Good question. I think I feel the same way that Will Rogers did about that."

"Which was . . . ?"

"He said that if there were no dogs in heaven, then when he died he wanted to go where they went."

Another hour went by. Passing headlights that illuminated the cockpit barely penetrated into the backseat. Jennifer watched their beams slide across Nathan's face. Did she love this man? She wanted to, but she wasn't sure. She'd been on her own a long time, long enough for it to become a habit. Change was frightening. Not changing was frightening. How could she decide when there was no easy choice to make?

Boomer groaned and shifted on the seat.

"I think Boomer needs to take a walk," she said.

Nathan nodded. "Want me to pull over?"

Jennifer shifted, too, and felt the pressure in her own bladder.

"No, I need to go, too. Better find a gas station."

It was cold outside. Jennifer stepped out of the truck and gasped. After five hours with a warm dog in her lap, the temperature difference was bracing.

Nathan reached in and unbuckled Boomer's harness.

"I'll take him," he said. "You go on inside."

"Can I get you something?" she said, fighting to keep her teeth from chattering.

"Maybe a Red Bull?"

"I'll see what they have."

Jennifer hurried inside and found that the women's restroom was occupied. Not surprising; she could wait. On the way out, she grabbed a couple of energy drinks and a bag of Oreos for the road. Convenience store comfort food.

As she stepped outside, she saw the two of them sitting at the far edge of the parking lot. Nathan was talking to Boomer and pointing at something in the sky. Jennifer tiptoed forward, wanting to hear what was being said, not wanting to disturb their private moment.

"See that bright star?" Nathan said. "That's Sirius, the dog star. Pretty soon, you're going to be up there, Boomer, running and playing with all the other dogs and looking down at us from that beautiful bright star."

The world blurred. Jennifer placed a hand over her mouth.

Don't make a sound. This is important.

Nathan's voice was thick.

"Do me a favor, will you, Boomer? If you see Dobry up there, tell him that I never forgot him and I never stopped loving him. Tell him . . . tell him that he was the best friend I ever had."

Jennifer smiled as the tears ran down her face. Of course she loved this man. Of course she did. How could she not?

Boomer never got to romp in the surf at Santa Monica Pier. In spite of the medication and supplemental oxygen provided by the emergency vet clinic, his heart simply wasn't strong enough to make it. In the early hours of the morning, on a lonely stretch of highway east of Cactus City, Boomer's breathing became labored, the stertorous sound an undeniable harbinger of the end. Jennifer asked Nathan to pull over and join her in the backseat, where they spent Boomer's final moments reliving the highlights of their trip, laughing and crying by turns. At the end, Dr. Samuels's prediction of a painless death was born out. A brief tightening of limbs and a final, peaceful release of air was the only indication that Boomer was gone.

EPILOGUE

The boardwalk creaked underfoot as Jennifer and Nathan walked to the end of the Santa Monica Pier. Pacific Park was closed for the season; the Ferris wheel looked like a giant eye, bearing silent witness as they passed. A handful of fishermen sat in folding chairs, making desultory comments and drinking beers as the sun went down, their poles propped against the railings like tired sentries. Curious glances noted the strangers' approach and quickly veered away.

Jennifer approached the railing, a shoebox in her hands. Sea foam swirled around the pilings below; the ocean was a slurry of sand and kelp and salt water. She inhaled sharply and stepped back.

"It's a long way down."

Nathan stepped up beside her and peered over the railing. "It is," he said. "But not when compared to how far Boomer's come already."

Jennifer gently patted the box's lid, then removed it and drew her fingers one last time through the smooth dollops of colored glass.

"Once we do this, he really will be gone."

For a time, it had seemed as if her plan to scatter Boomer's ashes off the pier would be impossible. Crematory ash was liable to fly up and cover everything in the surrounding area if released into the open air. Once again, though, Boomer's notoriety had paid off.

At the suggestion of a follower on Boomer's Bucket List, his ashes had been mixed with silica, melted down, and made into nuggets of glass that were indistinguishable from the ordinary sea glass found in every ocean in the world. The weight of the nuggets would take them to the bottom, where they would eventually erode, leaving his ashes to tumble among the waves. And if someone collected a few and took them home, well, that was okay, too, Jennifer thought. Boomer had always enjoyed making new friends.

"It seems so strange not to have a dog in my life."

Nathan nodded silently, and Jennifer swallowed, grateful for his forbearance. How many times had she said that in the two months since Boomer had passed? Too many, she thought, and yet Nathan had listened without complaint, understanding without being told that she needed, once again, to say it. His patience meant more to her than all the declarations of love ever could. What Boomer had sensed in Nathan Koslow, Jennifer now knew. Here was a man who would love and cherish her if only she was willing to trust him. If Boomer had had a bucket list of his own, she thought, finding someone for Jennifer to love would have been the only thing on it.

"We can get another dog, if you'd like."

She shook her head. "I could never replace Boomer."

"That's not what I meant."

"I know that," she said. "But it's still hard. He was so young. I guess I'm still grieving the time he didn't have."

Nathan indicated the box. "If you're not ready to let him go—"

"No." She shook her head. "It's time to move on. I know that. It's just . . . hard."

He nodded and stepped back. It was up to her now. There was nothing more to say.

Jennifer held the box out over the water, tipped it slowly, and watched its contents stream over the side. A waterfall of glass slipped silently beneath the waves.

"Bye, Boomie."

As she replaced the top, Nathan slipped his arm around her waist. She nodded.

"Let's go," she said, her eyes sparkling.

Seagulls wheeled overhead as they retraced their steps back to the parking lot. As the sun crept closer to the horizon, the air cooled; the wind was picking up. Jennifer zipped her jacket and thrust her free hand deep into her pocket.

"Thanks for coming with me," she said. "I couldn't have done this alone."

Nathan drew her closer and kissed her hair.

"You don't have to be alone anymore," he said softly. "Remember? 'To have and to hold, from this day forward?'"

She bit her lip. "I still can't believe we did it. We must have been crazy."

"That's what Rudy said, too, until he met you." He grinned. "Now he says I'd have been crazy not to marry you."

Jennifer looked at him. "The Ice Queen and Mr. Poisoned Pen. Who'd have guessed?"

"That wasn't us," Nathan said. "Those were just the disguises we wore to keep from getting hurt."

"And now we will?"

"Not by me. Not if I can help it."

"No guarantees in life, I suppose."

"You're right," he said. "Better to make today count."

It was a phrase that had taken on new meaning for them in the last two months. Boomer's death had forced them both to take stock of their lives, and the changes they'd made since had been both radical and deeply satisfying. The success of Boomer's Bucket List had put Jennifer's career achievements in the national spotlight, and though that also meant that some of the more notorious episodes in her life had been brought into the open, they had not resulted in the sort of public embarrassment she'd feared. If anything, in fact, the opposite was true. She was working with Derek Compton to create her own boutique agency, a subsidiary of Compton/Sellwood, where she would have more control over her workload.

For Nathan, quitting his job at the *Trib* had only been the first step. It turned out that Jennifer wasn't the only one who was a fan of his writing, and when word got around that he was writing a book about Boomer, a friend from college put him in touch with an agent. Two weeks later, he'd signed a book deal.

Their personal lives had changed, too. The reminder that life was too short to spend stuck in the past had been motivation to take the plunge, and once they knew what they wanted, it made little sense to put off the rest of their lives. Two weeks after returning to Chicago, the two of them had walked down to the courthouse and gotten married. The sharp-tongued lonely boy and the coldhearted workaholic had found in each other the key that unlocked their self-made prisons. For the time being, they were living in Jennifer's town house, but they were looking for someplace outside the city to settle down.

A dozen yards from the end of the boardwalk, they stopped and turned back to look at the ocean one last time. The sun had dipped noticeably, forming tiers of yellow, orange, and red along the horizon. Jennifer laid her head against Nathan's shoulder and sighed.

"I think Boomer's going to like it here."

Somewhere behind them a board squeaked; they heard footsteps approaching.

"Would either of you guys like a puppy?"

They turned and saw a boy of about fourteen standing

behind them. The cardboard box in his arms said: *Puppy—Free to Good Home.* Peering over the top was a fluffy, squirming bundle of yellow fur struggling to pull itself up.

Nathan heard Jennifer's sharp intake of breath.

"Oh, he's adorable, but—"

She took a step back, shaking her head.

He reached out, patting the softly rounded head, and the pup struggled harder, his urgent licks and gentle nips on Nathan's fingers a silent plea for assistance.

"May I?"

Sensing that a deal might be struck, the young man nodded eagerly.

"Go ahead. He's real friendly."

Nathan lifted the pup from the box and gently cradled its hindquarters, feeling the little dog tremble under its velvety softness. *So much trust,* he thought as its tail beat an excited cadence against his hand. *We're all like this puppy,* he thought, *every one of us. Taking our first steps into the world, asking nothing more than a kind word and a gentle touch.* He held the little dog to his chest and ached for all the creatures whose hopes went unfulfilled, counting himself lucky for having finally found love. Nathan drew his chin back, and for a moment the puppy's brown eyes regarded him solemnly. Then it lunged, planting a kiss on Nathan's unguarded mouth.

Jennifer stepped closer.

"Can I hold him?"

Nathan transferred the tiny bundle into her arms and looked back at the boy, still holding the empty box, watching them hopefully. He was a head shorter than Nathan, with a tangle of blond hair falling over one eye and the loose limbs and outsized hands and feet that said he had more growing to do.

"He's had all his puppy shots," he said eagerly. "And he's paper trained, too. Mostly."

"How old is he?" Jennifer said.

"Eight weeks today."

Her eyes widened. Boomer had died just a little over eight weeks before. Nathan smiled and shook his head.

"Just a coincidence," he whispered.

"There were five puppies in his litter," the youth said. "This guy's the last of the bunch."

Jennifer turned the pup in her hands, examining him from all angles.

"He looks like he's part golden retriever."

"Must have been his father. His Mom—that's our dog, Daisy—is mostly yellow Lab."

"I thought so. He looks like—" Jennifer's chin dimpled. "He looks like my old dog."

"And mine," Nathan said.

"It's a good combination," she said. "Smart, even tempered."

As if acknowledging the compliment, the puppy craned its neck and delivered a sloppy kiss to her cheek.

"What do you think?" Nathan said. "Is it too soon?"

She shrugged. "It isn't that. I mean, in a way I think it'll always be too soon, but wouldn't it be better to get an older dog? A puppy takes so much time."

"I can watch him," Nathan said. "I'll be home working on my book anyway. It'd be good to have an excuse to take a break, take him out for a walk . . ."

"Clean up poop, put down puddle pads."

"An older dog would need some of that, too, at least for a while."

"Please take him," the boy pleaded. "If you don't, my mom says he'll have to go to the pound."

Jennifer sighed and looked back toward the end of the pier. Nathan gave her shoulder a squeeze.

"I don't think Boomer would mind," he said.

A horn honked. Nathan looked up and saw a Chevy van pull into the parking lot. The woman inside was rolling down her window.

"Uh-oh," the boy said. "That's my mom."

Nathan looked at Jennifer. "Well, what do you think?"

"I don't know," she said. "I mean, I wasn't even thinking—"

"Dobry!" the woman in the van yelled. "Time's up. Put the puppy back in the box and let's go."

Nathan felt Jennifer grab his arm. He stared at the boy, the brown eyes that crinkled in a ready smile, the golden hair a near match to the puppy's.

"Your name is *Dobry?*"

The boy thrust his chin out, his look defiant. "Yeah, so?"

"It's the name my *babcia* wanted for me, but my parents . . ." Nathan shrugged. "It's a good name."

"Yeah, I like that it's different. So," Dobry said. "What about the puppy?"

Nathan looked at Jennifer, who gave him an encouraging nod, and the two of them answered at once.

"We'll take him."

ACKNOWLEDGMENTS

Once again, I am greatly indebted to the team of professionals who made this book happen, especially my editor, Gary Goldstein, his saintly assistant, Liz May, the rest of the team at Kensington, and of course, my wonderful agent, Doug Grad. And to Chris, who makes everything better.

AUTHOR'S NOTE

In writing *Boomer's Bucket List,* I drew upon childhood memories of traveling across the United States in the back of the family car, many of which found their way into the book. Should you decide to follow in Jennifer and Boomer's footsteps, however, please be aware that some of the places they visit exist only in my head. There is, for example, no squeaky-toy factory in Santa Rosa, New Mexico and no fire hydrant museum near Atlanta, Illinois. (There is, however, a giant fire hydrant and museum in Beaumont, Texas, and several fire hydrant collections across the country that are open to both the human and canine public.) And if you do take that road trip, prepare to be amazed. The vastness and diversity of this beautiful country is truly beyond description.

*Keep reading for a special excerpt from Sue Pethick's
witty and heartwarming novel, where a sweet dog in need
of an owner brings together the perfect candidates. . . .*

PET FRIENDLY

"A light, heartwarming read perfect for a wintry afternoon
at home or a sunny beach vacation."

—*RT Book Reviews*, **4 Stars**

"A funny and sweet book with plenty of howls!"

—*The Parkersburg News and Sentinel*

Available now from Kensington Books.

Visit us at www.kensingtonbooks.com.

CHAPTER 1

It was odd seeing a dog at a man's funeral, Todd thought as he glanced at the little mutt sitting in the pew, but that was Uncle Bertie for you—odd. The dog's name was Archie and he was the fourth dog with that name that Todd's uncle had owned over the years, every one of them a well-trained part of Bertie's stage act.

Todd's mother liked to say that her brother was the only person she'd ever known who actually carried out his threat to run away and join the circus. Uncle Bertie had spent three decades touring the world, and when living out of a trunk became too much for him, he'd begun a second career performing at kids' birthday parties and volunteering at nursing homes. In his handwritten will, he'd asked that there be no tears at his funeral.

On the other side of the pew sat Todd's sister, Claire. She'd flown in to help their mother clean out Uncle Bertie's apartment and make arrangements for the funeral, and she'd be leaving after the reception. Claire had been in a snit ever since their mother agreed to give Archie to Todd, and he didn't want her to leave town if there were any hard feelings.

He nudged her with his knee.

"You mad at me?"

She shook her head. "But I still think you're making a mistake. Gwen's never going to let you keep him."

"Will you cut it out? She's always saying she wants a dog someday."

"Someday, sure, but not today and not a dog like that, either."

"What's wrong with him?"

Todd looked down at the little fur ball lolling in the pew beside him and smiled. Archie had a mass of unruly white fur and a patch of tan that looked like the faded remains of a black eye, but there was a warmth about him that was as comforting as a hug. Todd reached out and patted him protectively.

"Nothing," Claire said. "But I'll bet he's not the pedigreed pooch Miss Gwendolyn Ashworth had in mind."

Todd ignored the barb. If his sister thought Gwen was a snob, there was nothing he could do about it. He decided to change the subject.

"Did the boys get my present?"

She rolled her eyes.

"Yes, and it's driving me crazy. Did you have to do *all* the dogs' voices?"

Todd had sent his nephews a prerelease sequel to his megahit game app, Pop Up Pups, and he'd been anxious to find out what they thought. Claire's eight-year-old twins were his most reliable product testers.

"So they like it?"

Claire couldn't suppress a smile.

"Of course they like it. Their friends think they've got the world's coolest uncle."

Todd grinned. "No argument there."

"I thought Gwen was coming," Claire said.

"She was," he told her. "Something came up at work."

"You pop the question yet?"

He shook his head.

"But you're going to."

"Of course."

Claire nodded tactfully, but Todd knew he'd be getting an earful later. She glanced back at the rest of the mourners.

"So, what do you think?"

He smirked. "What a bunch of clowns."

It was true. With the exception of the immediate family, every person sitting behind them had come in greasepaint to honor Bertie Concannon, a man who'd been clowning longer than many of them had been alive. Though barely five-six, he'd always seemed larger than life. He had an Irishman's gift of gab, a voice that could fill a theater clear up to the cheap seats, and hair a shade of orange unknown in the natural world. Uncle Bertie had never had much, but he never seemed to need much, either. He was funny and carefree and utterly ridiculous, and Todd had admired the hell out of him.

The service began and the mourners stood for the first song. As the opening strains of "Just a Closer Walk with Thee" rose from the pipe organ, Archie sat up and looked around. He cocked his head and whimpered; his chin quivered and his eyes grew misty. Then, as the organ music swelled, the little dog began to howl.

Claire's comment continued to weigh on Todd's mind at the reception. As he passed through the crowd, accepting condolences and offering homemade *hors d'oeuvres,* he wondered if adopting Archie was a mistake. His relationship with Gwen was serious—serious enough that Todd was planning to propose to her that weekend—but they'd been living together for only a few months and there'd already been a few bumps in the road. Would adding a pet at this point really be a good idea?

A succession of clowns was coaxing Archie to do the tricks that he and Uncle Bertie had used in their act. As Todd watched the little dog dance, play leapfrog, and give high fives, he felt his anxiety start to lessen. He'd spent the last five months creating virtual dogs for his game app; it was going to be fun having a real live dog again. And once Gwen met Archie, he told himself, she was going to love the little guy, too.

A clown in a pink wig sidled up and took a crab cake from his tray.

"So, you're Bertie's nephew," she said. "What is it you do?"

Todd hesitated. The success of Pop Up Pups had been a pleasant surprise, but he wasn't comfortable with the public attention it had brought him. The billion-dollar acquisition of his previous start-up hadn't garnered any interest outside the business world, but thanks to his game app, he was on the verge of becoming a household name.

"I write game apps for smartphones," he said.

"Anything I might have heard of? My kids play a lot of those."

She popped the crab cake into her exaggerated mouth.

"Ever heard of Pop Up Pups?"

She swallowed. "That's *you?*"

He nodded.

"Wow. My kids would play that game all day if I let them."

A hobo clown with a pile of cheese puffs on his plate gave Todd a curious look.

"Hey, I know that game. Isn't one of the pups named Archie?"

"That's right." Todd smiled. "It was sort of a tribute to Uncle Bertie."

Inspired, he said a few words in the virtual Archie's voice, a sound *GamePro* magazine had described as "a Rottweiler on helium."

"Right," the hobo said, his eyes narrowing. "You do the voices of the dogs, too. I think I read something about that."

"So," the pink-haired clown said as she shifted the last two crab cakes onto her plate. "I hear you're adopting Houdini."

Todd frowned. "Who?"

"Houdini." She pointed at Archie, whose ball-balancing act was getting cheers from the guests. "Bertie's dog."

"You mean Archie?"

"I guess." She shrugged and brought another crab cake to her mouth. "But Houdini's the only thing Bertie ever called him."

When the last guest had departed, Archie was passed out under the coffee table. Todd took the trash out to the Dumpster and headed back inside. Claire and their mother, Fran, were in the kitchen, cleaning up.

"It was a good service," Fran said. "Nice reception, too. Bertie would have liked it."

Claire slipped on a pair of rubber gloves and started washing the serving dishes.

"A few of them cried, though," she said. "Bad form."

Todd popped an olive into his mouth and grabbed a dish towel.

"They were sad clowns. That doesn't count."

"Too bad Gwen couldn't come," his mother said. "Another big project at work?"

"Mmm. Something like that."

"Well, I suppose work comes first," she said. "You know what they say: 'The difference between ordinary and extra-ordinary is that little extra.'"

"Right," Claire said. "And hard work never killed anyone, but why take the chance?"

Fran took out a stack of Tupperware containers and began lining them up on the sideboard.

"Are you sure you want to take Archie?" she asked Todd. "Claire says there's room for him on the plane."

"I'm sure," he said, setting the turkey platter back in the cupboard. "And even if I wasn't, there's no room for a dog on one of those little puddle-jumpers."

"But you and Gwen just got settled. Don't you think it'd be better not to add another complication?"

Claire was scraping the last of the Jell-O mold into the sink. "Give it a rest, Ma."

Todd gave his sister a grateful smile. He loved his mother, but it was hard to get her off a subject once she got started.

Fran was indignant. "Why? What did I do?"

"You're butting in."

"Who's butting in? I just think it's the considerate thing to do, especially if he wants to marry this girl."

Todd shot Claire a dangerous look. "Who says we're getting married?"

"Oh, don't blame your sister," Fran said. "Anyone could see you're crazy about Gwen, and why not? A girl like that doesn't come along every day."

"I agree," he said. "But I'd still appreciate it if you'd let me handle this my own way."

"Well, I suppose you know best," Fran said, looking doubtful.

"I do," Todd said, kissing her cheek. "And don't worry. Gwen'll be thrilled."

Archie was quiet on the way to the airport. As the car inched its way through traffic, he lay on the backseat, shifting his gaze between the two people in front. Todd watched him in the rearview mirror.

"I think Archie misses Uncle Bertie."

Claire glanced back over her shoulder.

"What makes you think that?"

"I don't know. He just looks kind of sad."

"He's probably just carsick. Bob says dogs don't really have feelings like we do."

Todd held his tongue. Bob was all right as a brother-in-law—he was a good provider and he loved Claire and the boys—but he had a habit of stating his opinions as facts, and God help you if you disagreed with him. If his sister wanted to believe that Archie had forgotten Uncle Bertie, that was fine, but Todd knew a sad face when he saw one.

Claire opened her purse and started rifling its contents.

"So, why didn't you call Gwen?"

"I didn't want to bother her at work," he said.

"There's still time to change your mind, you know."

He shook his head. "No, thanks."

As he waited for the cars around them to start moving again, Todd's mind began to wander. In a little over forty-eight hours, he'd be asking Gwen to marry him. If she said yes, he thought, he'd be the happiest man on earth. If she turned him down . . .

"I see you've bought your girl a ring."

He jumped. It was like his sister had been reading his mind.

"How'd you guess?"

"You've had your hand in your pocket all day, Todd. I just *hoped* it was a ring you were holding." She held out her hand. "Can I have a look?"

He took the velvet box from his pants pocket and passed it over. Claire snapped the lid open and gasped.

"Holy moly! Where'd you get this, Buckingham Palace?" She took the ring out and watched it catch the light.

"Gwen saw it in a jeweler's window a couple of months ago," Todd said. "I'm going to pop the question this weekend."

He stuck out his hand. "Now, give it back."

Claire kept the ring just out of reach.

"Not so fast. I haven't had a good look yet."

Todd's embarrassment turned to pride as he watched his sister's reaction.

"You like it?"

"Of course I like it," she said. "But, Todd, it must have cost a fortune."

He shrugged. "Not quite."

She put the ring back in its box and handed it over.

"Are you sure about this?"

"Why, you think she's too good for me?"

"No, I think you're too good for *her.*" Claire tapped her forehead. "You've got a *brain.* All she does is gossip about people she doesn't know and prattle on about the stuff she owns or wants to buy."

Todd felt his lips tighten. "How can you say that? You've only met her once."

"Once was enough. I don't know what you see in her, but I certainly know what she sees in you."

Todd pretended he hadn't heard. If Claire thought that Gwen cared only about his money, there was nothing he could do to change her mind.

"Sorry," she said. "I know it's none of my business. I just don't understand the attraction. There was a time when you would have seen right through a girl like that."

There it was, Todd thought. The unspoken accusation that he suspected Claire had been holding against him for years. When was she going to let it go?

"This is about Emma, isn't it?"

She crossed her arms and looked away. "Not necessarily."

"When are you going to get it through that thick noggin

of yours?" He reached over and tapped her temple playfully. "That girl doesn't exist anymore."

Claire's eyes flashed. "How would you know?"

Todd felt a stab of guilt. Things had happened back then that his sister wasn't privy to, but if she was going to blame him for something he didn't do, he figured she should at least know the truth.

"Maybe I should have written to her," he said, "but when Dad died, things changed. I had to get a job. Then there was the house to take care of, and you and Ma. I don't remember hearing any complaints about that."

Todd swallowed the lump in his throat. Looking back, it felt as if losing his father had cut his life in two. He understood why it had happened, knew he hadn't been the only one forced to adjust to a new reality, but he resented it when Claire accused him of being heartless.

Claire's voice softened. "I know that, *dearthàir.*"

"And don't go all Irish on me," he snapped. "Emma's home life was a mess; things were never going to work out between us. Ma said it'd be better if I didn't write to her, so I didn't. End of story."

"I'm sorry," she whispered. "I didn't know."

"It was a long time ago," he said, gripping the steering wheel tighter. "I've got a good life now. The last thing I need is to be pining for Emma Carlisle."

He heard the scream of jet engines; Archie dove for cover as the 747 passed overhead. Todd reached around the seat and patted the little dog's head.

"It's okay, boy," he said, grateful to be changing the subject. "That's just how civilized people fly: with reclining seats and restrooms and tiny bottles of booze."

Claire craned her neck, taking note of the bumper-to-bumper traffic that jammed the Interstate in all directions.

"Oh, yeah. This place is real civilized." She took out her ticket. "Terminal D, smart guy."

They pulled up to the curb and Todd grabbed his sister's

luggage. As he closed the hatchback, a cold blast of air nearly knocked him over. He set her bag down on the sidewalk.

"You want help with this?"

"I'll be fine." Claire's hair was buffeting her face. "But you'd better roll up that window. Feels like a storm's moving in."

Todd glanced back at his car. Sure enough, one of the back windows was open.

"Thanks for telling me," he said. "I didn't realize I'd left that down."

They hugged briefly.

"Call me when you get home," he told her.

Claire grabbed her bag and smiled. "Call me when Gwen says no to the dog."

"She won't," he said. "But thanks."

"I'll talk to you later," she said. "And, Todd? Good luck."

Todd waited until Claire had disappeared into the crowd before getting back into the car. Archie was sitting up in back, an expectant look on his face.

"How you doing back there?"

The little dog tipped his head and whimpered.

"Must have been cold back there with the window down. You want to move up here?" He patted the passenger's seat. "Be my guest."

As Archie settled down on the seat beside him, Todd started the car. Claire was wrong, he thought. Gwen was going to love Uncle Bertie's dog just as much as he did.

CHAPTER 2

Emma Carlisle was not having a good day. In fact, at that very moment she couldn't remember the last time she'd actually had a good one. When she inherited the Spirit Inn from her grandmother, she'd thought her life was finally turning around, that all the lousy relationships, rotten jobs, and just plain bad luck in her life had been payment in advance for her once-in-a-lifetime windfall. Instead, it seemed as if karma was once again having a big ole laugh at her expense. *You thought you were out of the woods?* she heard it snickering. *Ha-ha! Fooled you again.*

This latest bout of karmic deserts was being served up by Harold Grader, her up-until-now friendly local banker, who'd apparently decided that loaning her more money to maintain and upgrade her hotel would be throwing good money after bad.

"I'm sorry, Emma," he said, looking anything but. "The committee just isn't going to approve another loan when you're only making the minimum payments on the one you have."

"I understand," Emma said, "and I know it doesn't look good, but business has really been picking up."

"Yes, I can see that," he said, prodding the financial statements on his desk with the tip of his finger. "But your overhead has also increased. If anything, it looks as if you're making less on a per-guest basis than you were before."

Emma closed her eyes in silent acknowledgment. It didn't make sense to her, either, but she'd been over the figures a dozen times and every time it came out the same. It was as if her profits were vanishing into thin air.

Maybe I'm just incompetent.

No doubt that's what her banker was thinking. Emma had worked at her grandmother's inn every summer since she was six and could do any job on the property, yet when people heard that it had been gifted to her, they just assumed she was a neophyte, a manager in name only who left the real work to her older, more experienced staff.

It didn't help, of course, that Emma didn't look like the kind of businesswoman a bank was used to dealing with. She was a little below average height; her figure was more boyish than buxom; and she considered makeup to be a waste of both time and money. She liked the convenience of shorter hair, but had grown hers out after being mistaken once too often for a preteen boy. At work, she wore a suit and the highest heels she could walk in without breaking an ankle, but her days off were spent in T-shirts and jeans.

Grader was fiddling with his pen. "What does Mr. Fairholm think of your proposed changes?"

Emma tried not to resent the question. Clifton Fairholm had been her grandmother's assistant manager since the Spirit Inn opened, and Gran's will had stipulated that he be allowed to keep his job when ownership of the hotel changed hands. He was as stumped by the inn's problems as she was, but his fondest memories were of the hotel in its heyday, and convincing him to modernize the place was like forcing a fish to fly.

"I'd say he's on board with most of them," she said.

"Most, but not all?"

Emma chewed her lip. She'd only said "most" because she wanted her answer to sound plausible. The truth was, Clifton Fairholm didn't think much of any of the changes she was proposing. But then, she thought, her assistant manager probably wouldn't agree to add indoor plumbing if there'd been a choice.

"Well, you know Clifton." She chuckled. "Always a stickler for historical accuracy. Anything new puts his knickers in a twist."

Grader pursed his lips. "So, he's had some objections?"

"A few. Yeah."

She squirmed. *Don't ask, don't ask, don't ask.*

"May I ask which ones?"

Emma sighed. If she hadn't been so desperate, she'd have gathered up her financial statements, told Grader what he and his committee could do with their money, and walked out. As it was, however, she didn't think she could stay in business much longer without it. If she didn't turn things around soon, she'd be forced to sell the Spirit Inn to pay her creditors. It'd be like losing Gran all over again.

"What about the coffee bar?" Grader prompted.

She realized that she'd dug her fingernails into the arms of the chair and released her grip. *Relax,* Emma told herself. There were good reasons behind every penny she was asking for. Grader was only doing his job. This wasn't personal; it was just business.

"He thinks it's unnecessary," she said. "He says we already serve coffee in the restaurant."

Grader considered that. "Does he have a point?"

"Yes, but people like coffee bars. Having to go into the restaurant, wait for a table, and then sit down to order is a hassle when all you want is a latte while you read a book."

The banker's face was impassive. "Anything else?"

She took a deep breath. "The automated key cards. Clifton thinks they'll 'diminish the historic ambience' of the inn," she said, making air quotes with her still-stiff fingers.

"Won't they?"

Emma frowned. She'd have thought that improving the hotel's security was a no-brainer. Was Grader just trying to be difficult?

"Did they have key cards in the nineteenth century?" she said. "No, but people want to know their stuff is safe when they leave their rooms. Plus, guests steal our keys all the time."

Grader seemed taken aback. "Surely not."

"Okay, maybe *steal* isn't the right word. Let's just say that a significant percentage of our guests leave without returning their keys, which means that before I can rent the room again I have to get a locksmith to come out, replace the lock, and make new keys for everyone on staff."

"You could charge the guest for that."

"I could," she said, feeling her temper rise. "But I'd have to spend a lot of time on the phone listening to them complain about it, and in the end we'd probably lose the chance to have them back. Believe me, the costs are significant."

"More than an automated system?"

Emma was losing patience. She'd gone in there with a simple business proposal. Why the inquisition?

"Obviously not," she said, "but there are some things that our guests want and need that can't be *amortized*."

She saw heads turning her way and shrank back.

"Sorry."

"That's all right," he said. "I know you feel strongly about this, but a well-run hotel shouldn't have to borrow to cover its overhead, and there's no guarantee that any of the changes you're proposing will improve your financial position. Unless and until the Spirit Inn can show a profit, I don't see how we can give you another infusion of cash. It's just too much of a risk."

Emma looked down, refusing to concede defeat. So
what if Grader turned her down? There were other banks out
there. She didn't care how long it took; she would not take
no for an answer. The Spirit Inn meant too much to her to
give up now.

She started gathering the papers from the loan officer's
desk.

"Thank you for your time," she said, placing them back
in the Pee-Chee folder that served as her briefcase. "I guess
I'll just have to find the money somewhere else."

Grader shifted in his seat and stared at the pen he was
twirling in his fingers.

"Look, maybe I could run your request by the committee again."

Emma's heart leaped; she could have kissed him.
Instead, she gave a dignified nod.

"Thank you. I appreciate it," she said, handing him the
Pee-Chee folder.

"Don't thank me yet," he said. "To be honest, I doubt
it'll make any difference."

"It doesn't matter," Emma said. "Just the fact that
you're willing to ask means a lot."

Grader waved away the compliment and set the folder
aside.

"I admire your spirit," he said. "But I think you're making a mistake. You're a young woman. Why hang on to a
white elephant like that? You could sell it, take the money,
and see the world. If she were still alive, I think your grandmother would agree."

"I know that," Emma said. "But I don't want to see any
more of the world than I've got right here. I know that
sounds crazy, but it's true."

"All right." Grader sighed and shook his head. "But
don't say I didn't warn you."

He walked her to the door and they shook hands.

"I'll submit your request tonight and call you when the loan committee makes its decision."

As the door closed behind her, Emma almost wilted with relief. Maybe things hadn't gone as well as she'd hoped, but at least he hadn't said no. Harold Grader was probably just making sure that she knew what she was doing. Why else would he have asked her all those questions? He was a banker, after all. Bankers were supposed to be careful with their money. If he didn't think the committee would approve her loan, he wouldn't have agreed to run it by them.

The more she thought about it, the surer Emma was that her loan would be approved. She could pay off her bills, give herself some breathing room, and start moving the Spirit Inn squarely into the twenty-first century. And after that, she thought as she got back into her truck, there'd be no stopping her.

Emma was halfway home when the first drops of rain hit her windshield. As she started up the winding road that led to the Spirit Inn, she congratulated herself for having put the studded tires on her truck the day before. Down in the valleys, they could wait until November to prepare for winter, but up here even a moderate amount of precipitation could quickly turn to ice, making the roads hazardous.

The inn her grandmother had left her was situated on a large plat in the middle of an evergreen forest. Ski resorts and newly minted tech millionaires had been snapping up the land around her fifteen hundred acres, but Emma refused to sell. To her, the towering trees were like the spires of a natural cathedral, the ferns and wake-robin as ethereal as stained glass.

I've got to find a way to save this place.

The box of supplies lurched from one side of the cab to the other as her truck continued up the hill. Emma was anxious to talk to Clifton about her meeting with Grader and hoped he wouldn't be upset that her plans were still alive.

After all, she told herself, his reluctance had nothing to do with her. Some people just had a hard time with change.

As her truck rounded the last curve, the road widened and Emma smiled. The inn's parking lot had filled in the time she'd been gone and people were gathered on the front porch, laughing and hugging the new arrivals as they hurried to escape the rain.

This would be the sixth time that the SSSPA had held their annual convention at the Spirit Inn and Emma saw several people she recognized from years past. A few of them spotted her truck and waved as she drove by. She smiled and returned their greetings, grateful for their loyalty. They were a well-behaved bunch who paid their bills and were easy on the furnishings, she thought. Who cared if they were a little strange?

Emma pulled into a parking space marked *Reserved* and hauled the box of supplies around to the inn's back entrance. Two small steps led to a concrete landing just outside the back door. Emma balanced her box on the cast-iron railing and fished the key out of her pocket. In the past, the back door had always been left unlocked, but since the inn's financial difficulties had begun, she'd had to ask the staff to be more conscious of who had access to the supplies. She didn't accuse anyone, and had no evidence even if she'd wanted to, but in the last few months both she and Clifton had noticed a sharp uptick in the restaurant's overhead. If someone had been helping themselves to the pantry, they needed to stop.

When the supplies had been safely put away, Emma walked down the path to her private quarters, a tiny cottage her grandmother had built shortly after buying the inn. She took a quick shower and donned her "uniform," the green blazer, white shirt, and green-and-gold ascot she wore to work. The tie had been Clifton's idea, ascots having been popular back when the inn was built, and her grandmother insisted it be standard attire for everyone on staff. Emma's black pencil skirt, which she wore instead of slacks, was one of only two things that distinguished her from the rest of her staff, the second being something else that Gran had insisted upon: a name tag that said *Emma Carlisle—Manager*. She ran a comb through her hair and headed back up the path to the inn.

The lobby was a hive of activity. Recent arrivals, still damp from their trip through the parking lot, stood in line at the front desk, anxious for a chance to freshen up after hours on the road, while those who'd checked in earlier milled about, looking for familiar faces and discussing the weekend's upcoming events. The bellboys were in constant motion, loading their brass carts and whisking them away before scurrying back like dandified Energizer bunnies.

At the front desk, Clifton Fairholm was projecting his usual air of unruffled efficiency, his movements as deft as a croupier's, but the new clerk, Adam, seemed harried. When Emma asked discreetly if there was anything she could do to help, the young man gave her a look of such gratitude that her heart went out to him. She suspected that Clifton, whose standards were as high as his patience was short, had been pushing the young man hard. When this rush was over, she'd have to speak with him about it.

When the line had been dealt with and the inflow of new arrivals had slowed to a trickle, Emma went out to visit her guests. The first-timers were usually satisfied with a brief hello, but repeat customers expected to be given a few minutes to talk about previous visits and fill her in on what had been going on in their lives since they'd been there last. Clifton had never understood her enthusiasm for the meet and greet, referring to it as "politicking," but Emma found it the most enjoyable part of her job. What was the point of owning a hotel if you didn't like people?

She was halfway across the lobby when the sound of tinkling bells alerted Emma to the approach of Viv Van Vandevander. Viv was in her late sixties, a full-figured woman with wavy salt-and-pepper hair that fell from a middle part to just past her shoulders. Her typical outfit was a version of what Emma thought of as hippie chic—peasant blouses and voluminous skirts in deeply saturated colors—and her signature sound came from the talismanic *suzu* bells sewn onto her velvet slippers. According to Viv, the ringing of the *suzu* bestowed positive power and authority to their possessor, while at the same time warding off evil spirits. An asset, no doubt, in Viv's line of work.

"Emma, dear, how are you?"

The older woman embraced her briefly, then studied her at arm's length.

"Your aura is very blue tonight."

Emma was always at a loss when Viv made one of her pronouncements.

"Uh, thanks?"

"However"—Viv frowned—"I see smudges of brown in the background, which are disturbing. Have you been troubled lately by distracting or materialistic thoughts?"

"Well, now that you mention it—"

The older woman clasped her hands together. "I knew it!"

"Knew what?" a hearty voice boomed.

Emma turned and saw Viv's husband, Lars Van Vandevander, approaching with a beverage bottle in each hand. Lars was a professor of parapsychology and the organizer of that year's SSSPA conference.

"They don't carry Kombucha," he said, handing a bottle to his wife. "I'm afraid you'll have to make do with Snapple." He smiled at Emma. "Nice to see you again, my dear."

Viv took a sip of her drink and continued her diagnosis.

"I was just telling Emma that she must free herself from her attachment to the material if she's to have any hope of clearing her aura."

Lars nodded and took a sip of his Trop-a-Rocka tea. "Mmm."

"If you embrace the things that are true and worthy in the world," Viv said, staring deeply into Emma's eyes, "whatever vexations you face will melt away."

Emma doubted it would be much help with the loan committee, but she thanked Viv for the advice.

"I see Dr. Richards is here," she said, pointing to an awkward-looking man standing by the fireplace.

Dick Richards was Lars's rival for the leadership of the SSSPA's local chapter, and the two men spent a large portion of every conference trying to win converts to their latest pet theories. Emma didn't know or care much about their research, but she preferred Lars's friendly, easygoing personality to the prickly, obsessive Richards, whose pointed nose and snow-white hair made him look like an irritated egret.

"Oh, yes," Lars said. "Dick's got himself another new theory this year. It should be fun helping him disprove it."

Viv swatted him playfully.

Emma glanced around. "Has Dee arrived yet?"

The other two exchanged a troubled look.

"She's here," Viv began. "But . . ."

"Dee isn't well," her husband said. "I fear this may be her last conference."

The news was sad, but not surprising. Dee was one of the older members of the Van Vandevanders' group, and Emma knew her health had been failing. Dee and her grandmother had been great friends, and when Gran passed away, Dee had transferred her affections to Emma. Sharing each other's company had been like a salve on the wound left by their mutual loss. Now Emma felt hot tears pricking her eyes.

"What's wrong, do you know?"

"Her heart, most likely," Viv muttered. "I told her years ago—"

"Perhaps she should tell you herself," Lars said. "Dee's always been a very private person."

"Of course," Emma said. "I won't tell her you mentioned it."

Emma made her excuses and walked off to continue welcoming the other guests, trying not to let the thought of dying make her feel weepy. It seemed wrong, somehow, for all the vitality that a human life contained to just disappear. She believed in heaven, but it still depressed her when someone she cared for died. Maybe that was why she was willing to put aside her skepticism for a few days every year when the SSSPA showed up. If it made losing someone less painful, she thought, why not believe in ghosts?

Visit our website at
KensingtonBooks.com
to sign up for our newsletters, read
more from your favorite authors, see
books by series, view reading group
guides, and more!

BOOK ‖‖‖ CLUB
BETWEEN THE CHAPTERS

Become a Part of Our
Between the Chapters Book Club
Community and Join the Conversation

Betweenthechapters.net